All the rules had changed

Clay felt both disoriented and acutely sensitized. And he was about to do something that he would probably hate himself for later, but he couldn't stop.

"Firstly, the decision to kiss should never be reached solitarily. A man should telegraph the move in order to allow the lady to prepare to enjoy it, or decline the suggestion."

His hand did nothing but simply lay against her face, yet it immobilized Janessa. "You don't believe in being forceful?"

He shook his head, his eyes looking into hers. "That causes the lady to tense, or to be annoyed," he said. "A man should gently make contact. Then, with gentle pressure he brings her into his arms." His hand slipped to cup her head, bringing her forward. He was trembling, he thought in amazement. Or was she?

His mouth came down, lips slightly parted, and met hers. Their touch was gentle, and Janessa, captivated by the wonder of kissing this man who had always been like a brother, slid her arms around his neck and leaned into him.

"Now, wasn't that better than being kissed without warning?"

Still mesmerized, Janessa whispered, "Infinitely..."

ABOUT THE AUTHOR

A native of Massachusetts, Muriel Jensen now lives in Astoria, Oregon, with her husband, who is also a writer, two calico cats and a malamute named Deadline. She also has three grown children. Muriel loves investigating restaurants and dress shops—all in the interest of research!

Books by Muriel Jensen

HARLEQUIN AMERICAN ROMANCE

Side
by Side
Muriel Jensen

Harlequin Books

TORONTO • NEW YORK • LONDON
AMSTERDAM • PARIS • SYDNEY • HAMBURG
STOCKHOLM • ATHENS • TOKYO • MILAN

Published February 1989

First printing December 1988

ISBN 0-373-16283-9

Printed in U.S.A.

Chapter One

Jake Knight wandered moodily across an office cluttered with newspapers, magazines and reference books, which were the tools of a journalist's trade. Stopping at the window, he turned back and frowned. "Well, you're the insightful, analytical reporter. What do you think of him?"

Clay Barrister shut down his computer terminal and leaned back in his chair. Jake's concern was genuine, even if his fears were unfounded. Deadline or not, Clay couldn't tell his lifelong friend he didn't have time to talk about Simon Pruitt.

He tried hard to adopt a concerned expression that would equal Jake's anguish. "Seems to me," he said reasonably, "that it doesn't matter what our opinion of Pruitt is. It's what Jan thinks that counts, and she appears to care for him."

"She doesn't." Jake denied the suggestion with quiet vehemence. "She just thinks she does. Anyway, they haven't even been intimate."

After a moment's stunned silence, Clay winced. "No wonder she isn't speaking to you. You actually asked her that?"

With a guilty glance at his friend, Jake sank into the cushioned chair on the other side of the desk. "Yeah."

Clay shook his head pityingly. "She's a grown woman, Jake. You can't—"

"She's my little sister."

"She's twenty-seven years old."

Sometimes that was hard even for Clay to believe. Three years younger than he and Jake, Janessa had trailed after them constantly as a kid. By age nine, she had developed a better pitching arm than any boy, and they let her play baseball with the team. It didn't seem so long ago.

"It doesn't matter." Accusing blue eyes glowered at Clay. "I remember when she meant as much to you as she does to me."

Clay rolled his eyes. Jake's tendency toward the dramatic always tried his patience, even though he found his friend fascinating to watch. "I still love her as though she were my own sister, and you know that. But you've got to let her lead her own life and make mistakes, Jake. We had to protect her from creeps when she was sixteen, but she doesn't need bodyguards anymore. She's a grown woman with good common sense and a successful business."

"That's another thing," Jake said doubtfully. "Custom-designed sweatshirts. That's not a serious business."

"The same could be said of saloon-keeping."

Jake took instant offense, as Clay knew he would. "I run a quality place with great food and have very satisfied customers. Yourself included."

Clay nodded. "True. But to some, your line of work might not be taken seriously. Of course, you're good at what you do and enjoy it. That makes all the difference."

Defeated, Jake expelled a martyred sigh and tried another tack. "You know how trusting and caring she is."

That did give Clay a moment's pause. Among family and friends, Janessa Knight's trusting nature was legend. She also brought home every stray that crossed her path, and donated her time and extra money to numerous charities.

"She's a giver," Clay said with a reflective smile. "You'll never change that part of her."

"I don't want that to change," Jake said, his temper rising. "I just want to protect her from what it could do to her in this particular case. Clay, Simon Pruitt's an opportunist—I know it. He's wormed his way into Jan's life because she's the daughter of ex-senator Ethan Knight. She'll be an asset when he launches *his* campaign for state senator." Jake's voice was quieter as he added, "And I've seen him in the company of Billy Calderon."

Clay looked at Jake and knew his friend wasn't lying, but the possibility of Jake's jumping to conclusions without facts was another matter.

"You know who he is?" Jake asked when Clay didn't react with appropriate indignation.

"Of course I do," Clay replied. "He's a two-bit hood on Santiago's payroll. But, you must be—"

"I saw them together at Escobar's," Jake interrupted calmly, "a block away from Jan's place. I don't want anybody like them that close to her, Clay."

Though he was not entirely sure Jake's implication was correct, the thought of someone associated with Salem's small criminal underworld that close to Janessa was not a thought he liked, either.

"All right. I'll see what I can find out," Clay agreed, "but it'll take a while. In the meantime, try to make up with Jannie, will you? If she backs out of our weekend at the cabin, you'll have to cook. You know how you hate to play chef on your days off. You'll be lousy company."

The three of them had bought the cabin together to have a place to relax far from the pressures of their jobs. They often used it separately, but the best times at the lake were spent together.

"She won't talk to me," Jake said grimly. "You'll have to call her."

"All right, I will, as soon as I meet my deadline." He rolled his chair up in front of his computer terminal in a not-so-subtle effort to get Jake to leave. But Jake seemed rooted in his seat.

"You never did tell me what you thought of him," Jake prodded.

Riffling through his notes, trying to recapture the thread of his story, Clay frowned absently. "Who?"

"Simon Pruitt!" Jake replied.

At the impatient sound of his friend's voice, Clay looked up, searching his mind for an answer that would be honest without encouraging Jake's hostility. The truth was, he didn't like Pruitt, either.

"He's...sort of...pretty," Clay said, remembering the wire-rimmed glasses, the styled blond hair and the colorful clothing. "But I guess a politician never knows when he's going to have his picture taken. You can't hold looks against somebody." He smiled frankly at Jake. "You're ugly and you've got lots of friends."

Jake rubbed a hand over his face in exasperation. "You've been a lot of help, Clay," he said dryly as he got to his feet. "It's been a real comfort talking to you."

Clay stood and walked his friend to the door. "Relax, Jake," he admonished seriously. "I'll check Pruitt out. But I'm sure Jan's smart enough to know if the guy loves her or not. And your father's shrewd. If he thought..."

Jake shook his head, frowning. "There's something wrong there."

"What do you mean?"

"I tried to talk to him about this, but...I don't know. It was like he wasn't quite with me."

"In what way?"

"Like he had some serious problem of his own and just wasn't hearing me." Jake shook his head and sighed. "I think the whole family is falling apart."

"Will you lighten up?" Clay clapped his friend's shoulder. "Everything'll be all right. I'll start checking on Pruitt and then I'll call Jan. Get back to work. I'll stop by the tavern tonight for dinner and let you know what she says about the weekend."

"Thanks, Clay." Jake stopped halfway out the door and turned. "I'm right about Pruitt."

"If you are, we'll find out."

"See you tonight."

Closing and locking his office door, Clay sat down at his terminal and tried to clear his mind of all but his story. After poring over his notes and making three false starts, he turned his chair to face the window and looked out onto downtown Salem, Oregon.

The golden Pioneer statue atop the white marble capitol building shone brightly against the cloudy March sky. Heavy city traffic moved against a backdrop of deep green lawns and deciduous trees in a state of winter undress. Horns honked and people hurried.

Clay stared moodily at the cityscape, thinking back to the first time he had ever seen it. He'd been six when his mother and father, both paleontologists, had brought him to Salem to stay with his grandparents. His parents were leaving to spend two years at Fort Ternan in the Olduvai Gorge in Tanganyika as part of Louis Leakey's team.

Having spent the first six years of his life on a farm in Connecticut, Clay had been frightened by the prospect of two years away from his parents in an environment so different from what he'd been used to. But meeting Jake Knight and his sister, Janessa, who lived in the big brick house next door to his grandparents, helped alleviate the loneliness and the strangeness of his surroundings. The three of them quickly became fast friends and went through a lot together. When he was twelve, his grandparents were killed in an automobile accident, and he began living with the Knights. And then there was Janessa's accident. For a year and a half, their lives had been completely disrupted, but they'd emerged from the crisis closer than ever.

After the better part of a lifetime spent in Jake's company, Clay could say without reservation that he was a good and honest man, and as much fun to be around as the boy had been.

Though every bit as precious to Clay, Janessa was a little more difficult to file. Ebullient and impulsive, she alternately charmed him and drove him crazy. But he loved her like a sister and so felt obliged to arbitrate this newest of many crises between her and Jake.

Though he felt certain Jake was overreacting to his sister's relationship with Simon Pruitt, he resolved to make the man the object of a thorough study. If he found anything that posed a threat to Janessa, no matter how remote, he would personally see the man registered for the first trip to Mars or the first cryogenic test, whichever came first.

Clay reached for his phone and stabbed out Janessa's number. The line was busy and he replaced the receiver, smiling as his mind created an image of how he had often seen her in the basement workshop of her home.

He could picture her with the phone cradled on her shoulder, her thick, straight, dark blond hair falling down her back. She would either be trading gossip and her most current sales information with one of the four women who sewed for her in their homes, or taking orders from her newly acquired sales representative. Granny glasses would be perched on her nose while she sewed an artful appliqué of an intricate pattern onto a sweatshirt.

He wrote Call Jannie on a gum-backed note and applied it to the top of his computer screen, then went back to work on his story.

"TELL ME THE TRUTH, Simon. Wasn't that the greatest space for a shop you've ever seen?" Across town in her basement, Janessa Knight had the telephone on her shoulder as she sewed, just as Clay had imagined. But her hair was tied back into a ponytail with a red bandanna. She was smiling as she talked to Simon Pruitt, who was on the other end of the line discussing the prospective new location of Knight Shirts.

"I stopped by this morning like you asked me," Simon replied carefully. "Isn't that waterfront area a little . . . seedy?"

"It's old," she corrected, "and historical. I thought the atmosphere was wonderful, with all the traffic on the river. And the shop next door sells jeans. Talk about business compatibility."

Simon was silent for a moment and Janessa could imagine him frowning as he tried to formulate a diplomatic reply. He was an ambitious young attorney who'd just earned his candidacy for state senator. With the goal of being elected in mind, Simon treated everyone, herself included, with the tactical care a prospective constituent deserved.

"I met your mom today at the Art Association fundraiser," he said, apparently deciding to ignore the issue of the new shop location altogether. "She invited us to dinner next week—Thursday night."

"She did?" Janessa paused in the act of smoothing out the sweatshirt front to check for puckers. Her mother had hardly communicated with *her* at all in the past few weeks. It was surprising that she would have extended an invitation to Simon. Particularly considering the way she usually behaved around him—bored and a little condescending.

"Yeah. You're supposed to call her and let her know if Thursday night's convenient." He paused, and when she said nothing, he asked quietly, "Is it?"

She glanced up at her calendar, squinting over her granny glasses to focus. "Thursday's fine. I'll call her tomorrow. Are you coming by tonight?"

"I'd love to—" he sounded genuinely regretful "—but I have a brainstorming session tonight with my campaign manager, and I should put together a speech for tomorrow afternoon. Are you free this weekend?"

She thought about the argument she'd had this morning with Jake and almost gave a heartfelt yes. But something stopped her. It had been a rough week, and she counted on going to the cabin on the lake and enjoying the usually uncomplicated company of her brother and Clay. If she refused to go with Jake and Clay it would be a case of biting off her nose to spite her face.

"Saturday night's the League of Women Voters' cocktail party," Simon reminded her with the intention of enticing her. She was grateful he couldn't see her make an ugly face at the very thought. She'd been dragged to too many of these social-political parties in the past few weeks. Suddenly her mind was made up.

"I'm sorry, Simon," she said, managing to sound genuinely regretful, "but Jake and I are spending the weekend at the lake. I promised."

There was a moment's silence. "With Barrister, too?"

Janessa folded her arms and frowned. "Yes. Why?"

"No reason," he said quickly, "except that he's always with you. More often than I am, in fact."

"That's because—" Janessa's voice was dry "—he isn't always going to board meetings and writing speeches."

Simon laughed softly. "You're a politician's daughter. You know what the grind is like."

"Mmm," she agreed. "I was very grateful when my father retired from public life."

Simon was silent for another moment, then he said solemnly, "But you could find yourself in public life all over again."

Janessa tried to let the remark pass without having to comment, but was sabotaged.

"Don't toy with my affections, Janessa Knight," Simon said, a smile in his voice. Then it became serious again. "You know how I feel about you."

Janessa massaged her forehead with the fingertips of her right hand. The truth was, she didn't know how he felt. She thought he genuinely cared for her, but she wasn't sure. She had no valid reason for suspicions, yet she entertained a few. She was ashamed of her doubts, but they wouldn't go away and it was impossible for her to think of his constant references to marriage with any seriousness.

"Jan?"

"I'm here," she said brightly. "Sorry, Simon. I've been working on a rush order all week and I'm getting a vicious headache. I've been dreaming of a bubble bath for hours now."

"You shouldn't work so hard," he admonished. She could imagine his blue eyes frowning at her. "You have people to do that for you." People. He said the word as though her employees were tool-and-die machines specially crafted to fit her specifications. She thought of the four women who worked for her and she had to smile.

There was Annie, Janessa's best friend, a single mother with a nine-month-old son named Mark; Jean, who worked at home so she could care for her elderly parents; there was Graciella, who was grateful for the job because her English wasn't great and she had no office skills; and finally Denise, who sewed in order to supplement the sporadic income she earned singing with a rock band. They weren't the experienced stitchers a famous designer would have making samples, but they were hard and dedicated workers, and those qualities fit Janessa's specifications.

"A couple of aspirins and a hot soak will fix me right up." Janessa moved her massaging fingers to the cords of her neck. "But I've got two more shirts to finish first."

"All right, I'll let you go," Simon promised, "but if you're on the brink of expanding your business, be prepared to delegate more. You'll be able to oversee things better if you're in a managerial position."

Actually, it had always been her theory that she best understood the problems of production when she was producing herself. But she was too spent to argue.

"Have a good time tonight, and a nice—" Janessa was interrupted by the peal of the doorbell, followed by a frantic hammering. "Got to go," she said hurriedly. "Call me next week, Simon. 'Bye."

As the banging continued, Janessa hurried to find diminutive, wild-eyed Graciella standing on the front step, a rainbow of sweatshirts spilling out of her arms.

"*Yo tengo un problema* with my *estupida* machine!" Graciella stormed past Janessa into the house. "*Permiso* to use yours, *por favor*?"

Despairingly pushing aside the image of her bath, Janessa struggled to match the little Spanish she knew to the English she had understood and turned to follow Graciella and offer assistance.

SURROUNDED BY A TUBFUL of gardenia-scented bubbles, Janessa groaned in relief as her muscles began to loosen. Thirty-dozen shirts was her largest order to date. Having to deliver them within a week had been her major crisis.

But a few quick phone calls to her employees assured her that three hundred and sixty shirts would be steamed and ready for shipment tomorrow afternoon. The crisis had passed. Her house was a disaster, but domestic chaos was a small price to pay for success in the rag trade. And there was no one but herself and a cat to notice the dust bunnies that had grown so large they looked like a radiation experiment gone wild.

She took a moment to offer a prayer of gratitude that Simon wouldn't have time to stop by tonight. He would have shaken his head at the disorder, groaned at the fabric and thread strewn from one end of the house to the other. The basement, where she assembled the finished product, was tidy. But the rest of the house where she designed—sometimes at the kitchen table, sometimes on the sofa, often on the floor—was impossible to keep tidy.

"Jannie!"

The masculine shout brought Janessa upright with a wild sloshing of water. For a heart-stopping moment she thought Simon had changed his mind after all and decided to fit her into his busy schedule. Then she remembered that he didn't have a key. Also, the voice was deeper and mildly raspy—not Simon's practiced, Shakespearean tones.

"Clay?" she shouted back.

"Where are you?"

"In the bathtub."

"I want to talk to you." His voice was coming closer.

"I'm soaking away an awful day," she said, then added aggressively, "and if you've come to plead my finky brother's case you can just leave."

She had left the bathroom door ajar, and as it opened a little farther, she crossed her arms over her breasts, expecting invasion. But a long, gray-wool-clad arm appeared instead, the hand at the end of it holding out three large cartons. The tantalizing aroma of Chinese food filled the small bathroom.

"I've brought egg rolls, honey-and-garlic ribs, and chicken chow mein with fried noodles," Clay coaxed.

Janessa maintained her righteous snit for a brief ten seconds, then stood abruptly, water streaming down her body. "Put the tea on. I'll be right out."

Wrapped in a white terry robe, the damp end of her ponytail hanging like a rat's tail, Janessa scuffed into the kitchen. With the ease of familiarity, Clay was setting the small round table, while tea brewed in a brown pot in the middle of it.

He looked up at her to smile, and she felt the day's residual concerns slip into unimportance. A good friend made up for a lot. "So you've come to soften me up." The accusation was cushioned by a warm grin. She closed her eyes and inhaled the restorative aroma of the food. "Lord, that smells wonderful. All my favorites. You're not very subtle, Barrister."

Dark eyes chided her as he pulled her chair out. "You've never appreciated subtlety and you know it. Sit down."

"Yes, your worship."

She felt his knuckles rap lightly on her head. "And keep a civil tongue. I haven't your brother's devotion to you, nor your boyfriend's patience."

He sat opposite her and passed her the carton of pork ribs. "What do you know about Simon's patience?" she challenged.

He took an egg roll and switched cartons with her. "You're still alive, aren't you? Proof enough."

Janessa grabbed for the chow mein before he could reach it and served herself a large portion. "Many people find me quite charming."

He studied her heaped plate with an arched eyebrow. "They'll soon be finding you quite obese. Now, will you please be quiet and listen to me. And hand over the chow mein.''

Passing the carton across the table, Janessa pursed her lips at him. ''Jake was wrong, Clay.''

''I know. I just want to try to explain to you why he comes on the way he does.''

''I know why he comes on the way he does,'' she said, her voice rising slightly, her hand gestures broadening. ''It's because he loves me and he still thinks I'm the seventeen-year-old who he helped to walk again after the accident and my coma. But that was ten years ago. I'm fine now!''

Clay smiled as she held two small hands against her small chest in emphasis. But her large winter-blue eyes attested emphatically to the truth of her claim. There was enough life and enthusiasm there for triplets.

''Even Mom and Dad don't treat me like the fragile flower he thinks I am. I'm strong. I'm clever. I'm—''

''Careful,'' Clay cautioned soberly. ''If this is a two-out-of-three, you're already two down.''

With a groan, Janessa retreated into her dinner.

''He worries about you,'' Clay said quietly. ''He feels responsible for you.''

Janessa nodded while she chewed and swallowed. ''Because I was riding on the back of *his* Harley when he took a turn on loose gravel and tossed me headfirst into a rhododendron.''

''He'll never forget that he was wearing a helmet and you weren't.''

''It was just supposed to be a spin around the block. I had begged and pleaded and whined until he had no alternative but to take me for a quick ride to shut me up.''

''He feels he should have stood firm. Or at least given you his helmet.''

"I climbed on behind him while he was still trying to argue me out of it. Anyway, that was so long ago. And I'm fine now."

Clay paused to study the slight shadows under her eyes. "Except for the headaches and dizziness when you get tired. Is one coming on right now?"

"No." She smiled at him, rubbing at the spot at the base of her neck that had been constricting before she finally got into the bathtub. The soak had relaxed her. She was tired, but fine. "Anyway, I've told him a million times that I blame myself and not him. And I can live with the headaches. I wish he'd just mellow out a little."

"He loves you, Jannie. And he'll always blame himself. That makes him overprotective. Try to understand." He laughed softly. "He does everything with drama and flair."

"And you're so calm and analytical." Janessa folded one hand over the other, her fork hanging down as she contemplated Clay with thoughtful gravity. "It amazes me that you've remained friends for so long."

Clay dipped an egg roll in hot mustard and shrugged. "We believe in the same things and want the same things. Our personalities are different, but at heart, we're the same."

Janessa watched him bite off the end of the egg roll, and she smiled as she remembered his column in that day's paper. "I read your verbal caricature of Senator Dawson. It was perfect. I got to know him pretty well when I was in college and worked summers for my father."

Clay laughed, remembering the brief but profane call he'd received from the senator just before Jake had arrived. "Dawson didn't like it. At this very moment he's probably trying hard to get me fired."

"Well, you really can't expect him to like seeing himself called 'the greatest political airhead since Neville

Chamberlain,' do you? Airhead.'' She repeated the word he had used and grinned at him. "Would a *Washington Post* reporter have used that term, do you suppose?''

"The big-timers have to be polished," he said, downing the last of the egg roll. "I just have to be accurate.''

"Speaking of big-timers..." Janessa paused to pour tea into two glass mugs. "Before we started fighting, Jake told me the *L.A. Times* has asked you to go down to talk.''

He nodded, sugaring his tea. When he offered nothing more, Janessa prodded, "Well?''

"I'm not going.''

"Why not?'' She felt instant relief, but it was tinged with indignation. Clay had been within arm's reach of her for as long as she could remember, and there was so much about him she'd hate to lose. Yet she felt angry that he had apparently given such an important offer so little thought.

"This is home," he answered simply. "And Los Angeles is too far from the cabin." He laughed again, wickedly this time. "But I told them they were welcome to syndicate me.''

Janessa's eyes widened. "Do they want to?''

"It's a possibility. Now, could we get back to Jake? He felt badly that you'd decided not to go with us this weekend because you were mad at him.''

Janessa gave him a knowing look over her glass mug. "You mean, he doesn't want to have to cook.''

"*I* don't want him to have to cook. He'll be a bear all weekend, and I need a few days of peace and quiet.''

"You know," Janessa said, mockingly earnest, "you could learn to cook, Clay. It's really pretty painless. Then you wouldn't be dependent on others to feed you.''

"Pardon me." He indicated the lineup of empty cartons and asked pointedly, "But who is feeding whom?''

"Suzi Ling's fed both of us.''

"Why do I continue to try with you?" he asked, frowning darkly at her. Only years of exposure to his unflappable good humor and his propensity for teasing prevented her from drawing back. "You're an ungrateful, unsympathetic brat."

She smiled, secure in his affection. "And that's why you love me."

"If you were my little sister," he assured her, stacking up the cartons, "I'd have drowned you long ago."

Leaning her chin on her hand, Janessa watched him work. "Mmm. That's why you spelled Jake and my parents at the hospital and spent hours at my bedside while I was in a coma, and then when I came out of it helped with my exercises so I could walk again."

"I was living with your family while my parents were away," he reminded her. "I figured I was earning my keep. And you were a lot easier to deal with comatose."

"But I wasn't easier to deal with when I was learning to walk again." Her voice became grave as she thought back to the gritty darkness of that long, frustrating year of recovery. "You put up with my tantrums with more patience than anyone—even Mom."

With his thumb, Clay stroked the small scar on his cheekbone acquired when she had hit him with her crutch. He'd been coaxing her to do her exercises and she hadn't wanted to. That evening he had shown up at the dinner table wearing a catcher's mask. "I was grateful to simply live through them." He got up to toss the cartons in the trash bag under her sink. "About the weekend . . ."

Still sitting, Janessa offered a proposition. "I'll come under one condition."

Suspicious, Clay moved slowly back to the table, hands in his pockets. "What?"

"That you and Jake meet me at the bridge tomorrow after work."

"We going hunting for trolls?"

"Cute." Janessa rolled her eyes. "I want to show you a shop I'd like to move my business into. It's 321 Bridge Street. Six o'clock."

"All right." Clay's answer was affirmative but his tone, cautioning. "But be prepared for Jake to warn you about all the expenses involved in moving Knight Shirts out of your home."

Janessa grimaced. "I know. But he's made such a success of the Crown and Anchor, and he started with so little. He'll have good advice, even if I have to put up with a lot of brotherly flack."

"Well—" Clay patted her cheek in approval and headed for the living room "—very mature of you, Jannie. So I can tell Jake you're coming fishing?"

"Yes." Janessa followed him. "But you might also tell him to suspend the subject of Simon Pruitt for the sake of a peaceful few days."

"All right." Clay leaned over the back of the sofa to retrieve his jacket and found a large, indiscriminately striped and spotted cat on it. Preposterously long whiskers bristled and large amber eyes dared him to remove her.

"My God, Mabel," Clay said in disgust as he reached intrepidly for the cat. "You're lucky newspapermen aren't expected to look tidy." Ten pounds of irritated feline writhed in one hand as he tried to extricate claws from his jacket with the other.

"Mabel!" Janessa shouted in the cat's ear as she offered assistance. "It's Clay!"

Held at eye level in Clay's hand, Mabel stretched her head forward like a turtle, myopic eyes blinking to get a closer look. Whiskers twitched as she peered at Clay. "Hi, Mabel!" he shouted. "It's me! The man who feeds you when your mistress is away."

Mabel cocked an ear as, almost deaf, she caught the faint sounds of a familiar voice. Amber eyes closed to slits and a raspy purr began.

As Janessa took his jacket to brush off the cat hair, Clay held the rumbling feline against his chest and stroked her. "You cussed old fleabag," he said with more fondness than annoyance. Mabel purred contentedly.

"There." Janessa traded Clay his jacket for the cat, who protested the disturbance but recognized Janessa's touch. After a moment of resettling, the purr began again.

"Thanks for dinner." Janessa watched Clay shrug into his sports jacket, then smiled to let him know how much she had enjoyed his visit. "I'd had an awful day. But you put me on an even keel again."

"Hey. Chinese food can fix anything." He leaned down to kiss her cheek. "See you tomorrow at six at 321 Bridge Street."

"What a memory," she praised.

"I've cultivated it because I usually can't read my notes. 'Bye, Jannie."

"'Bye, Clay." Closing the door behind him, Janessa walked back into the quiet living room and reached down to scoop Mabel up. Propping the cat's behind in one hand, she held her up at eye level with the other.

"Really, Mabe," she scolded. "You're half-blind, almost deaf and the most ill-temp..."

Indignant, Mabel gave Janessa a right to the nose with a very capable paw and an almost audible, "Take that!"

Janessa dropped the cat onto the sofa and watched her methodically grind a throw pillow into shape before lying on it. Her life, she reflected, was populated with eccentrics.

Chapter Two

"It reminds me," Jake said, standing in the middle of the cavernous, high-ceilinged room and inspecting it with a slow turn, "of a room that might have been used during the Spanish Inquisition, full of strange devices—" he leaned down and added with deep-voiced drama into Janessa's ear "—and the echo of long-ago screams."

"Will you stop it!" Janessa swung at his chest with her black leather clutch. Taking Jake's arm and walking him across the room, she pointed to the pulleys hanging randomly from the ceiling. "This was a plant-and-basket shop. My landlord, who owns the shop next door, says that large plants were hung on the pulleys, up out of the way, then brought down to water. Clever, huh?"

"What are you going to use them for?"

She gave him a pointed look. "Seems like a good solution to the problem of what to do with you."

Jake looked back at her in silence for a moment, then sighed in reluctant contrition. "I'm sorry about yesterday. I was out of line."

"Yes, you were." Hooking her arm through his, Janessa began to lead him toward the stairs at the back of the room. "But I forgive you. Actually, I'm going to take the pulleys down. Step into my office."

Running lightly up the stairs, Janessa went to the loft's spindle railing and looked down, already envisioning Knight Shirts in full operation on the lower level. As Jake joined her she pointed to the front of the room.

"The first fifteen feet to the right of the door will be our reception and sample areas, then I'll close off a small section as an outlet for seconds." Leaning out over the railing, she pointed to the middle of the room where Annie Chandler, her single-mother friend who'd been working for her since she'd first envisioned her business, was inspecting the sad state of the hardwood floor with Clay. "That'll be our packing area, and the sewing and steaming will all be done in the back of the room. I'm so excited."

Jake looked into her blue eyes aglow with plans and smiled wryly. "It's hard to tell." He wandered across the narrow loft and peered into a closet. He closed the door, then looked up at the loft's one bare bulb. "It's awfully dark up here."

"I know," she agreed, "but I thought I'd get one of those big brass hanging fixtures with the green glass shades. Then I'll get an old banker's lamp for my desk."

"You don't have a desk."

"When I get one."

He walked back toward her and smiled uncertainly. "Are you going to climb all over me if I ask you if you're sure you have enough capital to do this? If I point out that your expenses will probably be twice what you imagine?"

"No." Janessa handed him the notebook she carried along with her purse and opened it, flipping through the pages until she found what she was looking for. She pointed to her current financial statement. Jake raised an eyebrow.

"And this—" she turned the page "—is what the bank is willing to loan me. This week, I shipped thirty-dozen shirts out of my basement. In this place, I could triple production while greatly simplifying the process. I won't have to clear my dining-room table to do the cutting, then again to package. I'll still have to transport the work to my girls, then pick it up, but I'm closer to them here. And to a courier service. And on days when the girls are free of responsibilities at home, they can work here in the shop. I'll even have room for enough machines so that I can hire a few more stitchers. And—'' she drew a breath and took the notebook from him, closing it with a decisive snap ''—I can finally separate my work from my private life.''

Jake's first thought was that Simon Pruitt probably objected to being surrounded by the tools of her trade when he arrived for a romantic evening. Irritation rose in Jake, but he quelled it. He'd hate himself if he said or did anything to diminish her excitement.

''So, what do you think?'' she asked.

''I think it's great. And it sounds like you're going about it in a way that will guarantee success. Good luck, Jannie.'' Jake hugged her, then took her hand and headed for the stairs. ''When are you going to need a painting party?''

''I know how busy you are,'' she said. ''I don't expect you to help with that.''

''You helped me when I did the tavern.''

''My business wasn't quite off the ground then. I had time.''

''I have time. And so does Clay.'' Jake added the last loudly as they reached the bottom of the stairs and their two companions. ''Right, Clay?''

Clay looked up from a conversation with Annie. ''Time for what?''

''A painting party.''

''Depends,'' Clay said conditionally. ''Who gets to be job foreman?''

''I'm her brother,'' Jake pointed out.

Annie, small and slender with long auburn hair in curly contemporary disarray, said, "I'm going to be shop manager. I should be foreman."

"I'm the one with the most experience." Clay folded his arms with feigned self-importance. "Who set up the paint sprayer at the Crown and Anchor?"

"You," admitted Annie, who had also worked on that project. "'Course you painted Jake with it."

Clay shook his head. "He was in the way."

"I'll be job foreman," Janessa proclaimed. "And I promise good food for those who work well, ceiling painting for those who don't."

Annie frowned at Clay. "Is it too late for us to form a union?"

"Now, Annie," Jake said quietly but with malicious undertones, "You know you don't believe in unions—of any kind."

Silence fell as Annie and Jake looked at each other across the small space that separated them, Jake's blue eyes challenging, Annie's green gaze hardening. A startled Janessa met Clay's equally surprised expression.

For a protracted moment, the big empty room closed in on all of them, the air rife with an almost tangible hostility. Then, as though he hadn't made a rude reference to Annie's status as an unwed mother, Jake leaned down to hug Janessa.

"I've got to get back to the tavern, Jannie. For what it's worth, I heartily approve and I'm ready to sling paint whenever you need me." He smiled at Clay. "I'll give you a call tomorrow about the weekend." Then he turned to Annie and said with grave courtesy, "Good night, Annalie."

Annie replied formally, "Good night, Jason."

As the door closed behind Jake, Annie put on her coat, pulling her curly mass of hair out of the collar. Janessa noted that her cheeks flamed as brightly as her hair.

"Annie, I—" Janessa began to apologize for Jake, but Annie interrupted.

"It's going to be great, Jan," she said, taking one last look around. "When do you think we can move in?"

"I'll see the landlord tomorrow. I suppose it'll be ours the moment I say yes."

"Just let me know. Well...I've got to pick up Mark. I'll be by in the morning to help you package. Good night, Clay."

"'Bye, Annie." Clay opened the door for her, then closed it and watched her run several yards up the street to her red Toyota.

Janessa came to stand beside him, watching Annie drive off into the night. "I can't believe Jake did that. What do you suppose it was all about?"

When Clay didn't reply immediately, she looked up to find him frowning at the spot where Annie's car had been. "Love, I think," he finally said.

"What?" she demanded.

"Love," he said again, smiling down at her. "You know. The stuff you and Jake fought about yesterday." He pulled her long leather coat off the floor where she had left it and helped her into it.

"You mean Jake and Annie?" Her tone was incredulous.

"Didn't you notice the tension when we arrived and they saw each other?"

She had. "I just thought he was still angry at me."

"I think they developed a thing for each other when we were all working on Jake's place." Clay opened the door and waited while Janessa turned off the light and stepped out onto the street. A chilling drizzle was just beginning, and the air smelled of winter and the river. "That's all I know, except that it ended, and not happily. Where are you parked?"

She pointed up the street. "I knew they were seeing each other, but neither of them ever let on that it was serious. How did I miss all that?" she asked, looking up at him as they strode side by side.

He shrugged, his fine profile etched against the neon lights across the street. "You were just getting Knight Shirts going. Maybe you'd just met Pruitt, I don't know." He smiled down at her. "Anyway, you're usually too tied up with other stuff to get the little details into focus."

She stopped under a theater marquee. "What do you mean? She's a good friend—I would have noticed. Jake's my brother. I'd know if he was in love."

Clay walked on. "Sometimes love is difficult to recognize. Even for those involved."

"But Annie had an affair with a man in her building right after that." Janessa hurried to catch Clay, falling in step with him again. "The result was Mark."

"Rebound, maybe?"

Janessa stopped in front of her blue Volvo, lost in the thought that her brother and her best friend had been in love and she hadn't noticed. "You think so?" she whispered.

"Yes, but I don't know for a fact. Jake's never told me he was in love, but I think he was. I think he still is."

"Jake and Annie?" Janessa said again, smiling in wonder at the possibility. Then, remembering her brother's edged remark and her friend's icy glare, she frowned. "What do you suppose happened?"

Clay shook his head. "I don't know. People are too complex for other people to reach conclusions about them."

Janessa rolled her eyes at his philosophy. "You sound so paternal when you talk like that. I don't want to reach conclusions about them in the interest of gossip. I want to know what went wrong so we can fix it."

"It's up to them to fix it," he said. "Would you dig out your keys and get in your car so I can get in mine and go home?"

Janessa gave him a scalding glance as she routed through the clutch for her keys. "Where's your sensitivity, Barrister?"

He lifted an apologetic shoulder. "Sensitivities not included."

"Sure." Unlocking the door, she tossed her purse in the car and turned to smile up at Clay. "Then how come you noticed they were in love when I didn't?"

"I'm a reporter, remember? I *see* things."

He was teasing her, but she knew that was true about him. Even when they were children he would notice something seemingly unimpressive, a cloud, or a flower or an old man—and he would describe it to her in a few simple words that created a lasting picture in her mind. She folded her arms on the top of the car door. "And what did you *see* at 321 Bridge Street?"

"A dream on the brink," he replied, putting his hand out as the wind whipped a long straight lock of her hair across her face. He smoothed it out of the way, his smile full of fraternal affection. "Success even beyond your imaginings. The place looks tailor-made for you. You have my endorsement."

"Good." She had intended to rent the space whatever Jake's and Clay's reactions had been, but their approval heightened her excitement and fortified her determination to succeed. "Thanks for coming. I'll see you Friday night at the cabin."

"You driving up?"

"No." She got behind the wheel and pulled on her seat belt. "Graciella's going to come over and feed Mabel, and her husband's going to lube my car and change the oil while I'm gone. I'll ride up with Jake."

"Wasn't Pruitt upset that you'll be gone for the weekend?"

"He has an important cocktail party."

Clay looked doubtful. "How could a cocktail party be judged important?"

Janessa put her key in the ignition. "Politicians operate on a different plane than we do. You lived with us long enough to know that."

"Your father never played those games."

"It's the Salem League of Women Voters," Janessa said in plainer terms. "It's important to Simon that they get to know him."

"He didn't invite you along?"

"Yes, but I hate those things."

"I know, but as his wife, you'll have to—"

"As simply his friend," Janessa said, pulling her door closed and rolling the window down to finish the conversation, "I'm entitled to spend the weekend with my brother and my friend if I so choose."

"I did say the man has great patience with you." Clay reached inside the window and locked her door. "Drive carefully, Jannie. I'll see you Friday."

As Janessa pulled away with a squeal of tires and a whirl of street litter, Clay shook his head and walked around the corner to his car, allowing himself a moment to pity poor Pruitt.

THIS WAS WHAT LIFE should be all about, Clay thought as he held his pole loosely in gloved hands and stared at the tree-lined shore of the quiet lake. The cold on the water was bone chilling, but the sky was blue with an artistic smattering of clouds, the setting was idyllic and the company was perfect.

He enjoyed his work. There were beautiful and intelligent women in his life, and talented, stimulating friends. But when he wanted to find simple warmth and contentment and a reality more merciful than the one he dealt with every day, he came to the lake with Jake and Janessa. It was easier to see things in perspective in the company of those who cared most about him.

Clay turned in the Boston Whaler's chair, stretching his legs toward the stern as he waited for a bite.

Jake, in the stern chair, sat facing Clay, his feet propped on the lid of the cooler. Clay had noticed a mild tension in him, a subtle remoteness when things grew quiet. Jake took part in their customary teasing free-for-alls with convincing energy, but when he had time to himself, it was obvious things were preying on his mind. He and Jannie had made up, but the problem he had with Annie and his concern about his parents and Simon Pruitt remained.

Janessa appeared not to have a care in the world. Lounging back in the chair beside Clay's, her feet propped up on the brass railing, her pole tucked negligently in the crook of her arm, she looked out at the water from under the rolled brim of a gray felt hat.

Smiling, Clay took a moment to enjoy the sight of her. One would never guess that she had just made a major business decision and laid all her capital, along with her physical and emotional resources, on the line.

Even when they'd been children, her ability to enjoy the moment had fascinated him. When he'd felt hurt by his parents' absences, or troubled by some problem at school, he found it hard to enjoy whatever entertainment the three of them had chosen. But Janessa had always been able to compartmentalize her life and deal with things as she had time or strength to confront them—and that was never when she was having fun.

He remembered a time when she'd still been in a cast. He'd pushed her wheelchair several blocks to the local field so they could watch Jake pitch for a city-league baseball team.

Clay had been feeling sorry for himself that day. In his junior year in college, he'd received the Samuel Churchill award for outstanding achievement in journalism. It was a national honor, and he'd received a fair amount of local notoriety. But knowing that his parents wouldn't get the news for weeks and that even then they would simply smile at each other over their research results and say, "How nice for Barclay," had depressed him beyond his ability to describe to his second family.

Sitting in the grass beside Janessa's chair, he'd been forced out of his dark mood by a not very gentle fist to his shoulder. "Jake's on third, Clay," she'd sniped at him. "Get up and cheer him home for me."

Clay had looked up to find Jake crouching, one foot on the bag, ready to run for home. Jake had looked pleased with himself and the situation, determined to earn the cheers that were building by making the most sincere effort to score any man could make.

Janessa's undiminished loyalty, and Jake's unabashed delight in giving his all had brought Clay out of his personal slump and to his feet. Depression was impossible for anyone connected with those two.

But neither Clay nor Janessa had seen Jake score. She had cheered wildly when the bat smacked the ball and Jake launched toward home. But her gyrations had caused the wheelchair to roll. It had taken all Clay's considerable speed and strength to stop the runaway chair halfway down the incline to the field.

"You never set the damn brakes!" he had shouted at her, his reaction part relief, part terror. But she'd been laughing so hard he'd abandoned the scolding and laughed with her.

"What's so funny, Clay?"

Janessa's curious inquiry brought him back to the present.

"You," he replied, not taking time to explain as he glanced up at the suddenly murky sky. It was lowering, shaping itself over the surrounding evergreens like a collapsing canopy. Slowly he began to reel in his line. "It's going to rain," he predicted.

Janessa flicked her arm forward in an expert cast. Her line lashed out, snaking through the air, plunking her lure about twenty feet from the boat into the frothy surface of the lake. "You journalists are such a pessimistic lot. So the wind is picking up. It doesn't have to mean rain."

Unhurriedly Clay continued to reel in his line, then stepped off his seat to store his pole forward.

In the stern seat, Jake looked thoughtfully at the menacing cloud directly overhead, then began to grind on his reel. "I'm with Clay," he said in answer to his sister's frown. Storing his pole beside Clay's, he pulled up the hood of his rain poncho.

"Spending a weekend with you two," Janessa complained with a pitying shake of her head, "is like bunking with a pair of old maids, I swear! Where's your love of the outdoors, your spirit of—"

The lash of an instantaneous downpour cut off her appeal. Looking up at the traitorous sky with a gasp of indignation, she got a mouthful of rain, then a slap in the face with wet felt as the rain unrolled the brim of her hat.

Laughing helplessly, Clay sparked the motor to life as Janessa tore off her hat with a threatening glare at him.

Jake reeled in her line. In a moment the Boston Whaler roared through the water, headed for shore.

"We've been a day and a half without a catch," Jake pointed out as they tied up at the small dock. "We're down to macaroni and cheese for dinner."

Clay leaped out and offered a hand to Janessa. "Won't the rain make the fishing better tomorrow?" she asked.

"Beats me." Clay pulled the poles and tackle box out of the boat and laid them on the dock. "I think the fish go into hiding whenever we arrive, rain or shine."

Janessa sighed, picking up her pole. "Well, let's discuss it inside where it's dry."

"Dry?" Clay lifted both hands, palms up. "Why, this isn't rain, Miss Knight. This is just a little wind picking up."

Laughing, she shoved him toward the cabin. "You're going to need picking up, when I'm through with you, Barrister. Will you get moving?"

With a swift and dexterous movement, Clay slung Janessa over his shoulder, proving the absurdity of her playful threat. He headed for the cabin. Jake fell in step beside him with their gear as Janessa laughingly threatened ugly retribution.

"Why do we keep inviting her along on these trips?" Clay asked Jake as they sauntered through the rain.

"She got us the good deal on the boat and put down the deposit," Jake reminded.

Clay nodded. "Oh, yeah. I knew there had to be a reason."

ROLLING UP THE SLEEVES of a green-and-gray plaid flannel shirt, Clay walked from his room through the cabin's large living room to the kitchen. He detoured to stoke the puny fire in the deep stone fireplace.

Shaking his head over Jake's inability to get a decent fire going no matter how many times he showed him how, he took newspaper from the wood box and twisted several pieces, placing them strategically to feed the flames. Then he made a V out of the two logs Jake had placed side by side and added a chunk of fragrant cedar across the top. Almost immediately, the fire began to dance and leap toward the draft.

Straightening and brushing off the knees of his gray cords, Clay wandered to the rough wood bar that separated the kitchen from the living room.

Attired in an apron that read Me and My Chili Are Hot!, Jake read the directions on a box of macaroni-and-cheese while Janessa set the table.

"One of Salem's great kitchen masters," she said with a grin at Clay, "and he has to read the directions on the box."

Jake aimed a pitying look at his sister. "You have never known what it's like to follow directions—of any kind." He turned back to the box with a frown. "There's scary stuff in here, guys. Disodium phosphate and thiamine mononitrate. What are those?"

Before anyone could reply, the telephone rang shrilly. Clay turned toward the living room's long shadows to answer it. "For you, Jake. It's the Crown and Anchor."

Wiping his hands on the apron, Jake frowned and came around to take the receiver. After he listened a moment, his frown deepened. "How badly was he hurt?"

Excited conversation on the other end of the line filtered into the now silent room as Clay and Janessa listened from the archway. Jake heaved a sigh and looked at his watch. "Yeah, well, broken ribs are enough to make anybody crabby. Try to hold things together and I'll be there by eight. In the meantime, see if you can get hold of any of the relief cooks we've used. You know where the personnel info is in my Rolodex. All right. 'Bye.''

"Something happen to Stewie?" Janessa asked the moment Jake hung up.

"Yeah." They had to follow Jake to his room to hear the details. While throwing the few things he'd brought into his gym bag, he explained. "He got sideswiped on the bridge on his way to work and skidded into the guardrail. Broke a couple of ribs. Jeff's on vacation this week so that leaves us without a cook. Oh." He held one Reebok in his hand and looked around for the other. "Jannie's going to need a ride home, Clay."

Clay checked behind the door and, locating the errant shoe, tossed it at Jake. "Tempting as it might be to leave her here, I'll take her home. I'll put your fishing gear in the car. Anything else I can do?"

"Yeah, take this." Jake tossed the shoe in the bag, zipped it up and flung it to Clay.

Janessa headed for the kitchen, shouting back over her shoulder, "I'll make you a sandwich to eat on the way."

Ten minutes later she was handing Jake a sack and a thermos through the open window of his BMW while Clay slammed the trunk. As Jake stowed the things on the seat beside him, she leaned in to kiss his cheek. "Don't speed. They'll manage till you get there."

Clay's long arm reached in to land a light punch on his shoulder. "Take care," he said. "And look at it this way. You're spared the macaroni and cheese."

Jake smiled bleakly. "And the after-dinner cappuccino. I expect you guys to bring mine back in a thermos. See you next week."

Jake waved at his friend and his sister and pulled out onto the dark highway, honking as he disappeared into the void beyond the glow of the porch light.

Chapter Three

"No fives. Fish." Clay closed the splay of playing cards in his hand, then opened them again with grave concentration. He lay on his stomach on the mock leopard fur in front of the fireplace.

Janessa sat cross-legged, facing him, the firelight gilding the left side of her face. She studied her cards with a frown, pulling one out and moving it to the far side.

"I can't believe we're playing this silly game," she said. She picked up a card from the pile and with a groan placed it in the middle of her splay. "And you don't deal any better than you did when you were nine."

"If you could learn the difference between a straight and a flush," Clay said, "we could have an exciting game of poker. But you seem to have a mental block in that direction. Will you please discard?"

"Hold your horses, I'm thinking."

Clay rolled onto his back, placing his cards face down on his chest. "Wake me when you've made your move."

After several moments of listening to Janessa hum off-key, Clay heard the furious movement of cards, then the ominous rippling sound as they were fanned out on the rug.

"There!" Janessa said with satisfaction.

Clay turned over to see Janessa's hands outstretched to show their emptiness, her eyes alight with mischief, and the rug between them covered with pairs, triples and runs.

She consulted the pad at her knee. "You're into me for..."

He tossed the half-deck of cards in his hands onto the floor and asked accusingly, "Well, what was all that groaning and eye rolling about?"

"I may not understand straights and flushes," she said, getting to her feet while giving him a teasingly superior glance, "but I do grasp the strategic advantage of a poker face—even if I'm playing Fish. Another cappuccino?"

Sitting up, Clay handed her his empty cup. "Please. And if you tell Jake about this, your name's mud."

When Janessa returned with a tray bearing two steaming pedestal mugs and a small plate of crackers and cheese, Clay had cleared the cards away and put back the rustic coffee table they had moved to have room to play. He had placed another log on the fire and was now settled in a shadowy corner of the sofa, his feet propped on the edge of the coffee table.

It occurred to Janessa how quiet the evening had been, how still the room was now. The card game had been fun, their conversation lively, but the boisterousness that usually marked the cabin weekends had fled with Jake.

Studying Clay's profile as he stared into the fire, Janessa noticed a thoughtful maturity about him she'd never been aware of before. Of course, he was thirty. It was time for him to be mature. Still, the observation surprised her and brought on a subtle alteration of mood.

"Here, Clay."

"Mmm. Thanks." The delicious aroma of coffee combined with the fragrance of the fire as Clay took his mug from her. He held it up to hers in a toast. "To Knight Shirts's new location."

Drinking to that, Janessa then settled into the opposite corner of the sofa, kicking her flats off and stretching her legs out on the plump cushions.

Clay continued to stare into the fire, relaxed but thoughtful.

"It's quiet without Jake, isn't it?" Janessa asked into the silence.

Clay laughed softly and sipped his cappuccino. "Yeah. You can almost relax."

"You know—" Janessa leaned her elbow on the sofa back and rested her chin on it "—I've been thinking about him and Annie."

"Yeah?"

"It's scary to imagine him getting married one day."

Clay reached out to pinch the toes stretched toward him. "I think you can put that worry aside for a while. I said I thought they were in love, but as long as they're snarling at each other, we don't have to worry about them setting a date." Turning sideways to face her, Clay frowned. "But why do you find it scary?"

"Well," she said, gesturing with her mug, "it's been the three of us for so long. Everything would change."

"Isn't that what life's all about? If things didn't change, you wouldn't be moving your business to a larger location. Security's comforting, but it doesn't always allow for growth. In business or in people."

And that was what made him a great reporter, Janessa thought with reluctant admiration—the ability to explain the simple truth in simple words. But right now she wanted him to understand how she felt, not explain the mysteries of living to her.

"Thank you, Freud," she said, reaching sideways to put the mug down and pick up a cracker. "What I mean is— when I was growing up and my father was gone twenty hours a day and my mother had to spend so much of her time giving and going to parties, you and Jake were like my lifeline. Even after I recovered from the accident and could walk again I felt ugly and awkward at a time when girls are supposed to feel pretty.''

She smiled fondly, the cracker forgotten in her hand. ''But you two were always there to tease me out of it, or bully me out of it—whichever tactic was required. Remember the time you found me hysterical after Giselle Cunningham told me I was chosen valedictorian only because everyone felt sorry for me?''

Clay nodded. ''I remember.''

''You told me I was beautiful.'' Her voice reflected the wonder she had felt at the time. ''And you told me that the only reason you felt sorry for me was that I was silly enough to believe her. You said, 'Giselle Cunningham is jealous of you because even with a limp, you have more grace and sex appeal than she has.' That was the first time,'' she said softly, ''that I knew I could get completely over what had happened to me. Because you thought I had grace. I wonder if you'll ever know how much that did for me?''

''I do,'' he replied. ''You gave the best valedictory address Kennedy High ever heard.''

''No, it was more than that. Even limping and terrified, I think I turned the corner toward becoming a woman that day. I had a whole new pride in myself because of you.''

''It wasn't because of me,'' he corrected gently. ''It was because you'd been through a dark and difficult time and came out on top.''

''I'd have much preferred to sit on the sofa and wallow in my troubles than do my exercises. But you and Jake wouldn't let me.''

Clay grinned. ''We took great pleasure in making you miserable.''

Laughing, Janessa kicked out at his knee. "You did not. I remember your face when I'd cry." Her expression sobered suddenly as she thought of the way Jake's eyes looked then, dark and anguished and filled with guilt. "Jake is so emotional, so mercurial that he would cry with me. But you . . . you would just talk me through with quiet reassurance and encourage me to start all over again, determined to make me well, whatever it cost both of us."

Clay remembered those days with fresh emotion. At the beginning of the exercise regimen prescribed by the doctor, he and Jake had been so committed to their roles as Janessa's protectors that they both decided to do their junior and senior years at a local college so they could be nearby to care for her. Because Ethan and Elaine Knight led such busy lives, the responsibility of seeing that Janessa exercised daily fell upon Jake and him, and they had accepted it with fervor. She meant so much to both of them that the need to see her strong and well again was a burden each bore differently but with the same intensity.

The bravery that had carried Janessa through the months in the cast had been sorely challenged when it was time for her to rebuild her muscles. The doctor had warned the family that the pain would be intense and constant.

Jake, sensitive and emotional, hugged and coddled her through the long and painful workouts. Clay bullied her through because she saved her stubbornness and her tantrums for those times when it was his turn to help her work out. It hadn't taken him long to figure out that she considered him the weak link in the family's support system. If she could wear him down, she could be free of the agonizing exercises at least three days of the week.

"You can't make me do it!" she had screamed at him once from the mat on the floor of the den. "You're not my brother! You're not a Knight!"

Mercilessly but carefully bending her leg at the knee, he had applied pressure, pushing toward her chest. "Putting up with you, I think I've earned my place," he had replied quietly.

In pain she had cried out, "I don't want you here! Your own parents don't even want you or else why would you always be living with us?"

Pretending to ignore her, he had bent her other leg, methodically pushing toward her chest. Inside him, his heart was pounding and he couldn't swallow.

Her accusation was a conclusion he had reached years before. Of the twenty years of his life, he had spent six of those with his parents and the rest with his grandparents and the Knights.

He had been told that the remote parts of the world to which his parents traveled in their work were not suitable for children. As a young boy, he had understood and excitedly awaited their return to the United States every other year.

When the Knights took him in after his grandparents' death, his parents were located and they flew back to the States. He thought that finally he could join his mother and father, and that at last, when other children asked about his parents, he wouldn't have to say they were working in Africa and get those strange looks that asked why he wasn't with them.

When his parents explained to him that he would be staying with the Knights when they returned to Tanganyika, he had finally understood that he was less important to them than their work.

They were always happy to see him when they visited, and would sit for hours looking over all the things he had saved to show them when they came home—schoolwork, drawings, treasures he and Jake and Janessa had found in the riverbed. But they considered their work of prime importance, and within days of their arrival home, Clay could see the restlessness in them, the need to get back to the complete concentration their scholarly research required. He had found a way to cope with their casual attitude toward him, because Ethan and Elaine Knight gave him all the warmth and caring any child could hope for. But accepting their indifference was another matter.

It had come as a complete surprise to him that someone truly understood his situation—and knew that it hurt him enough to be used against him. He had thought his facade of carefree acceptance firmly in place.

"I'm sorry," Janessa had said finally as he continued to slowly manipulate the muscles in her legs. "I didn't mean it."

When he said nothing, just continued the exercises, she asked quietly, "Doesn't it bother you that they always go off without you?"

"It used to," he admitted, "but it doesn't anymore."

"Why not?"

"Because I'm more at home with your family than I ever am when my parents come home."

She had nodded. "Mom and Dad think of you like you'd been born Jake's twin, or something. That's weird."

He had smiled. At that point in her life, anything Janessa didn't understand was weird. "I know. But a lot of things are, and they work anyway. And a lot of things that should be perfect don't work at all."

"Like my leg." Her eyes followed the length of her slim but well-shaped limb as Clay moved it up and down. "It looks like it should work, but it doesn't."

"It will."

"But what if it doesn't?" she had asked with all apparent calm. Even then he'd been able to see things about people that they tried to hide. And he'd been afraid enough times in his life to recognize fear in someone else, particularly someone who had become like his own sister.

"It will," he had insisted firmly. "I don't think exercising your legs would hurt so much if they weren't ever going to work again."

There'd been silence for a long moment, then she'd sighed. "I'm afraid they won't get better and I'll never get to go dancing again, or run on the beach with you and Jake, or just stand to watch a parade. . . ."

Her voice had broken, and he had stopped the exercises to kneel beside her. As she lay on the mat, big tears slid down into her hair and she put an arm across her eyes. "There's nothing wrong with being afraid," he had said gently. "It's only wrong if it makes you give up. The doctor said there's no reason you shouldn't be back to normal if you keep doing the exercises. Just believe it's going to work."

"But it hurts so bad."

"I know. Pain is scary, but there's no way to build up your muscles again without making them hurt." He had given her several more moments to cry then handed her a box of tissues. "Now, are you ready to quit bawling and get back to work?"

Janessa had glared at him, ripped a tissue out of the box and blown her nose. "All right," she said. "But when my legs are well the first thing I'm going to do with them is kick you from here to California."

He had laughed and gently begun the routine again. "Why California?"

"'Cause when I'm done," she had replied reasonably, "we can go to Disneyland."

There had been something special between him and Janessa since that day, something even Jake didn't share. It was as though having inflicted pain on one another, and then soothed it, they had learned something important.

He felt an affection for her that was completely different from what he felt for Jake, and it wasn't different simply because she was a woman. Though gentle and sweet, Janessa was tougher than Jake, and he respected that and loved her for it.

Clay came back to the present to discover that he had Janessa's bare foot in his hand and was massaging it just as he had done all those years ago. She was watching him with a curious expression.

"Sorry," he said, taking hold of her big toe and swinging her foot off his thigh. "Force of habit. Did you say something?"

She folded her legs and rubbed absently at the foot he'd been massaging. "I've forgotten how deliciously pampered a foot rub makes you feel. Yes, I did. I was talking about Mom and Dad's fortieth anniversary. It's coming up in August, and I thought you and Jake might like to help me prepare something."

"Sure." There was no one he'd rather help and no cause he'd rather work for than Ethan and Elaine. "A family thing, or a major social event?"

"Something in between. Simon knows this restaurant, the Versailles, a short distance in the country that—"

Clay interrupted her with a frown. "You wouldn't have it at Jake's?"

For an instant she avoided his eyes, concentrating on sipping her coffee. Then she put the mug aside and explained, "Well, we thought we'd strive for something kind of elegant, you know? I mean, this place has chandeliers instead of track lighting, and crystal and china and all the special little accents that would make a memorable evening." Looking back into Clay's unaltered expression, she went on coaxingly, "And this way, Jake can enjoy the evening, too, without having to worry about and probably be involved in the cooking and setting up."

"I think you're going to hurt his feelings," Clay warned.

"Every time we have a family do, we have it at Jake's. Maybe he'd be grateful if we did this differently."

"I don't think so."

"Well, maybe you're wrong."

Janessa gave him one of her firm looks, one Clay recognized from their childhood. Prudently he considered the argument lost. The best thing to do was let her propose the idea, wait for Jake to blow up and come to him to arbitrate. Then he might be in a position to do something. "What would you like me to do in preparation?" he asked with feigned docility.

"Don't play your games with me, Barrister!" Janessa laughed as she took a corner pillow and threw it at him. "You're thinking Jake's going to have a fit and come crying to you and then you'll get me to change my mind. Well, it won't work. Having the party at the Versailles is a good idea. Besides," she said more quietly, "Mom and Dad like Simon. They've invited him to dinner next Thursday."

"Oh?" He took that news with a skeptical lift of his eyebrow. In deference to her feelings he wouldn't tell her what her father had told him he thought of Simon Pruitt, and what had happened with her mother at a retirement party Clay had covered for the *Salem Standard News*. Elaine had been standing behind Simon, who was holding court and talking at length about some proposed legislation regarding illegal aliens. Catching Clay's eye, she had opened and closed her right hand in a yak-yak motion. Then she had punctuated that with a descriptive roll of her eyes.

When Clay choked on his drink, Elaine had come over to pat his back. "Swallow the olive, dear?" she had asked with a wicked wink.

"How are your folks?" Clay said now, diverting the conversation before the memory made him choke again. "I haven't seen them since Senator Blake's retirement party."

"Actually—" Janessa frowned thoughtfully and put her mug aside, reaching for another cracker "—I'm not sure. If I didn't know them better, I'd think..." She paused and sighed, then shook her head. "I don't know."

"What?"

"Well...it's like they're having problems."

"Problems?"

"Yeah...you know." She hunched her shoulders as though the idea was painful. "Marital problems."

Clay remembered what Jake had told him about his father just the other day. "On the verge of their fortieth anniversary?" he said, his voice filled with denial to convince himself, as well as her. "I doubt that, Jannie."

"But they're both acting...strange."

"Janessa." Clay laughed softly and tossed the pillow back at her. "Can you really consider yourself qualified to judge strange behavior? I mean, unless it's a case of 'it takes one to know one.'"

"My mother's drinking," Janessa blurted.

Clay put his mug down. "What?"

"Annie and I had lunch at Escobar's the other day, and when we went in through the lounge, Mom was sitting at a little round table all by herself having a straight shot of something brown."

"That proves that she stopped for lunch," he said calmly, "and had a drink while waiting for her reservation."

"Mom's never sat in a lounge in her life," she said, scornful of his explanation, "and she certainly wouldn't sit in one and drink by herself if she didn't have some serious problem. She was staring into the glass and didn't even see us."

"Maybe she was meeting someone," Clay suggested.

Janessa's eyes widened at the ugly possibility; that was something she hadn't even considered. "Do you think so?"

He closed his eyes and shook his head at her misinterpretation. "I meant another woman—a friend."

"I peeked in before we left and she was still there. And still alone."

"All right, I give up," Clay relented. "I can't imagine why she was there. But I think it's foolish to jump to rash conclusions."

"I know, I know. People are too complex for other people to understand." Janessa brought her knees up and rested her chin on them, staring moodily into the fire. "But my mother is usually so straightforward. Her goal in life was always to be supportive of Dad and her family. Then when the three of us fled the nest and she took the job as docent at the museum, she seemed so happy. She had time for herself and she knew what to do with it." She heaved a deep sigh and lifted her head to look at Clay. "Do you think the problem is that she's working when Dad's used to having her at home?" Thinking aloud, she answered her own question. "But he's never been a domineering husband. I mean, she never worked when he was in politics because his job required both of them, and she seemed so suited to that life—attractive and outgoing, but strong enough not to let anyone push her around. You know?"

Valiantly struggling against a smile, understanding that he was required only to nod, Clay did so.

"But maybe now that Dad's retired," Janessa speculated, "he wishes she was home with him. Don't you think?"

Clay nodded again. "That could be."

Janessa frowned. ''That seems like something they could easily work out, though, doesn't it? It isn't something she'd be mooning over all by herself in a bar.''

''I know I'm going out on a new limb here,'' Clay said cautiously, ''but why don't you ask her what the problem is?''

Janessa stared at him thoughtfully, as though that course of action hadn't occurred to her.

''As you said, she's a straightforward lady,'' he went on. ''If she does have a problem, maybe she'd appreciate discussing it with you.''

''I don't know. She's spent her whole life trying to protect us from everything.''

''Well, we've reached the stage of our lives where those roles reverse a little. She might be needing you to help her.''

''Mmm.''

''Look.'' Clay got to his feet, gathering up their mugs. ''You can't do anything about it by worrying. And if we're going fishing in the morning before we head back home, we'd better get some sleep.''

''Right.'' Following him into the kitchen with what was left of the cheese, Janessa took out the plastic wrap, still ruminating as she snapped off a length of it. ''Has it occurred to you that the whole Knight family is in a kind of turmoil?'' she asked, fighting the end of the wrap that had folded in on itself. ''I mean, Jake with Annie, and Mom and Dad. At the moment, I'm the only stable one.''

Clay grinned at her as he helped her untangle the wrap and secure it on the plate. ''Now that's proof of a desperate situation if I ever heard one.''

The truth was he wasn't sure he'd ever known anyone more stable than Janessa. If she sometimes allowed her life to shift off balance, it was because she cared too much about people to worry about keeping herself on an even keel. Having been comforted by her caring nature several times himself, he had a great affection and respect for that particular foible.

Janessa gave him a scolding look as she put the plate in the refrigerator. "Thanks, Clay."

"Don't worry." He hooked an arm gently around her neck, pulling her along with him as he flipped off the light switch and walked through the living room toward the bedrooms. He found himself trying to reassure her as he had when they were children and she'd been concerned about something. Jake would try to tease her out of worrying, while Clay, understanding the reality of her fears, would try to be logical. "Your family is made up of special people with the sense and maturity to work out their problems. Everything will be all right. I promise."

"Maturity?" Janessa asked doubtfully. "Jake?"

"Yeah, well, we may have a problem there." Clay laughed and kissed her forehead then gave her a gentle push toward her room. "Get to bed. I'm going to check the fire."

He was right, of course, Janessa thought as she prepared for bed in her small, cedar-walled room. Clay was always right. She was probably more concerned than she should be about her parents, and Jake was certainly old enough to handle a relationship without her concern or interference.

On an intellectual level, she accepted that. But inside, where instinct and feeling lived, she felt as though her life and everyone in it was on the edge of upheaval. Subtle little changes were taking place she didn't understand. And she was afraid they might be setting the stage for more surprises.

Her brother, who often drove her crazy, but was by nature a caring, loving man, had come on like a Victorian father over her relationship with a perfectly nice man.

Then he had made an uncharacteristically rude remark to one of the sweetest women on earth.

Janessa's parents, always the stalwart foundation of her existence, were acting like strangers and doing things separately, instead of hand in hand, as they'd done everything for forty years.

At least Clay was the same, she thought with great relief as she slipped under the blankets. Thinking back over the evening and his alternately teasing and caring approach to being her friend, she closed her eyes and sighed. "Thank you, God, for Clay," she murmured.

"DID I MENTION that my largest bass was seven pounds?" Janessa smiled with superior satisfaction at Clay's profile as he took the exit off the freeway that would deposit them in her neighborhood. Streetlights were just going on in the early evening darkness.

"Seven times," he replied without taking his eyes from the road.

"And how large was your only fish again?"

Clay glanced at her to see blue eyes that were deceptively curious, backlit with laughter.

"A veritable guppy by comparison." He thought with grim humor of his two-pounder that lay packed in ice in the cooler in the trunk beside the robustly exquisite object of her boast and its three four-pound companions. "Only a mean-spirited woman would keep bringing it up."

She smiled again. "I know."

He turned onto a tree-lined street that was lit by front-lawn lampposts. Janessa unbuckled her seat belt as Clay pulled into her driveway. He reached into the back seat for her tote bag. "Want me to take this in for you?"

"No, I can manage. But I don't have room in my freezer for the fish."

"I'll keep it." He grinned. "We can have Jake over to share it, and rub in the fact that we had a catch after he left."

"Good idea." She arched an eyebrow. "Though he might not be too impressed with your... How many ounces was it?"

She winked at him and stepped out of the car, tucking her clutch under her arm and tossing her tote over her other shoulder. She pushed the car door closed with her knee. "Thanks, Clay." Blowing him a kiss, she ran lightly up the driveway to the steps of her small split-level. Clay watched her rooting for her keys, smiling to himself as he studied the straight length of her legs in her snug jeans under the short leather jacket. One would never suspect now that those legs had ever caused her pain.

Her front door open, Janessa turned back to wave. Tapping the horn, Clay waited until she had locked the door behind her, then shifted into reverse and backed out of the driveway.

Turning onto the brightly lit highway that would take him home, Clay reflected that he felt curiously mellow. Their usual boisterous free-for-all at the cabin always left him exhausted and dreading Monday morning.

But he felt comfortably in tune with things tonight, and he savored the feeling. It was probably because Jake had left early, he decided. Janessa, though an undisputed crazy, could be wonderfully serene company while fishing.

For a moment his mind entertained a vision of her leaning back in her seat to the right of him on the whaler, her feet crossed and propped on the edge of the boat, the rolled brim of her felt hat shading her eyes. He concentrated on that image the rest of the way home, curiously reluctant to part with it.

Chapter Four

The evening was not going well. Janessa, sitting beside Simon on the deep apricot love seat in her parents' living room, shifted uncomfortably.

"The loggers, longshoremen and the ports," Simon was saying, "all make money from the export of logs. I think we should encourage it, even offer loggers a tax break for doing it."

Janessa waited for her father to annihilate Simon's suggestion. Ethan Knight had long been opposed to the export of logs overseas because of the disastrous effect the practice had on local mills. The proposal should have launched him several feet out of his chair, but looking straight at his guest from the depths of his white leather recliner, Ethan seemed not to have heard him.

Janessa's mother, however, was paying attention. In a black crepe dress, she stood at the sideboard where a silver platter of fresh fruit sat beside a coffee service. With a toss of chin-length blond hair, artfully streaked to hide the gray, she popped a grape into her mouth and poured a cup of coffee.

"That's absurd, Simon," she said, bringing him the fine china cup. "If you propose a tax break for exporting logs, *if* you're elected—" she stressed the word as though she didn't consider it a possibility in her lifetime "—they'll string you up in the rotunda. Cream and sugar?'' Her hospitable smile belied the brutal way she had just decimated his suggestion.

"Please." Simon accepted the cup, smiling warmly at his hostess. "Actually I think if I could explain that . . ."

One of his strongest qualities, Janessa reflected in amazement as he went on to describe the details of his plan, was an extremely thick hide.

As Simon turned back to Ethan to make his point, Janessa looked up at her mother. Elaine Knight crossed her eyes in an expression of disbelief. Janessa bit the inside of her lip, unsure if she was holding back a gasp or a laugh. Her mother had been behaving like a society matron in a Noel Coward play who had chosen this particular evening to inflict her jaded, acerbic wit on her guests.

"Would you like some almond cake?" Elaine offered.

Simon interrupted his monologue to answer eagerly, "Please. Of course."

"Of course," Elaine repeated in an undertone with a pointed glance at her daughter. "You, Jan?"

"Yes." Anxious to get her mother alone, Janessa stood to accompany her to the kitchen. "I'll help you."

"You, dear?" Elaine turned to her husband. When Ethan continued to stare without response, she shooed Janessa in his direction. "You try, darling. If you get a pulse, ask your father if he wants cake."

With the only animation he had shown all evening, Ethan shook his head, his voice quiet. "No cake, thank you."

"Good decision, dear," Elaine said, turning to the kitchen. "You won't have to go to all that trouble of digesting it."

"Mother!" Janessa trailed her mother into the kitchen, whispering harshly. "What is the matter with you? What will Simon think?"

"Simon doesn't think, Jan." Elaine reached into a utensil drawer for a knife. "He must regurgitate ideas, or something. I doubt that there's any serious thought involved."

"Mom!"

"Well, did you ever hear anything so patently stupid in your whole life as that idea?" With a slash that would have cut an oak in half, Elaine sliced the cake.

Leaning against the white tile counter, Janessa folded her arms. She wasn't really angry with her mother. Though Elaine had been behaving outrageously all evening, Simon was too wrapped up in himself, and the fact that he was having dinner at the home of the former Senator Knight, to even notice. But Janessa was concerned. She thought she saw pain under the caustic facade.

"Why did you invite Simon tonight?" Janessa asked.

"As I recall—" Elaine held the knife over the cake for a moment, apparently thinking back "—I was studying a watercolor at the Art Association auction, and Simon came over, completely destroying the rapport I was developing with this lovely pastoral scene." She sighed in reflection. "After he introduced himself to the women I was with, he went on at great length about how long it had been since he'd seen your father and me. And I, trying to be polite, said, well, we'd have to have him over for dinner sometime." Arching an eyebrow, she made another cut in the cake. "He said he was free the next Thursday. I wasn't fast enough on my feet to make an excuse. What do you see in him anyway?"

"He's just a friend, Mom." Janessa moved a stack of Limoges dessert plates within her mother's reach. "We have a lot in common."

With the supporting tip of her broad knife, Elaine transferred a slice of cake to a plate, then licked her finger. "Like what?"

Janessa had to think. What *had* attracted her to Simon? She wasn't sure. Perhaps it was just that he had arrived on the scene at a time when she'd been working too hard and the only men in her life for months had been those in her family. "Politics, I guess. That was so much a part of my life for so long."

Elaine looked up from her task to smile at her daughter. It as the first genuine smile Janessa had seen on her face all evening. "But you were the one who was the most pleased when your father got out of politics."

Janessa shrugged. That was true. "He's just someone to spend my time with. He's good company when he's not trying to find alternate funding for schools."

They laughed together for a moment. "You don't get out enough," Elaine said, placing two more pieces of cake on plates. "You work far too hard, then spend your free time at the Crown and Anchor with Jake and Clay. You need some romance in your life. Trust me, darling." She put the knife down and took Janessa's chin between her thumb and forefinger. "You're not going to find it with Senator Silly."

"Mother!" Biting back a laugh, Janessa took her mother's hand and shook it. "You've got to stop this." Getting serious suddenly, she folded her arms and faced Elaine with the same firm look she used to get years ago when their positions were reversed. "I want to know what's wrong with you and Dad."

"Nothing is wrong," Elaine insisted, her laughter evaporating. She diverted her eyes to the drawer where she reached for dessert forks.

"You two are having problems, aren't you?" Janessa pressed.

Elaine looked up at her, surprise as well as pain now visible in her eyes. Then both emotions were replaced with denial. "After almost forty years? Of course not."

As Elaine turned away to place the plates on a tray, Janessa put a hand to her shoulder, frightened now by the distance her mother was putting between them. Honesty had always been the backbone of their family.

"I saw you at Escobar's, Mom."

Without turning, Elaine said lightly, "I eat there all the time."

"You were alone in the lounge." Janessa waited a moment, then asked cautiously, "Is there another man?"

Elaine turned around, her eyes wide, her lips parted in surprise. "What? You think I . . . ?" As Janessa waited, expecting to be scolded for posing the question, Elaine paused and then laughed. "I suppose I should be flattered that you think I could attract another man. Thank you, Jannie."

"Have you?" Janessa insisted.

"No," Elaine said firmly. Picking up the tray, she started for the living room. "Come along. Alone with Simon all this time, your father is probably comatose by now."

"Mom—"

Elaine kept moving, adding quietly over her shoulder. "Darling, this is not the time."

Janessa caught her at the door and stopped her. "I'm picking you up for lunch on Monday," she said, shaking her finger in her mother's face with what she hoped was a sternness that would be taken seriously. "And I expect you to be prepared to tell me what's troubling you. Remember what you used to say to me after the accident, when I'd sulk and wouldn't talk to anyone? 'I'll knock on that wall till you let me in.' Well, I will. So there."

Elaine shook her head sadly. "You remind me more and more of Grandmother Knight."

"You loved her," Janessa pointed out.

"I know," Elaine admitted, shouldering her way through the swinging doors, "but she drove me crazy."

"I THINK THE EVENING went well," Simon said, escorting Janessa up her front steps. "While you were in the kitchen with your mother, your father really listened to the details of my tax plan. When I'm elected and it comes time to propose it, I think I'll be able to say that it has the ex-senator's approval."

On the porch, Janessa opened her purse to search for her key, wondering if she and Simon had been to the same dinner. She was unprepared for his swift grab at her shoulders and the teeth-grinding kiss that followed.

"What I really want," he said, holding her away from him, firming his grip, "is your approval of me. When are you going to agree to marry me?"

Janessa usually found it easy to parry his proposals, but tonight she was worried about her parents. "I don't have time to marry anyone, Simon," she said frankly. "I know you're ready to launch your career, but I'm not ready to settle down."

"I can wait till you're ready," he insisted, giving her shoulders a squeeze. "But when I'm senator, I'll need you beside me. I'd be lying if I denied that your experience in politics would be a big help to me. But that's not the only reason I need you."

"I have a growing business," she said gently, unable to decide just how serious he was. "And I want to be able to give myself to it completely for a while. And—" she sighed "—I like you, Simon, but that's all. At least, for now."

"Some of the best deals in government," he said urgently, "are cut between factions who'd never share the same bed, but who realize that they're critical to each other's political health."

Suspecting that she'd just been deemed sexually unappealing, Janessa pulled away to unlock her door. "I'm beat, Simon," she said. "Let's talk about this another— Ah!"

As she pulled her door open, a tall figure dressed in jeans and a blue pullover appeared out of the shadows of her dark living room to stand on the threshold. "Hi, Jannie. Hello, Pruitt." Clay smiled at Janessa and offered his hand to Simon. As Janessa put a hand to her pounding heart, Simon hesitated, then shook hands.

"Clay, you scared me!" Janessa slapped his arm with unconvincing vigor. But, happy to see him, she smiled. "What are you doing in my house?"

"We're robbing you." Jake emerged out of the darkness to stand beside Clay. He nodded at Simon, not bothering to offer a handshake. "That is, we were going to, until we realized we'd get thirty, maybe thirty-five dollars on the open market for the entire contents of your place."

"Jake?" Janessa looked up at her brother in surprise. "What...?"

"We accepted a delivery for you," he said, pushing the door wider. "Are you coming in?"

Janessa turned to Simon. "Would you like to...?"

Looking into the eyes of the men standing intimidatingly in the doorway, one pair icy blue and staring, the other brown and shrewdly watchful, Simon declined, backing away. "No, thanks. I'll call you tomorrow."

As Simon ran down the steps, Jake pulled Janessa into the dark living room. "You get the light," he said to Clay, then stood behind his sister, holding her in place with one hand while covering her eyes with the other.

"What is going on?" Janessa demanded, half laughing, half suspicious. She'd been the object of their jokes before.

She heard a click, then squinted against the light as Jake dropped his hand. "Oh!" she exclaimed in a whisper. In the middle of her living-room floor stood an old oak office chair with a wraparound back and brass casters under the claw feet. It had been restored by an expert. Attached to a leather-padded arm was a bright red bow.

She looked from her brother to her friend. "For me?"

The men glanced at each other. "No," Jake said. "It's for Clay. That's why we brought it here. He wants to know if you like it with or without the bow."

Ignoring him, Janessa walked around the chair, running her hand over the smooth finish. Then she sat in it, crossing her legs and resting an arm loosely on each arm of the chair. "How do I look?" she asked. "Important?"

Clay nudged Jake. "You strap her in and put the cap on her. I'll plug it in."

Janessa pursed her lips at Clay as she stood. "Very funny." She put her arms around Jake's neck and held him, touched by this gesture of support and affection. "Thanks, Jake. I love it."

"You're welcome, Jannie. We spotting it in an antique shop window in Portland and it seemed perfect."

"*Who* spotted it?" Clay asked pointedly. "And *who* is getting all the credit?"

"I'll bet you spotted it," Janessa said, moving to loop her arms around his neck. "The reporter who never misses anything. Thank you, Clay." She kissed his cheek and held him for a moment. He laughed and hugged her back.

Pulling away, she experienced a tiny crackle of feeling, as though something inside her had short-circuited. Time was suspended as Clay released her and she felt the movement of his hands down every inch of her arms.

Clay stopped, his hands cupping Janessa's elbows. He was experiencing the strangest sensation. She felt fragile in his hands, warm and womanly. He felt a gentle jab at the heart of him, as though he'd just taken eighty volts.

Then he focused on her smiling, slightly questioning expression. The gentle jab held. Startled, Clay took a step back and headed for the kitchen. "I'll get the champagne," he called over his shoulder to Jake. "You bring the chair."

"Champagne?" Janessa asked. She turned to follow Clay, then changed direction when Jake picked up the chair and headed for the door. "Where are you going with my chair?"

"To your shop," he replied as though that should have been obvious. "To see how it looks."

She looked at her watch. "At ten o'clock at night?"

"Why not?" he challenged, standing in front of the door. "Could you open this for your favorite sibling?"

She complied and followed him onto the porch. Clay appeared behind them with a bottle of champagne and a package of plastic glasses. Before Janessa could offer an opinion on the advisability of such a plan at that hour, she was bundled into the front seat of Jake's BMW. Clay and Jake stored her first piece of office furniture in the trunk, then with her between them, drove to her new shop on the now deserted river front.

Clay carried the chair up the stairs to her office while Jake followed with the champagne, pulling Janessa behind him. At the top of the stairs, she stopped, unable to speak. She had not been prepared for a second surprise.

Under the feeble office light was an oak desk with a slate top. This was no ornate rolltop with slots and cubbyholes. This was a no-nonsense, fifteen square feet of desk designed for the user who needed room to spread out.

Janessa went toward it, contemplating it. She would no longer have to design on the living-room floor. There would be ample room on the desk for fabric swatches, patterns, and the ribbons, buttons and notions with which she detailed her designs.

Clay pushed the chair in behind her, forcing her to sit. "We checked for secret compartments, but couldn't find any," he said. "This probably belonged to some judge, or banker, who had no secrets to keep. What do you think? Too masculine?"

"No!" Janessa's denial was vehement, and she spread both arms across the desk as though daring anyone to try to take it from her. The slate was cool under her hands. She touched her fingertips to it and felt the most fractional indentations of the numbers and letters from all the paperwork that must have passed over it. She was touched beyond description.

"I don't know what to say," she whispered, her eyes filling. "I thought the chair was such a thoughtful thing for the two of you to have done. Now..." She shook her head, words and composure failing her.

Jake sat on the corner of the desk and smiled down at her. "We're both very proud of how hard you've worked and how far you've come. This seemed like the best way to let you know—short of buying a gross of your sweat-shirts."

Jake sat helplessly as her tears spilled over. He watched Clay pull her out of the chair and into his arms, urging her not to cry. Clay had always had a way with her Jake couldn't master, probably because the burden of blame for all she had suffered still sat so heavily on him, even after all these years. If he lived to be a hundred, he would never forget what it had felt like to look down at the hospital bed at the silent, unmoving shell of what only hours before had been his warm, laughing sister.

It was impossible for him to look at her now, beautiful, smart and successful, and not think about how his care-lessness had almost killed her. Even in the depths of her pain she had never once suggested that the accident had been his fault. But he was resigned to the fact that he would carry the blame to his dying day.

"Jake!"

"Yeah?" He straightened and found Clay looking at him over the top of Janessa's head.

"Pour the champagne."

"Right."

"To Knight Shirts." In a tight circle near the desk, they lifted their glasses and drank. Then Janessa offered another toast. "To brotherly love, and friendships that last forever."

Composed again, Janessa sat on the edge of her desk, looking back at it over her shoulder. "I can't believe," she said in wonder, "that you guys went shopping for me. How did you get this up here?"

Jake sat beside her. "We had it delivered. We wanted it to be a surprise, so we had to wait till you'd gone home. The owner of the building let us in."

"We were going to just surprise you with it in the morning," Clay explained, leaning a hip against the gallery railing. Then he added artlessly, "But we couldn't wait. So we brought the chair with us, bought a bottle of champagne and camped out at your place to wait for you." He frowned. "You weren't very late. Was Pruitt that dull?"

Janessa rolled her eyes, then covered them with one hand. "The evening was a disaster!"

Jake gave Clay a look of self-righteous smugness and waited for Janessa to explain. But what she said was not what he expected.

"Mom needled him all evening long." She frowned at Jake and took another sip of champagne. "And when she wasn't after him, she was haranguing Dad. Something's wrong. You can cut the tension with a knife in our very own parents' living room. I'm really worried.''

Jake nodded. ''I thought something was wrong with Dad the other day when I met him for a drink. But they're two strong-minded people. They've always argued.''

''This wasn't arguing. This was ... darker, more serious.'' She stood abruptly and walked around the desk to sit in her new chair. ''But I'm not going to worry about them tonight. I'm going to wallow in my small successes and my great good fortune at being so spoiled. Now, really. Tell me the truth.'' She planted her palms on the desktop and put on a stern expression. ''Do I look like the next cover of *Forbes* magazine?''

Standing side by side in front of the desk, Jake leaning an elbow on Clay's shoulder, they studied her.

When did she become such a capable woman? Jake wondered. It seemed only yesterday that she was following them everywhere. He kind of missed that.

Had she always been this beautiful? Clay looked at her blue eyes aglow in a delicately shaped face flushed with champagne and excitement. Her hair was wound in an intricate knot at the nape of her neck, wisps of it falling loosely to catch the light.

''The April issue,'' Jake agreed, his tone gentle. ''Definitely.''

Clay nodded, having a little difficulty coming out of his thoughts. ''And probably *Fortune* and the front page of the *Wall Street Journal*.''

''Well.'' Standing, Janessa pushed her chair in reverently. ''I'm going to keep flowers on it all the time, and I'm going to design the most wonderful shirts on it.''

''And make a profit,'' Jake suggested.

''Of course.'' Janessa smiled up at her brother and her friend, emotion still strong in her eyes. ''Thanks, guys. You've blessed my business, and made my whole day.''

Clay turned to Jake. "Then I'd say we've done our part and we're free to call it a night."

"Right." Jake corked the champagne bottle and, grabbing his jacket off the gallery railing, started for the stairs. As Clay fell into step beside him, they began talking and laughing, apparently oblivious to Janessa. She stopped them at the bottom of the stairs with a shout.

"Guys!"

They turned simultaneously to find her halfway down the stairs. Both looked innocently curious. "Yeah?" Jake asked.

She walked slowly down the rest of the steps, a grin acknowledging their teasing. "I need a ride home," she reminded.

"Oh." Jake turned to Clay. "You take her. I have to check in at the Crown and Anchor."

Clay shook his head. "I can't take her. My car's at the tavern, remember? I rode here, then to her place with you."

"You mean I have to take her?"

Janessa folded her arms in feigned indignation. "Well, I'm sorry to be such a thief of your time, but I'm not to blame. I was virtually kidnapped and brought here."

Clay nodded. "That's true. I'm a witness."

Janessa laughed at him. "You're a perpetrator!"

He shrugged. "A perpetrator, but also a witness. Could we go? I have a 10 a.m. deadline on a column I haven't even written yet."

"Do I have to do everything?" Jake demanded with a theatrically aggrieved air. "I mean there are three of us here, and who's always doing the cooking, and the driving, and . . ."

"The talking," Janessa added in a quiet aside to Clay as she locked the door.

Jake looked up from opening his car door. "I heard that." The friendly harassment continued all the way to Janessa's. Then she hugged Jake and kissed him soundly on the cheek. "Thanks again. I've never had a lovelier gift."

He squeezed her shoulders. "You're welcome. I've never enjoyed giving one so much. I'll be by to help you paint this weekend."

"Thanks. I love you."

"I love you, too," he replied. "Get outta here."

Outside of the car, Janessa looked at Clay and gave his arm a punch. "Thanks, old buddy. I love the desk."

"My pleasure." He leaned down to kiss her cheek as he had done countless times over the years. But she put a hand to his arm and something subtle in the contact changed. Just having convinced himself he'd imagined the episode earlier, he felt the same little zing of shock he'd felt when she'd thanked him for the chair.

He straightened, pushing her out to arm's length. "I'll be by Saturday afternoon. Have the paint sprayer ready." Then he was in the car and Jake was driving away.

Janessa let herself into the house, wondering about the little pulse ticking in her throat.

Chapter Five

"I think the quality of our clientele is deteriorating, Jake." Dexter Gordon, the Crown and Anchor's daytime bartender, poured a tomato juice, popped a stick of celery in it, and pushed it across the bar.

Clay, in paint-spattered jeans and sweatshirt, reached for it, stirring with the celery as he drew it toward him. "I'm on a mission of mercy, Dex," he said, "and how I look is of minor importance compared to the expertise I bring to the task of remodeling Janessa's shop."

Dexter leaned an elbow on the bar and exchanged a look with Jake, who was arranging clean glasses in an overhead rack. "I seem to remember an incident with a paint sprayer when this place was—"

Clay rolled his eyes. "Another one with a long memory," he grumbled, sipping his juice. "Make one mistake and no one lets you forget it."

In response to a beckoning wave from a customer at the other end of the bar, Dexter began to move away. He grinned at Clay over his shoulder. "Tell Jannie I said hi."

Jake leaned his elbows on the bar and looked at Clay expectantly. "Well? Did you get it?" he asked softly.

"Yeah." Clay took another sip of juice. "But it doesn't tell us anything. Simon Pruitt's service record is squeaky clean, if a little undistinguished. He held a lot of office

jobs, spent some time in the hospital, and scored misera-
bly on the rifle range. Not exactly the background of a
felon.''

Jake nodded thoughtfully. ''Did you find out why he
was in the hospital?''

''Hernia.''

''Is there anything else you can do?''

''I'm sifting through everything the newspaper library
has on him. Unfortunately, someone embarking on public life generates a lot of publicity. I don't think there's
anything there, but I'll keep looking.''

''Thanks.'' Jake straightened. ''Another juice?''

''I'd better get moving.'' Clay stepped off the stool and
reached into his pocket for change.

''Ah . . . Clay?''

''Yeah?''

''The juice is on the house.'' Jake's eyes went slowly up
and down Clay's disreputable attire. ''Save your money.
Buy a new sweatshirt. And next time you come by, try to
remember that classy people come here. I mean, we have
an image to main—''

Clay took the stalk of celery from his empty glass and
stuck it in Jake's mouth. ''See you later,'' he said, grinning at Dexter, who began to laugh but changed his mind
after a look from his employer.

THE MELODY WAS OFF-KEY, the harmony was definitely
off, though enthusiastic, and Clay couldn't recognize the
tune—at least not at first. But the choreography made up
for everything.

He found Janessa and Annie in a back corner of Janessa's shop, each wielding a roller spreading almond-
colored paint away from the corner. They were working in
opposite directions, singing at the tops of their voices.
With their hands occupied on the roller handles, they kept

the beat with their hips, each woman's style distinct and spirited.

Before making his presence known, Clay allowed himself a moment to observe. Annie, in slim jeans and an old T-shirt, swayed forward then back with the movement of the roller, then danced a fancy step as she stopped to dip the roller in the pan. Watching her slim hips move, Clay felt sure Jake would abandon whatever old grievances he held against her if he could just see her in action.

Janessa, in coveralls that must have once belonged to a giant, pranced in place. A tantalizing swaying motion in the middle of the baggy bottoms provided a rough idea of where her derriere was. For a moment he couldn't take his eyes from the undulation.

Then, apparently having reached the tune's lively chorus, Janessa dropped her roller to the pan and did a finger-snapping sidestep, ending in a pirouette. Then she saw Clay.

"You rat!" she accused, laughing. "How long have you been standing there?"

"Long enough," he replied. "Want to buy my silence?"

"Not unless you got pictures."

"You'd better be nice to him," Annie advised, dropping her roller in the pan and offering the handle to Clay. "I've got to leave. This torturous device is all yours, sir."

Clay took the handle and bowed with a flourish. "You're too good to me, my lady."

Annie rolled her eyes. "Only because it's such a relief to be leaving this martinet." She patted his shoulder pityingly. "Be sure that you overlap your strokes carefully, draw them down evenly, and don't waste paint or she'll be all over you. And you have to sing with her."

Clay pointed to the tape player at his feet with a smug smile. "I brought some tunes."

"Oh!" Janessa looked delighted and got down on her knees to investigate the box of tapes beside the player. "Billy Ocean, the Nylons, Carly Simon. Great!"

Annie shook her head. "I wish I'd thought of that. Well, I'm off. You two have fun."

Janessa got to her feet to walk Annie to the door. "Thanks a bunch for giving up your Saturday morning. I really appreciate it."

"Glad to help. I can't come tomorrow, but I'll be here bright and early Monday morning, probably with Mark."

"That's fine. Just bring his playpen and stuff and we'll find a comfortable place for him. 'Bye, Annie."

Janessa went back to her roller, dipped it in the paint-filled pan, then paused to admire the strong, smooth stroke of Clay's roller as it spread paint without apparent effort in a broad even stripe. Carly Simon was already singing on the tape player he had put under a sawhorse, out of the way.

Clay was working with the quiet confidence with which he did everything. Watching the stretch of his arms, the bunching then relaxing of his muscles, Janessa was reminded of her exercise sessions when she'd been recovering from the accident. He had moved in that same way then, carefully but with great strength. Her muscles had hurt her, but he never had.

He stopped to dip the roller and saw her watching him. "Are you here in a supervisory capacity?" he asked with a grin.

She was always aware of what a good friend he was and tried hard never to take him for granted. But now, as he forfeited a rare free day to help her paint, she realized how often he did selfless things on her behalf. "I appreciate your coming, Clay," she said gravely.

He looked back at her, noting her change of mood. "I know you do," he replied, his laughter ebbing. "That's why I'm here."

"I'll treat you to beer and pizza afterward."

"That's the second reason I'm here."

They worked in companionable silence for several hours. The Nylons followed Carly Simon, and Billy Ocean brought back all the wild moments of *Jewel of the Nile*, a film Jake, Clay and Janessa had seen together.

They stopped once in the middle of the afternoon to have tea Janessa had brought in a thermos. They went back to painting until it grew dark and Janessa had to turn the light on to enable them to see what they were doing.

What she saw when the light struck the newly painted walls made her walk to the middle of the room and look around in wonder.

"It's beautiful," she breathed, both hands joined at her chest as she did a slow turn. Three walls had been transformed from dingy beige to soft almond. It made a palace out of a dungeon.

Halfway finished with the fourth wall, Clay glanced over his shoulder then continued to work. "Beautiful may be a little strong."

"It is not," she insisted. "Come over here and look. You can't tell from over there."

Standing his roller in the pan and leaning the handle against the unpainted part of the wall, Clay joined Janessa in the middle of the room. He looked around while wiping a streak of paint from his face with the back of his hand. The lighter paint had made a big difference, he noted, but the biggest transformation was on Janessa's face.

If there was any one thing he loved about her, it was her great capacity for optimism. In the enormous, disreputable coveralls with paint all over her face and in her hair, she was radiant with the dirty work of making her dreams come true. With his hands on his hips, Clay looked around once more and had to acknowledge, "It is beautiful."

Janessa looped both arms around his left one and leaned her head against his upper arm. "I can't believe I'm finally going to have a place of my own," she said. Her voice was dreamy and tired. "With my business name on a sign, and a receptionist answering the phone with 'Knight Shirts.'" She expelled a dramatic sigh. "After all these years—my own place."

"All these years," he said teasingly. "You're only twenty-seven."

She looked up at him and made an ugly face. "I know, but how long have I been decorating shirts? I made one for you with a quill on it when I was only thirteen. I dreamed of this long before I ever mentioned it to anyone. Even when I was in the wheelchair."

He looked down at her in surprise. "I didn't know that."

"Actually—" she leaned away from him, smiling reminiscently "—in those days I dreamed of an elegant boutique with all sorts of fancy things specially designed by—" she paused to lend drama to the name "—Janessa."

"Then?"

"Then I decided that was too serious for me. I mean, I have sort of an intrinsic . . . lightheartedness."

"Silliness," he corrected.

She nodded grudgingly. "Maybe that's it. Anyway, signature sweatshirts seemed like fun as well as work, so I tried it, and sure enough, it is. And my customers love them. They're sort of a badge of individuality, a personal crest."

He laughed lightly. "Teddy bears rampant on a field of polka dots." She had made hundreds of shirts with teddy bears last year and he had even been rooked into helping her pack them one weekend when Graciella was ill.

She looked at him severely. "Don't laugh. Those shirts are buying your pizza."

"Now?" he asked hopefully.

"Right now." She gave the arm she still held a friendly pinch. "Want to go out for it, or do you want me to bring it back?"

He looked down at himself, then at her, and grimaced. "We're not very presentable. And I can probably finish this wall while you go get it."

She went across the room to the corner where she had left her purse and jacket. "The combination without anchovies, right?"

"Right," he answered, already dipping the roller. "And don't forget the beer."

"See you in twenty minutes."

"HAVE YOU GIVEN any more thought to the *Los Angeles Times* job?" Janessa asked. They were sitting in the middle of the shop floor on a blanket she had brought in from her car. The empty pizza box had been pushed aside. Clay reclined on an elbow, sipping his beer while Janessa sat, arms clasped around her bent knees, staring through the wide store window into the darkness beyond. The shop lights had been turned off to afford privacy while they relaxed.

"I think about it once in a while," he admitted, "when it's rainy and cold and a sandy beach seems so inviting. Then I remember that downtown Los Angeles is warmer, but probably no more inviting than downtown Salem. Maybe even less."

A car passed, its headlights slowly illuminating the room and Janessa's concerned expression before moving on.

"Don't you think you should at least go and talk to them?"

"I'm tied up right now with a couple of stories I'm working on." He looked down at his beer as he spoke, afraid that even in the dark she'd see the lie of omission in his eyes. His investigation of Simon Pruitt was beginning to work on his peace of mind in two ways. He was concerned about Janessa keeping company with the man if he was connected with Santiago in some way. Yet, he was beginning to feel guilty about digging into Simon's past without telling Janessa what he was doing. Of course, if he told her, she'd be furious. And he did owe a certain loyalty to Jake in this instance.

He took another sip of beer, thinking with bleak humor that he'd seen displays of his friends' tempers often enough to seek any other alternative.

"Another political investigation?" she asked.

He nodded, feeling safe in admitting that was true.

"Anyone Simon might know? I could probably talk him into doing a little sleuthing for you."

He bit back the swift no that sprang to his lips, waiting a moment to reply calmly. "I don't think so. In these cases, the fewer snitches involved, the better."

She laughed softly, the sound echoing musically in the empty room. "I don't think Simon would like to be known as a snitch. Bad for his political image."

"What would he like to be known as?" he asked easily. "Mr. President?"

"I'm sure he fantasizes about that." Janessa stretched out her legs and leaned back on both elbows, staring thoughtfully into space. "He'd like me to be known as Mrs. Simon Pruitt."

There was a moment's silence. Then Clay asked quietly, "Are you thinking about it?"

"No. I've got too much going on right now. I don't have time to get married and be a slave to politics."

"What if you didn't have the shop?"

She sighed, turning her head to focus on him. He could just discern her frown in the meager light from the street. "I don't love Simon. I keep telling him that. He said that some of the best deals in government are cut between factions who'd never share the same bed, but who realize they're critical to each other's political health."

When Clay made a scornful sound, she turned, leaning her weight on the elbow closest to him to look at him earnestly. "In view of what's happening to my mother and father, maybe he isn't wrong. They were the classic case of a love match, and now they're sparring partners. Maybe relationships based on being able to fulfill each other's non-romantic needs have a higher survival rate."

"You mean supply and demand?" Clay asked. "That's how you conduct a business, not a marriage."

"How do you know?" she challenged. "You aren't involved in either. You're paid to observe and philosophize. And you do it without a mate."

Clay frowned at her. "Would you want to be married to someone whose kisses you pull away from?"

Janessa was completely startled by the question. "Who says I pull away from Simon?"

Clay sat up, downing his last sip of beer. "I saw you," he said simply. Before she could accuse him of spying, he added quickly, a hand raised to stop her sputtering, "It was the night you came home from dinner at your mother's. Jake and I were inside your place with your desk chair. We weren't snooping, but you'd left the curtains open. Your clinch on the porch was impossible to miss." He was silent a moment, then smirked. "And not very impressive."

Janessa expelled a sigh of exasperation. "Nice of you to rate us. I suppose you have a lot more style."

He lifted a negligent shoulder. "I never lack for company."

"Perhaps," Janessa suggested with subtle sarcasm, "the long string of beautiful women moving in and out of your life suggests a dearth of ability rather than an abundance."

A pulse was beginning to tick in Clay's throat that had nothing to do with anger at her barb. It seemed to involve another emotion altogether. "No," he replied.

Janessa sat up as her heartbeat quickened. Within seconds of her becoming aware of it, it threatened to suffocate her. She felt strangely out of tune with what was happening, yet driven all the same toward something she didn't understand. "Well," she said, her tone and manner offhand as she sat on her heels. "Your readers may believe your every word, but I don't."

For someone who prided himself on always being in control of himself and the situation, Clay felt suddenly as though all the rules had changed. He felt both disoriented and acutely sensitized. And he was about to do something for which he would probably hate himself later, but he couldn't stop himself.

"I don't blame you," he said, an arm resting on his raised knee. "I always require proof before I make a judgment."

The earth tipped out of orbit and Janessa struggled for her grip on it. But she didn't fight the direction the tilt was taking her.

"All right, then," she said, her voice barely recognizable. "*I* require proof."

"Then you shall have it." Clay rose to his knees, only inches away from her in the darkness. Slowly he put one cool hand to her face. "First, the decision to kiss should never be reached solitarily, as Simon's was. A man should telegraph the move in order to allow the lady to prepare to enjoy it, or to decline the suggestion.''

Clay's hand did nothing but simply lie against her face, yet it immobilized her. She had trouble swallowing. ''You don't . . . believe in being forceful?''

He gave a small shake of his head, his eyes looking into hers. ''That causes the lady to tense, or to be annoyed. Either reaction negates the pleasure. A man should then gently make contact. A touch on the lady's arm, a hand to her face.''

''Contact,'' Janessa repeated in a whisper, her eyes locked with his.

''Then, with gentle pressure . . .'' The hand at her face slipped back to cup her head, bringing her forward with no more force than the pull of his eyes. He was trembling, he thought in amazement. Or was she? ''. . . he brings her into his arms. She must feel that no harm will come to her there so that, ultimately, when there is no longer time for escape, it will be the last thing on her mind.''

With that his mouth came down, lips slightly parted, and met hers. His lips were cool and tasted subtly of Italian spice and beer. Their touch was gentle, and Janessa, captivated by the wonder of kissing this man who had always been so like a brother, slid her arms around his neck and leaned into him.

With her body pliant in his arms, Clay became persuasive. His mouth moved along her cheek to her ear, his touch like a mere breath against her. Then, taking her face in both hands, he kissed her eyes closed, put his lips against her other cheek and drew back to her mouth to kiss her with tender fervor one last lingering time.

They drew apart slowly, Clay both amazed and horrified by what he had done, Janessa delighted and shocked that she had participated. Her heart pounded and she felt an emphatic beat under the hand she held against the sweatshirt.

Entranced and confused by the languorous downward sweep of Janessa's lashes, Clay cleared his voice, striving for a light tone. "Now," he said, holding her at arm's length. "Wasn't that preferable to being yanked and crushed without warning?"

Still mesmerized, Janessa replied quietly, but with heartfelt sincerity, "Infinitely." He was right. He had no dearth of style.

In a swift movement, he got to his feet and offered her a hand up. Then he scooped up the pizza box and the cans and tossed them into a large refuse bag in a corner.

"Think twice before you agree to marry Pruitt," he said, picking up the blanket and folding it while she retrieved their jackets and her purse, "unless you think he'll be so involved in his career that he won't have time for kissing."

Janessa had no idea how to answer him. For one thing, she hadn't completely heard him. Her mind was awash with sensation that made clear thought impossible, at least for the moment.

"Okay," he said, taking her arm and walking with her to the door. "Ignore me. Just don't ignore your feelings. What's the schedule for tomorrow?"

Forcing herself to think, Janessa followed him out the door and pulled it closed, locking it. "Putting on the second coat. But I don't expect you to give up your entire weekend. Surely Margie is awaiting your attention."

Margie worked in the *Standard News* library and he'd spent some time with her. But she had dreams of affluence and high living and he didn't. "What time?"

"I'll be here at seven," she said. When he winced she added with a coaxing smile, "with jelly doughnuts and coffee."

He sighed, won over. "I'm so easy."

Careful not to touch him, Janessa said good-night, got into her car and started the motor. To show him, and probably herself, that nothing outrageous had happened, she blew him a kiss as she drove away.

Wondering if she had fooled him, Janessa had to acknowledge as she drove through the dark, nearly deserted streets, that she hadn't deceived herself. A breathlessness that had begun when she first realized he intended to kiss her had not been relieved.

She put a hand to her mouth and found that her lips were curved in a smile. She felt as though she'd just done something unspeakably wicked and was depraved enough to have enjoyed it. Good grief, she thought in startled wonder, what was happening to her?

CLAY STARED AT THE CURSOR at the top of his monitor. It was demanding a brilliant lead, magic prose, surgical wit that would define the state's political problems and see a way toward solving them. But at the moment he could barely remember his name.

He had come to the office rather than go home when he left Janessa, because he knew he wouldn't be able to relax there. He'd thought he needed something to do, something demanding to divert his mind. But his mind refused to be diverted.

He could still feel Janessa in his arms, smelling of paint and pizza and the spicy floral scent that always surrounded her. Though she had probably long since gone to bed, her lips still tickled his, the touch of her cool, long-fingered hands at his neck lingering to make a mockery of his late-night attempt to work.

He was a useless hulk of anguish and remorse. He had taken into his arms the woman who had been a sister to him for almost as long as he could remember, and kissed her like a lover. Oh, there had been no blazing passion in the kiss, but the tender seduction of it had been almost as deadly. The desire to experience it again was already clamoring in him.

He hated himself. Janessa probably hated him, too. Although, thinking back on the incident, he remembered clearly the inclination of her soft body against his, and later, the lazy satisfied look in her eyes.

His heart gave an uneasy jolt. She had enjoyed the kiss as much as he had. Well, that had been what he'd intended at the outset of the playful experiment. That had been his point, though he hadn't planned to make it so effectively.

Tomorrow, he decided firmly, he would pick up Jake so they could arrive at Janessa's shop together. Then he would keep a careful distance from her until this glandular aberration he was suffering had passed. My God, he thought, as he finally turned off the monitor and shut down his terminal, deeming the effort to work lost. How could I have let that happen?

ELAINE KNIGHT REMOVED the cellophane-tipped toothpick that held her club sandwich together. With a careful jab into the heart of the green olive that sat on a patch of lettuce at the side of her plate, she removed the pimento, studied it in obvious anticipation, then popped it into her mouth.

Janessa looked around at the other patrons in the elegant Victorian glass-domed restaurant, wondering if any of them had noticed that the former doyenne of Salem's political society had just gutted an olive. But they all seemed occupied with their own lunches and conversations.

"Don't look so horrified, Jannie." Elaine now picked up the olive in her fingers and stuck it on the beautifully manicured fingernail on her left pinky. Then she wiggled it. "I no longer have a reputation to maintain. I can be wicked and outrageous and who's to care?" She bit the olive off her finger and chewed. "It makes life so much more fun. You should try it."

Janessa tried to remain calm. In the face of her mother's obvious list in the direction of insanity, she found it difficult. Guessing that Elaine was out to shock and upset her and thus divert her from finding out what was wrong, she sipped at her cream of asparagus soup. "Does that imply that Daddy doesn't care?" she asked.

Elaine picked up a triangle of sandwich and bit off a point. Grateful that she hadn't decided to take it apart and eat it with a toothpick, Janessa waited patiently.

"It implies that I see a whole new world opening up for me."

Janessa felt a mild stab of alarm. "I know how much you love working at the museum," she said, hoping that that was what she meant.

"Oh, that stuffy old place." Elaine dismissed it with a wave of her hand and took another bite.

Janessa sipped at her soup, refusing to succumb to panic. "Then what are you referring to?"

Elaine shrugged and looked up at the clear blue sky visible through the lead-stitched panes of glass that formed the ceiling. "Oh, I don't know," she replied dreamily. "Nameless things. Things I've had to push from my mind for years—almost an entire lifetime. Travel, excitement, romance..."

Janessa swallowed a spoonful of soup that was too hot and reached for her glass of water, which she gulped while Elaine nibbled at her sandwich. "Romance," Janessa repeated, sitting tall in her chair in an unconscious effort to intimidate. "I presume you mean with Daddy."

Elaine looked across the table at her daughter with a look that was level and completely serious. "No, darling, I don't."

Janessa could not hold back the gasp. "Just last Thursday you insisted that nothing was wrong, that . . . that . . ."

"That was Thursday." Elaine dabbed at her mouth with a pink linen napkin, then spread the cloth across her lap again with deliberate care. "I have since decided that there's no point in trying to protect you from the truth. The more I try to pretend it isn't happening, the less I'm able to cope with it."

Elaine took a swift sip of blush wine and angled her chin as she swallowed. The barest trace of a tremor at her bottom lip was the first sign Janessa had seen in her mother today that she recognized.

She reached a hand across the table and curled her fingers around Elaine's. "Mom, what's happening?" she asked in quiet desperation. "What's wrong?"

For one moment, Elaine's eyes filled with a kind of shocked misery. Certain that tears were going to follow, Janessa tightened her grip on her mother's fingers. But Elaine drew a deep breath. The misery was replaced with a quiet anger and the tears didn't materialize.

"Your father seems to have decided that he no longer loves me." Janessa heard the hurt surprise under the calm accepting statement. "I've made all sorts of suggestions about getting away, going to a counsellor or a therapist, but he refuses. And I won't live this way any longer."

"Mom." Janessa's whisper conveyed sympathy and horror and total disorientation.

Suddenly it was Elaine offering comfort with a squeeze of Janessa's hand. "I know, Jannie. I couldn't quite believe it at first, either. But denying it doesn't help. I think our marriage is over."

The calm conviction with which the words were spoken struck Janessa with the force of a wrecking ball. This was no melodramatic declaration made by her mother for shock effect. She was serious.

The slightly superior attitude with which Janessa had approached this meeting dissolved into helplessness. She had been so sure that if she just knew what the problem was between her parents she could tell them how to fix it. Her mother's grave acceptance made Janessa's confronting her seem like immature conceit. She swallowed, trying to find her voice. "Can you tell me what happened?"

Elaine shook her head, releasing Janessa's hand to take another sip of wine. "Not in detail." She smiled wryly over the tulip glass. "There are some fine points of a marriage to which even the children of that marriage can't be privileged. I can tell you only that we haven't formally agreed on a divorce, but I'm quite sure it will come to that."

Remembering vaguely that she had suggested something like this before, Janessa asked, "Does Daddy have someone else?"

Elaine smiled again. "When you're young, you're so sure that's the worst thing that can happen to a marriage."

Janessa blinked. "Isn't it?"

"Well, I wouldn't stand for it, of course." Elaine dabbed at her mouth again and pushed the plate with the other half of her sandwich away. "But that would at least be something I could confront. This ... is something I've tried to fight, but can't seem to win against. And it's wearing me out."

Janessa looked at her mother, saw the chicly styled hair, the blue eyes still so lively and usually mischievous, the beautiful pale skin lined in attractive maturity around her mouth and eyes, and had to strain to see the weariness there, the acute anguish.

Guilt plagued her. While she'd been building her business, planning the move, celebrating every little step forward, her parents' world had been falling apart. "What can I do?" she asked, the panic she'd been pushing back all through lunch taking over. "I mean...I know the details aren't my business...but I'm your daughter. I can't just let my parents break up without trying to do something. Can't you be a little more—" she groped for the right word and finally spoke it cautiously "—specific?"

Elaine shook her head, serene but resolved. "I can't, Janessa."

"I'll ask Daddy," Janessa said, the threat sounding petulant and childish.

To her surprise, a small smile curved Elaine's mouth. "Why don't you do that? Now—" she picked up the check and perused it thoughtfully "—since I've obviously spoiled your lunch and probably your whole day, I'll buy."

Chapter Six

Janessa spotted Clay on the far side of the city room. Ignoring the interested stares that followed her, she wove her way among cluttered desks and bustling people, trying to ignore the cacophonic ring of telephones, the sounds of spirited conversation and the general noise that fills a busy, metropolitan newspaper office.

The panic she had felt at finding his office empty and the receptionist's saying, "You might check the art department, because I think he was going to stop there before going home...." was beginning to recede when she found him.

Clay was leaning over a drawing table, his briefcase in one hand, his suit jacket slung over his other shoulder. He was laughing with the artist who was holding up a sketch.

"The Chamberlain umbrella is a nice touch," he was saying as Janessa approached. "If there's a lawsuit we may as well look as guilty as possible."

Distracted, Janessa caught sight of a sketch of Senator Dawson, Chamberlainlike umbrella in hand as he stepped out of a small plane labeled Fiscal Irresponsibility.

Clay's eyes looked up from the sketch and saw Janessa on the other side of the art table, her manner carefully controlled, her eyes frantic.

"Hi," she said. "Are you on your way home?"

He heard the frantic quality in her voice, as well. "Yeah. You need a lift?"

"Yes." She glanced from him to the artist and smiled apologetically. "I'm sorry. I can wait till you're finished."

"We're finished," the man assured her, then turned to Clay with a grin. "Don't keep her waiting."

"Thanks, Bill. It's perfect." Pulling the jacket from his shoulder and transferring it to the hand that held his briefcase, Clay put his arm around Janessa and led her away. They stepped into an empty elevator and he said gently, "I take it lunch with your mom didn't go well."

Holding on to him instead of the railing to steady herself as the elevator made its descent, Janessa shook her head. "They're getting a divorce, Clay. I can't believe it!"

Through the lightweight wool of her camel tweed jacket she felt his hand move up and down her spine. His touch both comforted and upset her. For the first time since she'd met her mother for lunch, she remembered the kiss she and Clay had shared in the shop on Saturday night.

Looking up into his eyes, she found the same slight restraint there that she suddenly felt and wondered if she had made a mistake in coming to him. It had been instinctive, a decision reached without conscious thought in that moment of dismay when she had finished lunch with her mother. She had run the five blocks to her old friend as though pulled there, caught in some magnetic force.

The elevator doors parted and Clay guided Janessa out onto the sidewalk and headed for the parking structure across the street. At midafternoon, the traffic was light, the usually busy streets of the state capital almost quiet. Janessa pulled against him just as he was about to enter the dark, cavernous building.

He stopped, looking down at her with a frown.

"Where are you going?" she asked.

"Home," he said, "where we can talk." When she continued to look at him with an odd uncertainty that was beginning to throw him off balance, he added, slightly impatient, "I presume that's why you came to find me in the middle of the afternoon."

She nodded, folding her arms in a defensive gesture. "I didn't stop to think that you might have other plans for the rest of the day."

"I don't," he replied simply.

Feeling oppressed by this uncomfortable constraint, Janessa pulled on the hand he was still holding. "I should just get back to work...."

He pulled her back, holding fast to her hand. "Jannie..."

The one soft word completely disarmed her. She put a hand to her head and sighed. "I don't know what's the matter with me. Could we just go to Georgio's and get a cup of coffee?"

"Of course," he said, drawing her into the darkness of the parking building. "Whatever you want."

Georgio's was a drive-in near the bridge, not far from Janessa's shop. A nostalgic remnant of the fifties, the place still had carhops on roller skates and food was still served on metal trays that affixed to the car window. Georgio's also still had the best onion rings in town. Janessa nibbled on one to satisfy the growling in her stomach.

"Did you and your mom fight instead of eat?" Clay asked, questioning her hunger. He'd tossed his briefcase and tie in the back and leaned in the corner behind the steering wheel, his suit coat and shirt collar open. He sipped at a steaming Styrofoam cup of coffee.

Janessa shook her head. "I didn't fight with her. I didn't even know what to say. She seemed so—" thinking back to her mother's stern chin, she closed her eyes, wishing she could blot out the entire morning "—certain that it's all over. They're getting a divorce. My parents. Your foster parents." Her voice rose in disbelief. "Senator and Mrs. Ethan Knight!"

"Easy, Jan," Clay cautioned quietly. "Did she tell you what's wrong?"

Leaning her head back against the passenger side window, she sighed. "She said she couldn't be specific. That there were some things her children couldn't know. It's not another man or woman, but it must be something awful."

"Have you talked to Jake?"

"No." She reached into the bag between them for another onion ring. She looked into Clay's dark eyes with aggressive challenge, presuming his reluctance to interfere. "I thought you would help me."

He began to shake his head. "Janessa, I can't meddle in their—"

"When Mom wouldn't tell me what the problem is," Janessa interrupted, "I told her I'd ask my father. She smiled and said, 'Maybe you should do that.'"

"The operative word being you," Clay said.

Janessa pursed her lips impatiently. "You know he won't tell me anything. We love each other dearly, and I know he's proud of me and all, but he'd never share that kind of thing with me. He's just too used to shielding his women from everything, particularly his little girl."

Feeling the trap tighten around him, Clay suggested feebly, "Then Jake should—"

"They'd be fighting before Jake had been there five minutes." Janessa's voice softened. "Clay, it has to be you. He loves you as much as he loves Jake and me, and he respects your honesty. He—"

"Stop!" he pleaded, defeated. "All right, all right. I'll talk to him, but if he throws me out and tells me never to darken his door again, I'll hold you personally responsible."

"He'd never do that to you."

Clay angled her a doubtful glance. "Famous last words."

CLAY GUIDED his Camaro up the curved drive lined with Lombardy poplars. But instead of going to the house, he stopped at the deep, four-car garage. Since his retirement, Ethan spent his free time working on an elaborate model-train setup in one half of the garage. Janessa's telephone call to Clay in the afternoon, advising him that her mother had a museum staff meeting that evening, had closed the trap. He'd come to talk to Ethan as he'd promised.

Before Clay was out of the car, Ethan was raising the garage door, squinting into the twilight to see who had arrived. "Hi, Ethan." Clay went forward, hand extended, feeling like a charlatan. In his left hand he held up a squat bottle. "I was working tonight," he lied, "and needed a break. Join me in an Irish cream?"

Ethan looked pleased if a little surprised. "Of course. Come on in." He shook hands then pulled on Clay's arm, closing the garage door behind them.

Beyond them, a highly polished blue Mercedes gleamed under the garage light. The spot beside it where Elaine's white one usually stood was vacant. But in this part of the garage, the width of two car spaces, was a roughly built table that supported a miniature turn-of-the-century town through which wove a seven-car train. Clay approached the table with a smile; it had been a while since he'd seen the layout.

When he'd first come to live with the Knights, he'd spent a lot of time in the garage with Ethan. Jake had never been that interested in the trains, but Clay had found their minute perfection fascinating.

Those had been important days for him. It wasn't that he and Ethan had spoken much. In fact, except for an eloquence that surfaced on the senate floor, Ethan was a quiet man. But he had been there when Clay's own father had been across the world, and he seemed to understand his loneliness and his sense of insecurity.

Clay put an arm around the shoulders of the man who was now a good half a foot shorter than he was. "You got that roundhouse yet?" Clay's eyes scanned the board, looking for it. Ethan had wanted a roundhouse since those days when Clay had worked with him.

"No," he grumped good-naturedly. "Still can't find a kit I like. They're all plastic now, you know, and I don't want that. Can't find a plan for one, either. Sit down, son. I'll get some glasses."

Sitting on an old peeling footlocker on which was folded a ragged army blanket, Clay watched Ethan's barrellike body disappear into the house. He took the moment of privacy to run a hand down his face and sigh disgustedly. The things he did for his friends.

"Now, then." Ethan returned, a brown-and-tan plaid flannel shirt hanging open over his bulky middle. He put two squatty glasses on the corner of the table. "Who sent you? Jake or Janessa?"

Clay laughed, both embarrassed and surprised. "How'd you know?" He handed over the bottle.

Ethan poured, glancing at Clay with a wry grin over the top of his glasses. "They've always conned you into doing what they couldn't. Here. To bends in the road."

Clay reached forward to touch glasses, but he didn't like the sound of that toast. "Actually," he said, as Ethan lowered himself into an old armchair, apparently relegated to the garage because of its age, "I'm here as much for myself as for them. We're all worried about you and Elaine, Ethan. Jannie had lunch with her mother today and came away very upset."

Ethan nodded, his lips tightening as he swirled the creamy contents of his glass. "We're all upset. You never think this kind of thing will happen to you."

Clay leaned his elbows on his knees, holding the glass in both hands. "Does it have to happen, Ethan?"

He continued to nod without raising his head. "Yeah. We don't have much in common anymore. Elaine's got a good job that she enjoys, and I...well..." Ethan shrugged and emptied his glass with a swift gesture. "Playing with these trains is about all I do anymore."

Clay straightened, alerted to the undercurrent in Ethan's voice. "You're retired after an illustrious career. You've done much more than your share. You're entitled to spend your time with your trains."

"Ach!" He made a disgusted sound that seemed to describe himself and his situation. "My bones creak, my muscles don't work, and I'm..." He shook his head wearily, pouring another drink. "I'm a useless old man, son. And my woman doesn't need me anymore." He held up the bottle. "Another one?"

Clay held out his glass. He needed one more to deal with this. "I don't believe that. In fact, according to what Jannie told me, it's Elaine who thinks you no longer love her."

When Ethan said nothing, Clay borrowed a tactic from Janessa and pushed. "Do you?"

Ethan turned to him with a look Clay remembered getting in his childhood whenever he had done something really stupid. "Do you honestly think I could ever stop?"

"Then why?" he asked desperately. "Why a divorce? Why not counseling or a therapist or—"

Ethan sprang from his chair. There was little evidence of creaking bones. "Therapist!" he spat. "I know my marriage, and I know my wife. It's over."

"The great Senator Knight just gives up?" Clay asked quietly.

Ethan spun on him, color flooding his face. "The six inches you've got on me won't help you, Clay, if you push me too far."

Bravely, Clay arched an eyebrow. "I thought you were a useless old man?"

Ethan glared at him for a minute, then turned to the table, downing the contents of his glass. "I am. Weaknesses aren't always visible."

"Then people who want to help can't if you don't tell them how."

Ethan turned back to Clay, his expression no longer angry, but fond. "Give Jannie a big hug for me, tell her that I love her, and the best thing all of you can do for Elaine and me right now is let us be."

Clay had been convinced of that when he'd driven over here. Now he wasn't so sure. Ethan's obvious pain made him desperate to do something. "All right." He stood and offered his hand again. "But you know where we are if you need us."

"Sure. Thank you, son."

All the way back to the Crown and Anchor, Clay kept remembering Ethan's hopeless, self-derisive expression as he'd called himself a useless old man. He sensed that there was more to it than that. Was he ill? But certainly that would be something that would draw Elaine closer to him rather than push her away. Unless he hadn't told her.

Then there had been that remark about not all weaknesses being visible. Clay remembered the way he had tossed off two glasses of Irish Cream. He wondered if the problem could be a dependence on alcohol, then dismissed the thought. How many times had Ethan told him that the endless round of meetings and parties to which he had been subjected for so many years had taught him to make one drink last all evening?

"Apparently something's gone wrong at the heart of the relationship," Clay said quietly in the small horseshoe-shaped booth in the back of his friend's tavern. Jake, looking bleak, sat across from him, rolling a tall, slim glass of soda between his fingers. In the bend of the booth, Janessa played with the straw in her lime-flavored mineral water. Clay had relayed his entire conversation with Ethan. "Whatever it is, he doesn't want to talk about it. I pushed a little and he got angry."

Jake glanced up at him, his eyes mildly condemning. "I'm not surprised. What did you think you were going to accomplish, anyway?"

Surprised by his criticism, Clay looked at him evenly. This had not been one of his best days. Senator Dawson was threatening the *Standard News* with a lawsuit; he had just done a distasteful job of prying, made tolerable only because Ethan had known exactly what he was doing; and when he was through here, he had to go back to the office and work on the information he was compiling on Simon Pruitt—for Jake. His patience was thin. "Janessa asked me to talk to your father," he said.

"I explained all that to you." Janessa frowned at Jake. "You're the one who's always saying you love Dad, but you just can't talk to him. It's easier for Clay."

Jake looked at his friend, saw the annoyance in his eyes and didn't blame him for it. That had been a stupid remark. He had never resented Clay's closeness to his father, because despite the volatility of his own relationship with Ethan, he loved him and knew his father returned his love. But the knowledge that Janessa had run to Clay instead of him rankled a little.

He wasn't sure why that bothered him so much tonight. Janessa's affection for Clay was of long standing and he had never resented that, either. The three of them had shared so much over the years that petty slights or misunderstandings were simply ignored, each knowing the offenses were unintentional and immediately regretted. But Jake sensed something developing now that he didn't entirely understand. The friendship was changing. He didn't know how or why, but he didn't like it.

At a time when he was concerned about just what Pruitt was up to, and when Annie Chapman had nothing civil to say to him after he had thought she'd already hurt him as much as any woman could hurt a man, he didn't need any more insecurities in his life. But that wasn't Clay's fault. He glanced up again, shaking his head. "Sorry. It's been a bad day."

Clay studied him levelly another moment and nodded. "Forget it. So what do we do?"

Jake shrugged. "Let them be, like Dad asked."

"No." Janessa's voice was firm, her posture stiff. "I can't."

Jake sighed and shook his head. "Has it occurred to you, Jan, that maybe it really is over? I know they're our parents and we think they're supposed to love each other eternally, but they're really just people. Maybe they've gone as far as they can go together."

Janessa turned on him. "They are people who have been devoted to each other for forty years! Remember when Mom had surgery and Dad held up a subcommittee meeting for three days to be with her? Remember when your scout troop got lost in the Siskiyous and they comforted each other for three days? Remember when I had my accident and..."

Jake stiffened imperceptibly, but it was a gesture Janessa recognized and had grown impatient with. "Oh, stop thinking about yourself," she said before she could stop herself, "and think about them!"

"Hey." The softly spoken, slightly surprised admonition came from Clay. In her frustration, she had leaned threateningly toward her brother. Clay pushed her gently back into her seat. "That's enough of that."

"I'm sorry," Janessa said grudgingly, glancing at Jake's stiff expression. "I didn't mean to hurt you, but you drive me crazy when you do that."

"Look," Jake said, picking up his glass, "I've got to get back to the kitchen. If you guys come up with a solution, let me know. I'll be glad to help. I just can't think of anything to do for them that they couldn't do better for themselves." He slipped out of the booth and looked at his sister. "I have a couple of hours tomorrow afternoon. Do you still want to hang that border paper?"

His offer swelled her remorse. "Yeah."

"All right. I'll see you shortly after one."

As Jake disappeared around the bar and through the swinging doors, his back stiff, his expression causing the bartender to do a double take, Clay turned to Janessa with a frown. "Good going, Madam Ambassador."

Returning his look, Janessa snatched up her purse, laboriously edged her way out of the booth and looked down on Clay. Her eyes were dark with the same unsettling disorientation he felt.

"Thank you for talking to my father," she said formally. "I owe you a favor."

As she turned to walk away, Clay dropped a bill on the table and followed a pace behind. "And a bottle of Irish cream," he said.

She stopped at the big oak doors and turned, her frown deepening. He shoved the door open and gently pushed her out into the night, keeping hold of her arm as he scanned the lot for her car and started toward it. "And we should probably discuss mileage and my consulting fee."

Understanding what he was doing, Janessa turned to face him when they reached her car. Leaning against the hood, she said, "I'm sorry."

"You should be," he replied without pause. "You're not the only one who cares, you know. So there's no need to get uppity with us."

She had to smile. "Uppity?"

The line of his shoulders softened. "Uppity. It describes your attitude very well. Jake and I feel as badly as you do. If you come up with an inspired solution, call us."

Janessa stared at Clay for a long moment, then reached up to kiss his cheek. "Thanks." She smiled. "Good night."

Clay stared after her as she drove away, rubbing his jaw where she had kissed him. And he had thought this day couldn't get any more complicated than it already was.

"PERFECT." JANESSA STOOD in the middle of the room, grinning broadly at the bright border of almond, dusty pink and soft blue wallpaper. It transformed the wall from one that was simply clean and painted to one that looked decorated, finished.

"Only three more walls to go." Jake climbed down, dusted his hands on the seat of his torn and stained jeans, and folded the ladder. His tone was intended to be jocular, but Janessa found it still stiff with resentment from their argument of the night before.

"I'm sorry about last night," she said, soaking another strip of border paper while he moved the ladder several feet. "I didn't mean to jump on you."

"Forget it." He set the ladder in place, tested its solidity, then waited patiently, an arm resting on a rung, while Janessa pulled the strip out of the water, making sure the adhesive back was thoroughly soaked.

She offered him the strip and watched him climb the ladder, judging by his grim expression that he certainly hadn't forgotten it. "We've never talked about the accident. I mean there was all that anguish over it at the time, but we were kids then and anxious to put it behind us. Maybe we should talk about it as adults.'' Janessa looked up at him, hands on her hips. She couldn't ever remember feeling this removed from Jake. A headache that had begun to annoy her this morning was now making itself felt more forcefully. She massaged the back of her neck, trying to relax it. ''Maybe if we did, you wouldn't shudder every time the subject comes up.''

The strip of border in place, Jake dabbed at it with the long wallpaper brush, then secured the bottom with the rubber roller. With just that simple stroke, the second wall began to come to life. He started down the ladder.

''That's the last thing I need to do right now,'' he said, pushing the ladder forward without looking at her. ''Let's not have any heavy discussions, okay? Let's just put up the wallpaper.''

Kneeling down to pull another strip out of the water, Janessa looked up at him in concern. She was beginning to suspect that his attitude resulted from more than just anger at her. ''Is it Annie?'' she asked, handing him the strip.

He climbed the ladder silently and applied the paper. When he came down again he looked less formidable but more miserable. ''Annie's a brat,'' he said, pushing the ladder with such force that it grated noisily on the floor. Janessa was grateful that new flooring was the last order of business.

''She's a good mother, a hard worker, and a great friend.'' Loyalty compelled her to correct him.

Jake laughed mirthlessly. ''A good mother to some biker's baby.''

''He raced bikes, he didn't terrorize towns on them. Anyway, that's her business, isn't it?'' Surprised by his caustic slur, Janessa concentrated on running a strip of border through the water. ''She wasn't committed to anyone at the time.''

"Not even the biker."

Janessa remembered thinking that, when Annie told her she was pregnant, her friend had lost her mind. She knew she'd been keeping company with John Kennett, the rough-looking man who lived in her apartment building, but hadn't realized their relationship was intimate. Whenever she'd seen them together, John's manner had always seemed offhand, more like that of a friend than a lover. But she hadn't felt it was her place to criticize.

When there was no talk of marriage and John moved away to take a job with a bike manufacturer in some eastern city, Janessa had tried to be supportive. Knowing Annie planned to raise the baby, she had given her the first opportunity at extra work.

The choice to have and raise the baby had been Annie's, and Janessa couldn't help but admire the determined, uncomplaining way she had worked and prepared. Despite violent morning sickness, she'd always produced her work flawlessly and on time. Even after Mark was born, Annie never used him as an excuse for being unable to work.

Hearing Jake dismiss all Annie had been through in such scornful terms sparked Janessa's temper. Handing him the dripping strip of paper, she said with quiet condemnation, "I wouldn't be so judgmental, Jake. You're fickle, and you yourself play the field a lot. The only thing that makes you different from Annie is that you can't get pregnant."

Fifteen years ago, that kind of verbal retribution would have earned her a good shove onto her backside. Grateful for the civility the intervening years had taught her brother, Janessa found her shoulder decorated with a slimy, sticky strip of wallpaper instead.

"I don't need this on my afternoon off," Jake said, dropping the brush and roller to the floor with a clatter.

"You need a good swift kick where your brains are! You don't want to talk about anything, do you?" Janessa shouted at him, weary of his mood and attitude and her headache. "We get involved in an accident *I* get mangled in, and nobody can mention it around you because *you* get your feelings hurt."

In the process of marching to the door, Jake stopped, turning in slow motion toward her, his face turning pale. Janessa swallowed but couldn't stop.

She moved closer to her brother. "It was an accident," she said, lowering her voice, though it still seemed to echo around her. "You were three years older than me, and maybe you should have known better, but I insisted. You told me there was only one helmet, and you tried to get me to put yours on, but I had already climbed on behind you and insisted we go. You were going to do one turn around the block just to shut me up." She drew a steadying breath and took another step closer. She saw him swallow with difficulty. "I'll bet even a Hell's Angel can lose it in the gravel. It was an accident."

"I shouldn't have let you..." he began in a barely audible voice.

"I made the choice," she insisted, jabbing the chest of her grubby coveralls. "I was sixteen. Kids make dumb decisions and have to pay for them. It wasn't your fault, it was mine."

He had stood quietly while she railed at him, as though spellbound by what she had to say. But he suddenly shook the spell off and turned back toward the door. "Yeah, well, I'll always feel that it was mine."

Frustrated, Janessa grabbed his arm and turned him around, shouting, "Then I absolve you. Forget it! Stop using it as a place you can withdraw to so that nobody can blame you for anything else!"

She hadn't planned to say that. She had certainly thought it enough times, but had never intended to speak it aloud. She caught a glimpse of his stricken expression before putting a hand to her eyes to shut it out. When she lowered her hand, Jake was gone.

Chapter Seven

Sitting in the middle of the shop floor, Janessa tried to force a cup of tea past the lump in her throat. Through sheer force of will, she had finished putting up the border paper after Jake left. The stiffness in her muscles from days of cleaning and painting had conspired with the tension of the past few days and her propensity to neck and shoulder pain, and now she had a headache of killer proportions.

Though she longed for relief, she could think of no solution that appealed. She was in such pain that she doubted food would stay down. Lying in bed would probably just worsen her headache, and a swift look around the room reminded her that despite today's progress there was still much to be done.

Then there was the matter of her parents' problems and the deep chasm she had opened between herself and Jake. All these things intensified her emotional as well as her physical pain, yet she couldn't stop thinking about them.

A knock on the shop door brought a groan to her lips. Not only did she not want to see anyone at the moment, she didn't want to have to get up and let them in. She rested her head on her knees in the vain hope of making herself invisible.

A firm rap sounded on the window, forcing her to look up. Simon was peering into the shop, his hands cupped around his eyes. She noticed for the first time that it was dusk.

Groaning as she rose to her feet, then walking slowly to the door so as not to increase the pounding in her head, Janessa admitted Simon. She smiled at him, though the bright color of his jacket increased the pain in her head. If he had come to help, she could use someone to paint the baseboards before she sanded and varnished the hard-wood floors. She had planned to stay and do it herself, but her head was pounding too hard to allow her to do any more work.

Simon dismissed that hopeful possibility almost instantly. "Hi, Janessa," he said, breezing into the room and looking around with a wince. "Still got a long way to go, haven't you? Look, I can't stay, I've got a meeting, but I wanted to talk to you about the Friends of Oregon party next week. I'd really like you to come with me."

She gestured vaguely behind her at the room. "I have so much—"

He nodded, interrupting her. "I know. But you've got to keep your contacts up. I'm sure a lot of your customers are women who know you and your family and want to support you."

It occurred to Janessa that he made it sound like her sweatshirts were being purchased by a small knot of acquaintances who were doing it out of charity. The twenty-two thousand shirts she sold last year couldn't all be attributed to friends of her family, but she was too tired and in too much pain to argue.

"Come on," he coaxed. "You have to do something besides paint, paper and sew. You really look a wreck." He shook his head in disapproval. "How long have you been at this today?" Without waiting for a reply, he went on,

"You have to stop working so hard. What's the point? When you're the wife of a senator you won't have time for this anyway. I'll pick you up at six. We'll have dinner first, then you'll have an entire evening with nothing to do but what you do best: be beautiful and charming."

There was a lot Janessa would have told him had she been able to think straight, but foremost in her mind was getting him out of the shop so that she could collapse and have a nervous breakdown in peace. And a nod would cause less pain in her head than shaking it.

"Great. See you at six on Tuesday." Simon leaned down to plant a kiss at her neck. "Promise me you won't stay too late tonight."

Clay pushed the door open just in time to see Pruitt, in a yellow blazer and gray slacks, lean down and kiss Janessa just under her ear. Rage rose instantly in him, and he checked his pace before he entered the room. Simple dislike and suspicion of Pruitt turned to a startling desire to kill him. He forced himself to close the door quietly and walk across the room at a slow, even gait. Over Pruitt's shoulder he saw Janessa's drawn and pale face, her tense hands held away from Simon. Then she spotted him and relief lit her eyes and sparked a thin smile.

"Hi, Clay." She pulled away from Pruitt, who turned around, obviously annoyed at the interruption.

Clay's eyes narrowed at the pain visible in her face. He recognized that look; she had pushed herself too far, worried too much, slept too little. He put a hand to her face and guessed gently, "Headache?"

"I told her not to stay too late." Simon frowned at Clay, his tone proprietary.

In all the nights and weekends Clay had helped Janessa, he hadn't once seen Pruitt wielding a broom or a brush. He dropped in often to check on her progress, but never offered to help. Clay gave him a cursory glance. "Have you come to help?"

Simon hesitated a moment, pulling out the lapels of his jacket in a defensive gesture. "I'm meeting with my campaign director at seven."

"Then go ahead," Clay said, "I'll see that she gets home. It must be time for you to leave anyway."

"Yes. I'm late." Galvanized into action, Simon turned to the door, waving in Janessa's direction. "I'll call you tomorrow. Maybe you should take the day off. Call the—"

Clay pushed the door closed behind him, effectively shutting off Pruitt's advice. He returned to Janessa, the anger in his expression curiously blended with tenderness. "Certainly it's occurred to you that if you kill yourself remodeling, you won't be here to enjoy what you've wanted for so long." The brief lecture was administered along with the movement of his fingers into the hair at the base of her neck. He began to massage at the tension knotted there.

Janessa felt her brittle will, which had taken her through the afternoon, shatter at his touch. Large tears filled her eyes and spilled over, the result of pain and anxiety rather than self-pity. "I've had a hell of a day," she said feelingly.

Clay pulled her closer and she leaned her forehead against his shoulder as his fingers worked at the stiff tendons. Silently he listened to her recount the argument with Jake that had resulted when she'd tried to make peace.

"He was so nasty about Annie," she said, pulling away from Clay to look into his eyes, her own tired and grim. "I couldn't stop myself. It just came out. I can't believe I said that to him."

Clay raised an eyebrow, also finding it hard to believe. But then, all three of them seemed to be behaving out of character. Jake, the perennial bon vivant, was now dark and brooding and barely civil. And Clay found his own behavior difficult to understand. He felt murderous toward Pruitt when that kind of reaction was hardly called for, and Janessa continued to have the damnedest effect on him. Even now, when she was in pain and in need of comfort, he was having difficulty feeling fraternal.

He'd been grateful when she'd walked right into his arms, free of the strange uneasiness that had plagued them both since the afternoon she'd come to the newspaper to find him. But while she rested comfortably against him, pouring out her story, he was very much aware of every point where their bodies made contact—her breasts against his chest, her thigh against his, her hands pressed into his waist for balance. In his massaging fingers, her slim neck had twisted and turned with disarming trust.

He didn't understand what was happening. Feeling unsure of which direction to move, he took refuge in old habits. He'd never been uncomfortable being a big brother to her. "Did you take a pill?"

She nodded, indicating the bottle of muscle relaxants on the floor beside her thermos of tea.

"Have you had anything to eat?"

"Breakfast."

He shook his head at her. "It's nearly seven-thirty in the evening, Janessa."

She smiled, a small glint of humor in her eyes. "I wonder if Simon made his meeting."

Clay reached down to pick up her thermos and handed her her jacket. "He's such a jerk. I'm surprised you let him get that close. Come on. We're getting something to eat."

"My car is..." Janessa pointed in the opposite direction as Clay took her arm and led her up the street into a night that smelled of rain.

"I'll pick you up and bring you down in the morning," he said, unlocking the passenger-side door of his Camaro. "Driving won't do anything for your headache."

She leaned back against the headrest, turning to grin at him as he got in behind the wheel. "Being bossed around isn't going to do much for it, either."

"What do you feel like eating?" Clay ignored her complaint and turned the key in the ignition. The high-powered engine came to life.

"Nothing appeals to me." She opened her window and drew a deep breath of the cool air. "I've had so much fast food since I've been working on the shop that my palate's ruined. At this point I'd sell my soul for a homemade peanut-butter-and-jelly sandwich."

Clay pulled out into the street, stopping at the corner then turning in the opposite direction from Janessa's house.

"Where are we going?" she asked.

"My place," he replied, a corner of his mind wondering if it was wise. But he'd been looking after her too long to put any other considerations before her safety. "No peanut butter, however. Will you settle for corned beef and Swiss cheese and sauerkraut?"

Earlier she had thought to make herself something bland when she got home, something that would go down easily and stay there. But now, though she still had a raging headache, Clay's company made her feel more human somehow, more willing to challenge the fates with an indigestible sandwich. She said, "That sounds wonderful."

Clay's condominium stood on a hillside that overlooked a parklike neighborhood just outside of town. From his living-room window, Janessa looked down on a thin scattering of lights and, beyond them, on a dense bright band of light that marked downtown Salem. She and Jake had helped Clay select this place right after the *Standard News* had offered him his own column.

"Hot mustard or sissy mustard?" Clay called from the kitchen.

Smiling, Janessa went to stand in the doorway of the small, Spartan black-and-white room. "How hot is hot?"

Clay picked up the small bottle from the array of sandwich makings before him. The counter looked as though Dagwood Bumstead were at work. "It's the sweet-hot stuff you put in my Christmas stocking. It's got enough bite to make it interesting without scalding your sinuses."

"I'll try it."

With an affection that warmed her and diminished her concerns, at least for the moment, Janessa watched him work. Whistling a Carly Simon tune, he spread mustard liberally on a broad slice of rye bread, applied a steaming clump of thinly sliced corned beef, two slices of Swiss cheese, then several forkfuls of sauerkraut. The sandwiches constructed, he buttered the outsides of the bread and put the sandwiches on a hot iron griddle. They spat and sizzled and filled the room with a mouth-watering aroma.

Clay worked in the kitchen with the quiet skill with which he did everything else. He seemed to expend so little effort, yet the product was delicious.

Sitting across from him at a small round table in a glassed-in nook off the kitchen, Janessa groaned in approval of her first bite.

"See?" he said with a teasingly superior lift of an eyebrow. "Jake's not the only one who can cook. 'Course, he turns out an elegant fish chowder, and I make sandwiches, but..." His shrug denied any difference in the level of their skills.

Janessa chewed and swallowed her second bite. "I love to eat someone else's cooking."

"Is Simon aware that he might have to share kitchen duties?"

"I'm sure he wouldn't care." Janessa savored the taste of another bite and relaxed against the ladder back of her chair. "My domestic abilities are not what appeal to him about me."

Clay sipped at a glass of ginger beer. "What do you suppose does appeal to him?" he asked, as though completely baffled himself.

She gave him a dry glance, acknowledging his teasing, before getting back to her sandwich. "Part of it is my father's connections," she admitted easily, "but part of it is just that he likes me."

"Do you like him? You looked a little tense when he was holding you and nibbling on your neck."

"He wasn't nibbling." She took a sip of the nonalcoholic beer. "And he's not always hovering, like the other men in my life." She smiled at him including him in the number.

"He doesn't hover," Clay said deliberately, "because he doesn't care about you. He only cares about himself. When I walked into the shop you looked about to fall over and he was feasting on your collarbone." He spoke quietly, but there was a sharp undercurrent in his voice. "And you looked glad to see me," he reminded. "Not offended by the fact that I was, uh, hovering."

"I was glad to see you." She looked surprised that he thought to even bring it up. "You're my best friend. Next to Annie." After a moment's thought, she corrected, "Maybe even before Annie. But that doesn't give you the right to be rude to Simon. Just because Jake doesn't like him . . ."

Clay shook his head. "It has nothing to do with that. *I* don't like him."

"I don't care," she said amiably. "I sold twenty-two thousand sweatshirts last year."

Clay blinked, trying to understand the significance of that unrelated detail. "Commendable," he said.

"Look," she said. "You write a wonderful column, and you make a great sandwich, but you can't see into my head."

He might have disputed that, but his intention in bringing her here had been to help her relax and get rid of her headache. He pushed away from the table. "Done with your sandwich?" At her nod, he stacked their plates. "Why don't you sit down in front of the fire and I'll bring you a cup of tea."

Janessa knelt on a small Oriental rug in front of the marble-framed fireplace. Her shoes off, she bent over, letting her forehead touch the rug. Her head protested, but the stretch the position allowed in her back and neck outweighed the discomfort. Puttering sounds came from the kitchen while she tucked her head farther inside the arch her body created.

Carrying a tray bearing a cup of coffee, tea and a plate of ice-cream nuggets he kept on hand because Janessa loved them, Clay rounded the corner into his living room and stopped. It wasn't the sight of the neat, jeans-clad bottom that quickened his pulse, but the puddle of dark gold hair on the rug in front of the fire. It slipped from the collar of Janessa's shirt, over her head and the arms crossed under it to the floor, like some rich, sun-shot waterfall.

Then she heard him and rose to her knees, sitting back on her heels while the brilliant mass settled around her in seductive disarray. *It's messy,* Clay told himself staunchly as he forced himself to breathe and swallow. *Her hair is messy. You've seen her with messy hair a million times.* But the reasonable man he was trying to reach inside himself had apparently fled. In his place was a man who saw Janessa's hair as provocatively appealing, not messy.

"I was trying to stretch out my back and neck," Janessa explained, oblivious to his shift in mood as he set the tray down. "I spent so much time this afternoon with my hands over my head, hanging the wallpaper border..." She put a hand to her shoulder, slowly rotating it. "I just can't do it for myself like you do it."

Janessa turned her back to him, pulling her hair to one side to bare the vulnerable nape of her neck. She knew without asking that he would perform the task he had done for her hundreds of times since the accident.

Clay hesitated just a moment, taking in the artful curve of her neck and shoulder. There was open trust in the way she offered her back to his ministrations. What unsettled him was that he'd never been aware before of how utterly feminine the gesture was, and how completely undeserving of her trust he felt at the moment.

Janessa began to feel the release of tension the moment his hands touched her. Her mother tried hard to perform this massage, but her fingers were slender and she was always concerned about applying too much pressure. Her father's hands were short and thick, their touch too strong, the span of his hand too small.

But Clay's fingers seemed to know just where the knots were—hiding along her spinal column with stiffening persistence, and tangible at the base of her neck where they were strongest.

He was quiet as his thumbs worked up and down her back, his fingers moving along from the back of her waist, up just to the sides of her breasts, then farther up to her shoulders, bringing soothing, blessed relief. And something else.

Janessa sat still as Clay's fingers climbed into her hair, rubbing behind her ears. A startling gooseflesh was rising all over her. And something else. She drew a deep breath and decided she must have imagined it. It couldn't have happened.

But Clay's hands began to move down again, his thumb kneading the base of her neck while his fingertips worked her shoulders. Then they slipped to the middle of her spine, his long fingers spread out against her back, their limber tips a fraction of an inch from the sides of her breasts. And she froze, closing her eyes as she realized she hadn't imagined it at all. Her nipples had pursed, their tips beading against the pressure of the lacy bra and the cotton sweater that confined them.

Sensation played along a fine string that seemed to run the length of her, vibrating as though plucked by a knowing finger. Then his hands moved to her shoulders again, pulling against the sudden stiffening there.

"Relax," Clay coaxed, his voice as soft as his touch. "You're getting tense again. Don't think about the shop, or your parents, or Jake. Just clear your mind and let yourself go."

With the sharpened senses of one who has made an alarming discovering, Janessa knew those were dangerous instructions. But she seemed capable of little else. Her mind refused to focus on anything but the tingling awareness along her spine and across her shoulders—and in places Clay hadn't even touched.

Frustrated because she had begun to relax but was now tightening her muscles in stubborn resistance to what he was trying to accomplish, Clay took a firm grip on her shoulder and pushed with a little more force than he'd intended between her shoulder blades. She reacted with a startled gasp, arching backward, and he found himself with a left hand full of soft breast.

He drew his hand away as though something had bitten it. Janessa clambered to her feet, her eyes wide, her hair still trapped over one shoulder. As he rose beside her she opened her mouth to speak, her head shaking in denial of something she obviously understood no better than he did.

Her look of dismay caused a sudden rise in that niggle of guilt he'd felt so much lately. But rising right beside it was an elusive glimpse of truth. His mind dove for it, but it was gone. He stood staring at Janessa, unable to recall a single word in his extensive vocabulary.

"Thanks for the sandwich and the tea," she said in a voice too ordinary for the circumstances. Then she lowered her eyes and added on a regretful note, "Oh, no, it's all over the floor."

Clay followed her gaze to see the cups on the carpet, stains spreading as he watched. Beside them were the melting ice-cream nuggets. Janessa must have upset them when she stood. Or maybe he had.

Despite the apology in her voice, Janessa made no move to pick them up. She went to the sofa for her jacket and purse and snatched them up in an agitated movement, retreating toward the door. She turned the knob before he could reach her, yanking the door open and giving him a broad, false smile, her eyes denying everything. "Thanks again. I've got to get home to Mabel. She must be starving. And I have to be up early tomorrow. Dinner was great. Well, thanks again...." Realizing she'd already said that, she pulled the door closed.

Clay remained where he was, a breath he couldn't expel held in his lungs. Staring at the door, he watched it open again. Janessa walked in, a frown between her eyes that was part confusion, part embarrassed aggression. "You drove me," she said, dropping her things on the sofa, the tone of her voice accusing.

"I know," was his quiet reply.

"What the hell was all that?" she demanded, stopping several inches from him, her hands on her hips. "Why did you...? How come I...?" Unsure of the questions, she found herself unable to finish them. And Clay was watching her with a steadiness and a concentration that rendered her speechless and unable to move.

I'm getting a grip on it, Clay thought as his mind fumbled through the confusion, chasing the flicker of truth once again dancing just beyond his reach. It seemed to draw nearer as he stared at Janessa, her blue eyes searching his brown ones with the same desperation he felt. Her cheeks were hectic with color, her lips parted in dawning surprise, her hair a riot of gold in the firelight.

It occurred to him that he was seeing her not as a friend, not as a sister, but as a woman. And not just any woman. His woman. He put a hand to his stomach as though he'd been struck there.

Janessa understood the look. The dark eyes she had looked into for years while seeking comfort, strength, laughter, even challenge, now offered something she felt herself leaning forward to accept.

Clay read acceptance in Janessa's eyes and reached for her with a resolve that pushed all caution aside. With an arm around her waist he held her against him, and time arrested for a moment as he watched the wonder there, the eagerness, and the beginning of a smile.

Feeling rose in him so strong that the tautening of his arm that had brought her closer lifted her off her feet. Her breasts were high against his chest, her knees against his thighs when he closed his mouth over hers.

Her response was immediate, eager. She had a vague notion of something important being dangerously out of balance: their friendship. How would this affect their relationship? But rising with undeniable strength beside her concern was a need to follow this path and see where it would lead.

Twining her arms around his neck, Janessa gave herself over to the strong hands that held her against him, to the lips moving on hers, to the tongue venturing into her mouth, exploring with debilitating boldness.

Clay felt drunk with sensation, overwhelmed by the soft warm woman in his arms. She clung to him with a fervor as strong as his, one tantalizing fingertip circling the rim of his ear while her mouth ran over his face with paralyzing tenderness. He kissed her ears, her throat, the soft silky skin above the round neck of her sweater. She breathed a small gasp in his ear as he rested his mouth against the curved swell of her breast. She lay quietly in his arms, her hot cheek against his.

"Clay," she ordered on a whisper, "stop."

He had to surrender to reason, he thought, the effort to focus on that truth forcing him to lift his mouth from her fragrant skin. But he didn't want to. "No," he said, turning to press a kiss just under her jawline.

"I have to think," she pleaded, groaning softly as his lips moved to her ear. "You have to..."

His lips wandered across her cheekbone. "I don't want to stop kissing you...holding you..."

"But...I'm your friend."

"That should make it..." His words blurred as his lips settled on hers again, threatening to plunge her back into mindlessness. But the last word came out clearly as he drew his head back to look into her eyes. "Magic."

With a ragged sigh, Janessa let her head fall against his shoulder. "Our friendship is magic." She tightened the arms wrapped around his neck and wriggled to be free. "Put me down, Clay."

Struggling against the new wave of sensations caused by that little undulation of her body against his, Clay complied.

Her eyes dark and grave, Janessa tried to think logically. "I..." she began. "We...God!" She abandoned the effort immediately when nothing intelligent took form in her brain. "I'd better go home. Maybe in the morning this will make sense." Easing out of his arms, she snatched her purse and jacket up again and headed for the door.

"Jan—" Clay tried to call her back as she turned the knob.

"Not now," she said with the first indication of impatience. "Neither one of us is making sense. We have to—"

"Jannie—"

"Good night," she said firmly and closed the door behind her.

There was something amiss here, Clay knew, but his brain couldn't quite focus on it; his body was overwhelmed with longing, his mind cluttered with confusion.

The door opened. Janessa did not appear, but her voice, firm though a little high, reached him through the opening. "So I forgot again. Big deal. Are you coming?"

Clay sighed as he dug in his pocket for his car keys.

Chapter Eight

"I don't know if this means anything . . ."

Clay looked up from his monitor as Bill Sutton, a reporter, appeared at his desk, brandishing a manila file folder. Bill was tall and thin with a curly mass of red hair.

"I remembered what you said about watching for anything related to Simon Pruitt." Bill spread three black-and-white photos across the desk. Clay leaned over them.

In one photo, a policeman had a young man by the collar of a denim jacket and was leading him away. In the other two, the man was being handcuffed before being put into a police car. The background was dark, almost indistinguishable.

"What kind of a bust?" Clay asked.

"Pirated videotapes."

Clay nodded. Illegally reproduced copies of videotaped movies were a big business in the United States, and the profits tripled for pirates who sent the tapes overseas. He studied the photos closely, looking for whatever had made Sutton think this could be connected with Pruitt.

At the same moment that Sutton put a freckled finger to an indistinct blob in the corner of the photo, Clay saw it. Sutton pulled a magnifying glass out of his shirt pocket and put it under Clay's nose.

Clay took the glass, lowering it onto the photo until the image began to blur, then raised it until it was as clear as he could get it. Revealed under the glass was the distinctive front fender of a light-colored Corvette. He felt a cautious stir of professional excitement. Pruitt drove a Corvette. Of course, many people in Salem did.

Sutton moved his finger to the left corner of the blurred image. It was a license plate with two of the three numbers on it just barely visible. The first figure was either an eight or a three—the grainy texture of that part of the photo made it impossible to tell. The last number was clearly a one.

"Pruitt's license plate," Sutton began, "is—"

Clay had memorized all the details of the investigation he had launched at Jake's request. "LUC 531," he finished for him. He looked up into Sutton's face. "You remember the color?"

"No," he replied.

As Clay looked back at the photo somewhat disappointed, Sutton added, "But the photographer did. It was yellow. He noticed the car particularly because it pulled away in a hurry right after the cops got one of the kids."

Clay smiled at Sutton. "Can you get me prints?"

"They're yours," he said, with a small quirking of his lips. "I'll keep you posted."

"I owe you a beer," Clay promised, closing the folder.

Walking away, Sutton turned to accuse over his shoulder, "You're cheap, Barrister."

After closing the door against intrusion, Clay stared at the photos. So far, an investigation conducted with all the resources at his disposal had failed to provide any serious evidence to incriminate Pruitt, but these photos were another matter entirely. Though only a suggestion of proof, the blurred image of the Corvette and its license plate ignited the drive at the heart of Clay's reporter's soul. He was onto something.

Then, unbidden, the fresh memory of Janessa in his arms, her body suspended against his, her kisses running over his face, undercut his professional objectivity in finding out why Pruitt was at the scene of a bust. The possibility that she might be in danger because of her association with him lent a deadly intensity to the plans he made for stepping up the investigation.

JANESSA FOLLOWED JAKE across the Crown and Anchor's large, aromatic kitchen. A pot of chili bubbled on the stove, soup simmered on a back burner, and the special glaze on the finely seasoned corned-beef brisket Jake had just put out to slice filled the air with the tang of orange.

"I told you to stop worrying about it." Jake stirred the chili, then the stew, then crossed to the butcher table where the brisket awaited. He snatched a carving knife from the storage block.

"Will you stop!" Janessa grabbed his arm and turned him around, tired of his skillful avoidance of her apology. "I've been here for ten minutes, and you haven't looked at me once."

"You're ugly," he said, pulling away from her and picking up a carving fork. "And you bug me."

"If you don't put that knife down," she threatened, "I'll drop that corned beef in the chili!" Her last sentence was louder than the rest and delivered with a vehemence that he had learned to respect.

With an exaggerated sigh, Jake put the carving knife and fork down carefully and wiped his hands on the white apron around his waist, then turned to lean a hip on the counter and look down at her. He folded his arms, trying to look as forbidding as possible. Unfortunately his little sister had never found him particularly frightening.

"Jake, I'm so sorry I said what I did back at my shop." She folded her arms, knowing she didn't have to be specific. The stubborn, aggressive movement of Jake's hands to his hips assured her of that. "The only excuse I can offer is that I'm tired and overworked at the moment, and worried about Mom and Dad. Certainly you can understand that. And I hate to see you continue to beat yourself with stupid . . ."

As he stiffened she put a hand out to him, hastening to correct herself. "Not stupid. I didn't mean stupid. I meant unnecessary guilt. If you don't want to talk about it, we won't talk about it. But if it's going to keep coming between us, we'll have to deal with it."

Looking into his implacable face, his blue eyes unreadable, his shoulders stiff and unyielding under the white T-shirt, she shook her head and rolled her eyes heavenward. "Well, I tried. If you come to life sometime in the near future, call me and maybe we can do something together."

She turned on her heel, but Jake caught her arm before she could take a step toward the door. He pulled her back, his fingers biting into her arm.

After what Clay had told him about Pruitt's car and the video pirating, he was angry with her for putting herself in danger, even though she didn't know she had. Unable to explain his fear at the moment, he satisfied himself by giving her a punitive little shake.

"Just try to remember that you don't know everything," he said, his expression thawing despite the scolding quality of his words. "I know you love everyone, but that doesn't necessarily mean you know what's best for them, or even that you understand them."

"I understand Annie." She looked back into his eyes, her voice quiet. "And she's nothing like you implied yesterday. If you're judging her that way, you're wrong."

He maintained his grip on her for a long moment, emotions she couldn't quite analyze at war in his eyes. Then he dropped his hands and picked up the knife. "Then I apologize, but that's how it looked to me."

"You should look a little closer sometime," she suggested, remembering the longing she had glimpsed under the anger with which he and Annie had confronted each other. "I'll bet you'd find it worthwhile."

Jake turned away from the brisket to fix her with a look of exasperated indulgence. The expression was so familiar to her; he'd used it on her scores of times since they'd been children. It told her that she was an indescribable, unremovable pain, but that he loved her anyway. Satisfied that the decision to see him this morning had been a good one, after all, Janessa stood on tiptoe to kiss his cheek. "I love you, too," she said. She winked and turned to leave.

"I SAID I WASN'T GOING." Ethan looked over the top of his *Wall Street Journal* and stared. Elaine stood at the foot of his recliner, adjusting one of the pearl-and-diamond earrings he'd given her for their last anniversary. Over her arm was a filmy rose wrap that matched the knee-length, deep V-necked dress she wore. He lifted the paper up again. "Have a good time."

"All your friends will be there," Elaine coaxed.

He shook the paper. "That's why I'm staying home."

"You're turning into an old coot."

"Retirement gives a man new choices." Ethan saw a twirl of pink over the top of his paper as Elaine put the wrap around her shoulders.

"Don't wait up," she said, walking to the door. "I'm going to try to entice the governor's bodyguard into a tryst."

"Don't forget all the safe-sex warnings," Ethan cautioned.

The door slammed with a force to wake the dead.

"MRS. JOHNSON, may I present Senator Ethan Knight's daughter." Looking elegant in a dark suit, Simon introduced Janessa to the wife of Congressman Steve Johnson.

Reaching for the slim hand extended to her, Janessa bit down on temper and smiled.

"Of course. Janessa, isn't it?" Rochelle Johnson asked. She was dark-haired and pretty in a bright red dress that showed off perfect curves.

"That's right." Janessa was glad the woman remembered. Simon seemed to have forgotten tonight that she had a given name, as well as a surname. Expecting the woman to ask about her parents, she was pleasantly surprised when Rochelle said instead, "My daughter Holly has three or four of your shirts. For Christmas she gave me one with an elf wearing a sign that says 'I've been good.'"

A handsome sandy-haired man appeared behind Rochelle, putting his hands on her shoulders. He winked at Janessa. "Unfortunately it wasn't true. Would you excuse us for a moment? Rocky, there's someone I want you to..."

As the congressman lead his wife away, Janessa turned to remind Simon that she had an identity of her own, but he was in conversation with Mrs. Goodwin, the president of the League of Women Voters. Sincerely wishing she was washing windows or hanging new light fixtures, or doing one of the dozen or more tasks demanding her attention at the shop, Janessa wandered to the champagne fountain and helped herself to a glass.

As she made her way to the French doors that closed out the rainy night, she saw that the cream of Salem's political life was out in force. Men in dark suits and women in colorful gowns moved among tables laden with food and drinks under the sparkling chandeliers of the elegant hotel.

Although she hadn't kept abreast of the latest political intrigues since her father had retired and she'd immersed herself in her business, Janessa was a little surprised to find herself bored. She was glad that her life no longer revolved around politics, but she had never thought of it as uninteresting before. Business was becoming such a challenge to her that political wheeling and dealing seemed pale in comparison. She admitted a little grimly that life itself was becoming such a challenge that the invasion of Normandy seemed like light work. Then one of her most exacting challenges appeared at her shoulder. "Mom. You look lovely."

"Thank you, dear." Elaine examined Janessa's simple, white, full-skirted gown. "So do you."

"Did Daddy come?"

"Heavens, no. I left him home, completely captivated by T-bills and pork bellies and exhilarating things like that." Elaine waved a dismissing hand, her eyes roving the room. "No matter. I'm going to try to pick up the governor's bodyguard, anyway."

"Mom . . ."

"There he is now. Lighten up, Jan. This is a party!" Elaine walked away in the direction of a small group surrounding the governor. At his shoulder was a burly young man with Hollywood good looks.

Before Janessa could recover, two tall, elegantly dressed men came toward her through the crowd around the champagne table. It couldn't be. She cocked her head sideways, straining to see as a woman stepped in front of them, reaching for a tray of hors d'oeuvres.

Clay and Jake emerged from the crowd, walking shoulder to shoulder like men who had moved side by side for much of their lives.

Tenderness touched her at the same moment annoyance did. And a peculiar nervousness made her voice sharper than it should have been. "What are you two doing here?" she demanded when they reached her.

The men exchanged looks over the tone of her voice. "I'm a political reporter, remember?" Clay deftly reached for a glass of champagne from the tray of a passing waiter. "This is my beat."

"You hardly ever cover this kind of thing," she challenged, frowning at him. "You get your information from . . . well, nobody knows where. Anyway, where are your notebook and photographer?"

"Those are bourgeois touches at such an affair." Clay looked around surreptitiously. "We try to be inconspicuous. It makes eavesdropping easier."

Fixing Clay with a look of open skepticism, she turned to her brother accusingly. "And why are you here?"

His eyes widened with an innocence she found unconvincing. "Clay and I played handball this afternoon. He wanted moral support, so I came along." He looked around and winced. "Deadly dull, isn't it? Did you see Mom?"

She glared from one to the other, ignoring the question. "Are you watching me?"

Jake's eyes widened further. "What do you mean?"

She rolled her eyes. "Don't play dumb, Jake."

"He's not playing," Clay said in defense of his friend.

Turning on Clay, intending to reprove him for making light of the complicity she was beginning to suspect, she found herself facing Simon instead. To his right was a paunchy gentleman in a gray striped suit. A cigar protruded from his breast pocket and perspiration beaded his forehead.

Putting out a hand to Janessa, Simon brought her closer. He acknowledged Jake and Clay with a brief nod, then dismissed them as he focused on Janessa. "Darling, this is Joseph Dugan, president of the Salem Longshore Workers' Union. Mr. Dugan, this is Senator Ethan Knight's daughter."

Clay noted the tightening of Janessa's jaw despite her smile as the union president beckoned his wife over and introduced her. Unnoticed, he and Jake disappeared through the French doors.

"Interesting how he can't remember her first name." Jake took shelter from the rain under an awning in the corner of the patio.

Clay, sipping at his champagne, followed him. "He doesn't need her first name tonight." His tone was quiet but sharp under the loud rhythmic sound of rain falling onto the awning and dripping down in sheets only inches in front of them. "Sleaze," he muttered.

Jake turned to his friend with a raised eyebrow. "So I've made a convert."

"The Corvette in the photo did that."

"Mmm. That's your fourth glass of champagne."

"Leave me alone. I can still drive."

"We rented a car to tail Pruitt, remember?" Jake pointed out. "So we wouldn't be recognized. If you wrap us around a pole we are no longer inconspicuous, nor too healthy, probably. And Rent-a-Wreck would not be pleased. I'll drive. You're better at taking notes and pictures anyway."

Clay looked at Jake, saw the defensive glare in his eyes and knew the issue rankling his friend wasn't the amount of champagne he'd consumed. "Haven't you come to terms with Annie, yet?"

Jake needed to pace, but he didn't want to get wet and spend the night drenched, trailing Pruitt and catching pneumonia. Instead he folded his arms and stared darkly ahead at the rain cascading off the awning. "Forget Annie. Right now I'm worried about Jan. She's special," he said. "Delicate."

Clay laughed softly. "She is special, but except for the headaches, she's strong as a horse."

Still staring straight ahead, Jake nodded. "And you've always been the one who could help her deal with those. You were the one who could get her to exercise when no one else could. You could make her stop crying and smile."

Clay turned to Jake, recognizing that that had not been a list of his accomplishments, but rather a list of grudges. "I'm sorry. We have a certain . . . rapport."

"And you didn't cause the accident."

"Oh, Jake." Clay pushed away from the wall in exasperation, taking two agitated steps forward before he was stopped by the rain. He turned on his friend, his patience gone. "Will you get over it? You're wearing the hell out of all of us. She doesn't blame you, so stop beating yourself with it."

Jake turned, glaring, and Clay went on, "Janessa was right, you know. You use the accident as a place to hide. You don't know what to do about your parents, you don't know what to do about Annie, and you're jealous of the relationship I have with your sister. You feel left out. Admit it, Jake, you're not as worried about her as you are about yourself." They stared at each other a moment, the only sound, the harsh drum of the rain.

"Is something going on between you two?" Jake asked, something in Clay's eyes surprising him into asking the question.

Clay expelled a sigh, shaking his head. "I don't know."

"What the hell kind of an answer is that?"

"The only one I have at the moment."

Jake looked at the rain still falling torrentially and turned up the collar of his jacket. "And you accuse me of hiding." He snickered and ran to the French doors. Clay followed him through the crowded dining room and out of the hotel to the car.

FROM THE OPPOSITE CORNER of the room, over the bald head of a small man who had spent the past half hour recounting the details of his uneventful tour as ambassador to Liechtenstein, Janessa watched Jake and Clay leave the cocktail party. She frowned at the anger on Jake's face and the grimly determined set of Clay's shoulders. As good friends who spent a lot of time together, they disagreed often, but always managed to retain a certain tolerance for one another's opinions.

Janessa found herself no longer able to consider what had caused the apparent rift between them, because someone across the room was calling her name.

As she straightened up, startled, to focus on the small stage area, there was a loud drumroll from the orchestra, and Simon was standing at the microphone. He was holding out a hand and the entire assembly had turned to her, applauding.

"Will you come up here, darling?"

A little panicky, Janessa went toward him, wondering if she'd just been elected to office. Simon was looking at her with indulgent affection as she made her way up the few stage steps. Embarrassed and confused by the attention, she whispered, "What's going on?"

He drew her toward the microphone, settling an arm around her shoulders. Since a lot of these people were acquaintances of her parents, Janessa thought perhaps he was going to mention the expansion of her business, or the location of her new shop. She began to feel seriously uneasy when he extracted a small jeweler's box from his breast pocket.

"Janessa and I have been seeing each other for five months now," he said, then added with quiet humor, "one week, two days, and about an hour and a half." The guests laughed, Janessa shifted uncomfortably, and Simon went on. "I've passed her parents' inspection and think the world of them. I'd say it's time to make it official."

Paralyzed with horror, Janessa watched him remove a ring set with a marquise diamond, lift her hand reverently, and put the ring on her finger. The crowd cheered and applauded and the band offered another drumroll as Simon leaned down to kiss her.

For a moment she heard and felt nothing. Strobe lights flashed, and Simon waved at the applauding crowd. Then years of being taught how to react in public came to her defense. She smiled at her parents' friends, spotted her mother's face in the crowd and quickly turned away from her expression of disbelief. She remained still while Simon leaned down to kiss her again, deciding magnanimously that she wouldn't embarrass him in this room full of people, but she would kill him slowly later.

Janessa had no delusions as to why Simon had chosen this particular time and place to propose. Everyone present had worked with her father in one way or another, and though not everyone who knew Ethan Knight loved him, they all respected him. Simon's engagement to Janessa Knight proved to everyone just how close he was to the ex-senator. And Simon knew Janessa was too refined to turn him down publicly.

In the crush that surrounded her later, Janessa received a hug from her mother. "You're out of my will, Jan," Elaine whispered. "And I'll see that your father gives his pork bellies to charity. Good night."

As her mother left the party, salvation came to Janessa in the form of Mr. Dugan, who wondered if Simon would consider spending an hour or two after the party with him and several of his union members. With the very real possibility of a union endorsement bright in his eyes, Simon stayed for the meeting, putting Janessa into a cab.

"I've got meetings in the morning and afternoon," Simon said, leaning into the back seat. "But I'll call you for dinner."

Janessa leaned forward and grabbed hold of his tie, pulling him closer. Thinking he was about to be kissed, Simon's eyes widened in anticipation. His expression changed quickly when Janessa glared at him, nose to nose. "You had better call me before your meetings, Simon," she threatened quietly, "or you are dead in the water in November. Is that clear?"

Half fascinated, half alarmed, Simon cleared his throat, a difficult task with his tie tightening around it. "But, darling..."

"Is that clear?" she asked again.

"Yes. Of course."

Janessa leaned back against the seat. "Good." She had a sinking feeling that he was more tantalized by her behavior than frightened.

JAKE, WHO'D BEEN SLOUCHED behind the wheel of a dusty blue Pinto, straightened in his seat, elbowing Clay.

"I see," Clay said, frowning as Janessa got into a taxi across the street. He saw Simon duck his head into the cab, it was too dark for him to see anything else. "What's he doing?"

Jake strained to see. "I can't tell. Jan appears to be choking him."

"What?"

"Could be a trick of the shadows." He watched Simon pull his head out of the cab, adjust his tie, then turn back to the hotel as the taxi sped away. "Now, why's he sending her home alone?"

"He's probably found a constituent he can get something out of and wants to work him." Clay leaned his head back against the seat and groaned. "Hell. This waiting around is a pain in the classifieds. I'm glad I'm a reporter and not a cop."

"Quit complaining. You're worse than an old lady."

With a sidelong glare at Jake, Clay reached into the paper McDonald's bag that sat between them on the console. Cold French fries didn't do much to alleviate the boredom, but they helped kill the taste of caviar he had sampled earlier in the evening at the party.

He offered the bag to Jake, who reached in and pulled out a Chicken McNugget. A hostile peace had settled between them after the argument on the hotel patio. Allied in the common cause of Janessa's safety, they were determined to follow Pruitt when he left the party. Though tailing him the past two nights had revealed nothing, the fact that he'd put Janessa into a cab looked promising.

More than an hour later, Clay shook Jake awake when Simon parted company with two men in front of the hotel and got into his Corvette. They slouched down in their seats as he drove past them. Then Jake straightened and turned the key in the ignition, executing a sloppy and illegal U-turn while Clay turned in his seat to keep an eye on Simon's car.

"Left on the highway," Clay said as Jake drove down the street that fronted the hotel. "There!"

Streetlights gleamed off the sleek lines of the highly polished car stopped a block ahead at a red light. There were three cars between when the light turned green and the Corvette sped away.

Clay, straining to see around the cars in front to keep his eye on Pruitt, called instructions to Jake. "Right at the theater marquee. Watch the truck!" Brakes squealed as

Jake followed instructions, changing lanes to make the turn and cutting off a small green pickup.

"You told me to turn!" Jake snapped back as Clay made a rude remark about his driving.

"You should have rented something that *could* turn!" Clay grumbled. "Only you would rent a Pinto to chase a Corvette."

"It was all that was available. Just keep your eyes on Pruitt."

"Right again at the blinking light."

This time Jake checked his rearview mirror. He made the turn, then braked when he found himself on a commercial street in a seedy neighborhood. The Corvette was nowhere in sight.

"Pull into that parking lot," Clay directed, squinting through the darkness. "I think he went down that alley."

Jake guided the Pinto into a spot in a small empty lot in front of a dilapidated shopping mall with few stores.

"Look!" Across the alley was a large, low warehouse-like building. Clay and Jake got out of the car, and Clay pointed up to the neon sign. In pink and purple letters, the sign flashed South City Video.

"I'll be damned," Jake said with quiet fervor. "He *is* involved in pirating."

Quietly Clay made his way to the top of the alley, flattening himself against the front of a Laundromat and peering around the corner. The Corvette was visible in a square of light that came from an open loading bay door at the back of the video shop. Voices, angry but indiscernible, could be heard from somewhere inside.

"What's happening?" Jake whispered, melting out of the shadows at Clay's right. "See anything?"

"Nothing," Clay replied softly. "I'm going closer."

Jake pulled him back just as Clay was about to round the corner into the alley. "What?" Clay demanded impatiently.

"There's nothing to cover you," he pointed out, also impatient. "What if he comes out?"

Clay held up the camera in his right hand. "I'll take his picture. Saving my skin'll be up to you."

Just as Clay prepared to turn into the alley, the voices grew louder. Jake and Clay plastered themselves against the Laundromat wall and waited while a string of invectives stung the air. Then there was the slam of a car door followed by the roar of a powerful engine. The Corvette burned rubber as it catapulted backward out of the alley. It screeched to a halt in the street as Simon stopped to shift gears.

"Oh, God," Jake whispered as the car's powerful headlights went on, lighting the alley and the Laundromat wall to within an inch of Clay's shoulder. If Simon turned left, they'd be safe, but if he turned right, they'd be in the path of his lights. After a moment of torturous suspense, the sleek car turned left, disappearing with a roar into the darkness.

Jake and Clay sagged against the wall. "What now?" Jake asked. "You didn't get a picture. We still don't have any proof."

"I'm going to the police anyway," Clay said, levering himself away from the wall. "We're reputable enough that they'll listen to us even without proof." Then he paused a moment, giving Jake a cursory glance before walking back to the car. "At least I am."

"Somebody's got to tell Jan."

Clay nodded grimly. "I will."

Chapter Nine

Clay rapped loudly on Janessa's front door. He had awakened that morning determined to tell her he'd been investigating Pruitt, to show her the photographs and tell her what he and Jake had discovered the night before. He would stand fast against her wrath.

His determination wavered as he waited for a response to his knock. When no one came to let him in, he raised his hand to knock again but stopped, hearing the unmistakable shriek of an unhappy baby. He tried the doorknob, found it unlocked and let himself in. As he stepped into the small hallway, Mabel darted past his feet, apparently desperate for escape. He didn't blame her. Even for something as deaf as the cat, the din was enough to sand teeth.

Following the sound into the kitchen, he found Janessa stirring something in a bowl with one hand, while holding Annie's squalling son, Mark, with the other. For a moment the sight amused him so much that he forgot the purpose of his visit and allowed himself a moment to watch.

Janessa had many qualities he admired and could list at length, but he had never thought of her as particularly domestic. As far as he knew, she seldom cooked or baked. She sewed, of course, but with the flair of an artist, not with the practical skill of a woman who darned socks and made curtains.

He had never imagined her with a child. The sight of her disheveled and a little frazzled as she swayed from side to side, cooing nonsense to the baby, touched something inside him he hadn't known was there. It made him feel strangely weak and filled with a longing he couldn't quite identify.

He advanced into the kitchen, pulling off his jacket. Finally aware of the sound of his footsteps on the tile floor, Janessa whirled, a wooden spoon raised and dripping some sticky substance. She closed her eyes in relief at the sight of him.

"Clay," she said, her voice barely audible over the sound of the baby. "Thank heaven. I hope you're here for breakfast."

"Ah...sure." That wasn't strictly the case, but he could save the details of his real purpose for later. The important thing now was to establish a tolerable decibel level.

"Good." She smiled thinly, her relief visible. "You can hold Mark or make pancakes."

He took the baby, clad in fuzzy blue sleepers, from Janessa. Annie brought the child with her occasionally when she came to help Janessa with extra work, and whichever member of the crew had been free when Mark needed feeding or changing had stepped in to do the job. Clay had taken his turn like everyone else and had even earned a smile or two for his efforts. Settled in Clay's arms, Mark stopped crying as though something mechanical had turned him off. Large, tear-filled blue eyes studied Clay with methodical thoroughness.

Janessa leaned her weight on one hip, feigning disgust. "He's been screaming ever since Annie left him here an hour ago. I've done everything but stand on my head for him."

Clay gave a superior shrug. "It's obvious that he needed another man to talk to. Lucky for you I came along to bum breakfast. Get moving with the pancakes. Mark and I will set the table."

By the time they sat down to pancakes and sausages, it was obvious to Clay that Janessa's harassed air was caused by something more than her impromptu offer to baby-sit for Annie. Her expression seemed to alternate between anger and sadness. With Mark happily straddling his knee and greedily eating small bites of pancake from the tip of his fork, Clay tried to find his way around Janessa's mood.

"How late did the party go on?" he asked casually. "I had to leave early."

She gave him a dark glance that doubted the reason he had offered for being there last night. "How can a good reporter write a story if he doesn't stay till the bitter end?"

"Those parties are all pretty much the same." He concentrated on Mark as the baby helped himself to a syrupy bite of pancake from Clay's fork and guided it, sort of, to his mouth.

Janessa dipped her napkin in her water glass and offered it to Clay. "Then why did you bother covering it?"

"I was assigned to cover it," he replied patiently, wiping Mark's hand and face. "I do have a boss, you know."

"And Jake just tagged along because you two had spent the afternoon together."

"That's what I said."

She put a hand under her ponytail and flicked it. "I don't believe you."

Smart woman, he thought. But she looked so fragile this morning, as though one more worry would put her over the edge. He gave her a look of complete innocence. "That's your prerogative, of course. Did you have a good time with Pruitt?"

She looked at him levelly, then sighed and stood to get the coffeepot from the stove. "So you haven't heard? We're engaged."

Cold surprise pinned Clay to his chair. He drew a breath, swallowed, dabbed at Mark's mouth with the napkin—anything to buy time. Fear, real and jagged, coursed along his spine.

Janessa topped off his coffee, then hers, and replaced the pot on the stove. Then she gave a strange little laugh and paused before sitting down to take something out of the back pocket of her jeans. She placed the ring on the table beside his plate, the large marquise diamond reflecting the light from the kitchen window in a blinding flash. Mark reached for it with a squeak of excitement. Clay picked it up, holding it out of the baby's reach, and his fear intensified—until he remembered that she had taken it out of her jeans pocket. He frowned at her. "I doubt that that's where he hoped you'd carry it."

She rolled her eyes expressively. "I don't love Simon and I'm not going to marry him. You know that. I think even he knows that. He announced our engagement from the stage last night at the cocktail party and presented me with the ring in front of everyone." She sipped at her coffee, regretting her decision to save his pride. "I'm sure he just wanted everyone to think my father truly approves of him—and he knew I wouldn't make him look like a fool in front of all those people."

He was feeling as relieved as she had looked when he'd walked in an hour earlier. "Well, apparently you didn't straighten him out when he took you home," he said, pressing for information on why she and Simon hadn't left together. "You still have the ring."

"He sent me home in a cab." She let him drop the ring in her palm, stood to put it back in her pocket, then sat down again. "He stayed to talk to the president of the dockworkers' union. I'm sure he sensed an endorsement there. I told him to call me first thing this morning so I could tell him what I thought of what he did.''

"Did he?"

"Somebody called shortly before you came, but I was trying to pry Mark off of Mabel, who was determined to scratch his eyes out, baby or not. I didn't get to the phone in time.''

"Call him now. I'll keep an eye on Mark."

"Simon had a couple of meetings today and wasn't going to be free until this afternoon. I'll just have to wait.''

Bored with eating and worn out from his terrorist activities of the morning, Mark began to whine and rub his eyes with sticky hands. Clay carried him to the sink and held him while Janessa washed his hands and face. The child protested loudly.

"So Jake was right about Simon," Clay said loudly, to be heard over the baby. He wanted to hear her admit it. That would somehow justify his deception.

"No, he wasn't," she shouted back, as much with impatience as the need to make herself heard. "He sincerely has feelings for me. He just doesn't mind using my family's connections. He considers them a bonus of caring for me.''

If he told her what he thought of that, she'd throw him out, so he held his peace, pacing with Mark against his shoulder while Janessa cleared the table and put their things in the dishwasher.

By the time Janessa had finished, Mark was asleep. Clay put him in a corner of the sofa, covering him with the ragged blue blanket that accompanied the baby everywhere. The small disturbance roused Mark and he began to fret, face contorting, a protesting whine about to shatter the quiet. But Clay leaned over the sofa, rubbing a finger along the baby's plump cheek, shushing him until he slipped back into his comfortable doze.

Janessa watched him, intrigued. Clay's facility with Mark had been a surprise to her before. Now it warmed her and made her long for things she'd never thought of seriously.

He straightened and they stood facing each other in the middle of the room. Tension rose. "Thanks, Clay," she said, forcing a lightness of tone that belied the nervousness she was beginning to feel. "I'd probably still be stirring pancake batter if you hadn't come along."

"When's Annie due back?"

"She didn't say. I'm not even sure where she went. She just showed up on my doorstep at eight o'clock, said she had an important breakfast appointment and asked if I would watch Mark."

"Well, I'm on my way to the office." Clay took several steps toward the door. "If you need help, call me." He reached for the doorknob, then stopped and turned, "Jannie, we..."

Janessa took a step forward. "Yes?"

He didn't know what he wanted to say, didn't know why he'd even started. Confused, impatient with himself, he yanked the door open. "Never mind." He stepped out onto the porch and almost collided with Ethan Knight.

Ethan carried two apparently hastily packed suitcases, one in each hand. His eyes were sparking anger and his jowly face was red with it. He looked around Clay at Janessa. "Can you put me up?" he demanded gruffly. "I've left your mother."

"I DIDN'T RUN AWAY," Jake denied, straining to hold his temper in the face of Annie's accusation. She sat across the table from him, her wild auburn hair pulled back in a knot that made her look soft rather than forbidding. But her hazel eyes were frosty. "I just . . . stepped back to take an objective look at our relationship."

Annie bristled like an indignant cat. "How can you take an objective look—" mockery underlined the words he had used "—at someone you claim to be in love with?"

He nodded, knowing his argument was thin. At the time, he'd just opened the Crown and Anchor and he'd been frightened by the responsibility. Annie's suggestion of marriage had terrified him. "I needed time."

Annie broke a huge bran muffin in half. "So I gave it to you."

Jake sighed heavily and pushed the untouched plate of omelet and toast away. He was beginning to doubt the wisdom of having invited her to breakfast. She had sounded eager when he'd called, but she'd done nothing since she'd arrived but heap accusations and abuse on him. He acknowledged that he probably deserved it, but he needed desperately to know if she still felt anything for him. About to pose the question, he looked up and found her watching him. It was there in her eyes so he blurted, "I still love you, Annie."

She pulled her hands from the table as he reached for them. "Is that an objective opinion, or is there personal feeling behind it?"

He slammed his fist on the table and the crockery shook. "Damn it, Annie! Yes, it's got feeling behind it—sincerity and passion and anger!"

When she gave him a cool questioning look, he leaned back in his chair, his eyes accusing. "Don't look so outraged. While I was trying to think things through, you had some biker's baby."

Annie stiffened, half of the muffin in her hand, the butter knife poised over it. Her eyes met his, their frost dissolving under a temper finally let loose. "John was a friend!"

Jake arched an eyebrow. "What kind of friend leaves you with his baby?"

Annie sprang to her feet, her chair falling over on the carpet. Jake deemed himself lucky when she threw the muffin at him instead of the knife. As she grabbed her purse, he reached across the table to stop her from leaving. He closed his hand over the first thing he could reach—the lapel of her jacket. Across the table, they glared at each other with hurt, angry eyes. "Well, answer me!" he demanded.

With a strong shove, Annie slapped his hand away, tearing the fabric. "You answer!" she screamed at him. "John left me with *your* baby!"

Rooted to the spot with shock, Jake watched her run from the restaurant.

"I CAN'T BELIEVE you've let it come to this." Janessa was changing sheets in the spare bedroom while her father put his belongings into the three drawers of the dresser she had hastily cleared of her things. "Almost forty years invested and you just walk away?"

"Forty years or forty days," Ethan said glumly. "What's the difference? When it's no longer working, it's foolish to hold on."

"Maybe you could get it working if you tried a little harder."

Ethan turned from the dresser to face his daughter across the narrow expanse of her guest room's single bed. "You have no idea what I've put into this. It isn't fair of you to judge me. If I'd had any other alternative, don't you think I'd have taken it?"

Janessa folded her arms, touched by his sadness, yet remembering her discussion with her mother. "Mom says you just don't act like you care anymore." She made the accusation quietly, hoping it would force him into revealing the real problem at the heart of his estrangement from her mother.

But he simply shook his head and turned to slap the T-shirt he held into a drawer. "Well, you know your mother. If you don't do things her way, she considers it a personal affront against God and mankind."

Janessa fought back the smile. That was slightly exaggerated, but true. "But you've worked around that for forty years."

He sighed and pushed the drawer closed. "Maybe I'm just too tired to think about spending what's left of my life doing what she wants instead of what I want."

"But you used to both want the same things." Janessa was beginning to feel desperate. With her father moving into her spare room, she had to confront the reality of her parents' split. And her father looked so tired and despondent she began to consider for the first time in her life that he was mortal. The realization that her parents had made the decision to spend what remained of their lives apart left her feeling grim.

"Well, we don't anymore," Ethan said firmly. "That's proof that it's over, my girl. Accept it." He turned to hang a few things in the closet. "Just try to go on as though I'm not even here. I just need a couple of days to look around for an apartment and get myself together, then I'll be out of here."

Janessa went around the bed to hug his broad middle. "Don't be silly, Daddy. You're welcome to stay as long as you like." She clung to him like she used to as a child, as though that very act would prevent the dissolution of life as she had known it.

"CLAY BARRISTER." Cradling the phone on his shoulder, Clay took a sip of coffee and perused his notes. He had twenty minutes until deadline; he wished he had turned his calls over to the switchboard. The business with Pruitt and his confusing feelings for Janessa were making it hard for him to concentrate.

"Barrister, this is Bill Chance at the *Los Angeles Times*."

Clay put down his cup and diverted his attention to the deep voice of the caller. "Good morning," he replied.

"I'd like to discuss a position here with you face-to-face."

"I—"

"I know you've turned us down," Chance interrupted, "but we hadn't even gotten around to discussing salary and benefits. Can I send you a ticket to fly down next week to talk to us about it?"

Clay hesitated. Surprise and the undeniable flattery of the prestigious newspaper's insistence on seeing him rendered him speechless.

"We read you every day," Chance pressed. "We all admire your guts, your insight and your style."

"Ah . . . thank you."

"If you prefer, you can make your own reservations. Maybe you'd like to tour L.A. while you're here. We'll take care of everything. Can you be here next Friday?"

Clay looked at his calendar. There was nothing written in for next week, but then there never was. Work took most of his time, except for what he set aside to spend with his friends. "I can be there."

"Ten-thirty?"

"Fine."

"Good. Looking forward to meeting you, Barrister."

Clay hung up the phone and stared at it. The *Los Angeles Times* had called him. Twice. He couldn't help a moment of cocky pride. Then he remembered his deadline.

Frantically running through his notes again, he swore in frustration when the telephone rang a second time. "Barrister!" he snapped.

"Hello, son!"

"Dad?" Clay dropped his notes and strained to listen. The connection was very poor.

"Your mother and I are coming to the States for a..." The last word was lost in the crackle of static.

"I didn't get that, Dad," Clay said loudly.

"A fund-raising tour!" Robert Barrister shouted. "We're starting in L.A. on Monday. Thought we'd try to make connections with you in Portland."

"Thought we'd try..." Clay picked up on those words with long-standing resentment. His parents had made his high-school graduation, but missed his graduation from college. Since he'd become an adult, their visits every two years had stopped and he hadn't seen them in over ten years. Now all they were going to do was try?

Somehow he hid his resentment and spoke civilly. "Coincidentally I'm supposed to be in L.A. at the end of next week. I'll just come a few days early. Then you won't have to make an extra trip."

"Great!"

"Hi, darling." Sharon Barrister's voice came over the noisy line. "We're anxious to see you."

"Me, too, Mom."

"We're staying at the Ambassador." The voice was Robert's. "Can you meet us for lunch, say, at one, on Wednesday?"

"I'll be there."

"Wonderful. See you then."

Both his parents' voices called goodbye in chorus, and Clay imagined them hanging up some outdated phone deep in the heart of Africa.

Before anything else could happen, he asked the switchboard to hold his calls. He glanced at his watch. He had fifteen minutes to make his deadline, then he had an appointment at the police department in half an hour. A visit to sunny Southern California became more and more appealing.

THE POLICE STATION was caged chaos. The office where he was told he would find Lieutenant McMullin, a friend from the days when Clay had been a crime reporter and the lieutenant a sergeant, was noisy and frantic. Telephones rang, officers and perpetrators walked in and out, and two men fought over the last doughnut in a box near a coffee-pot.

McMullin leaned out of a cubicle and waved him in. Clay sat facing the desk, surprised that there was an office in the city smaller than his.

The lieutenant, dark and thickly built, took his place in the swivel chair. "Read the report you gave about your pursuit last night." He slapped a hand on a stack of papers on his desk. "Very thorough. You investigating Pruitt for the *Standard*?"

"No, this is personal. A friend's...involved with him, and I'm keeping my eyes open."

"Janessa Knight," McMullin said. He grinned at Clay's look of surprise. "Their engagement's in the morning paper, and I know you grew up with the Knights." The grin faded. "Your instincts are good. It looks like he's in some bad company, so keep her away from him. We got a tip that a shipment of tapes is scheduled to go out weekend after next. Santiago himself is supposed to show. After our last bust, the guy wants to make sure this one gets to the docks. His connections in the Orient are getting upset and he stands to lose a bundle."

"When specifically is this going down?"

"I'll let you know." McMullin's expression sharpened. "Meanwhile, don't get in my way, Barrister."

"Come on, Mac." Clay leaned forward in his chair. "I provided you with good information. Tell me what you know."

McMullin shook his head. "Can't. But I have a copy of one of the porno tapes going out. Guys in the precinct are having a showing after the bust. You're invited. Supposed to be real quality stuff."

Clay grinned broadly. "What's it called?"

McMullin leaned over his desk and replied in an undertone, "*Wicked Wanda's White Water Whoopee.*"

ANNIE BURST through Janessa's front door in the middle of the afternoon, obviously near hysteria. She ran to the sofa where she began throwing things into the diaper bag. The elegant chignon with which she had left this morning was now a wild tangle of auburn around her shoulders. Her mascara was running and the natural canvas jacket Janessa had loaned her was rumpled, its lapel torn.

Janessa came up cautiously behind her while Mark strained in her arms, calling authoritatively for his mother. "Annie, what . . . ?"

"Thanks for . . . for watching Mark," Annie sobbed, zipping the bag closed and turning to force Mark's tiny jacket sleeve onto his flailing arm. Her movements were unconsciously rough, and her son, already upset by her neglect, protested loudly. "I've . . . got to hurry."

"What happened?" Janessa demanded, trying to hold the baby still while Annie battled with the second sleeve. "Who did you meet?"

"I don't have time now, Jan." Tears slid down her cheeks, and when Mark's jacket was finally in place, she swiped them away. She shouldered the diaper bag and tried to take her baby.

Janessa took a step back. "I'm not letting you leave like this. You're too upset to drive. You'll kill both of you. Sit down. We'll have some coffee—"

"Jannie!" Annie pulled on Mark, her eyes pleading. "Jake's probably right behind me. I've got to hurry!"

"Jake?" Surprised, Janessa let go of the baby, ran around Annie and placed herself between her friend and the door to block her escape. "He did this to you?"

"Not exactly. He got mad and I wanted to leave. He tried to stop me and I . . ." She began to sob again, brushing a hand over the torn lapel. "I'm sorry about your jacket."

"Forget the jacket!" Janessa shouted. "What happened?"

Annie held Mark against her and rocked from side to side, trying to shush him. "When he said he wanted to talk, I agreed to meet him. I've loved him for so long, Jan."

Janessa nodded, trying to draw her back to the sofa, but she resisted. "He made a remark about John and we got into a fight and I . . ." Her face crumpled and she hid it in the baby's shoulder. "I told him about Mark."

Janessa began to ask, "What about Mark?" when the door burst open behind her, throwing her against the wall. Sandwiched in the corner with a doorknob in her back, Janessa decided that this game the fates were playing with her had gone on long enough.

Straightening to confront the intruder, she saw the formidable, tweed-jacketed back of her brother bearing down on Annie, who clutched Mark to her and backed away.

"How dare you have my son," he shouted at her, "and not tell me!"

Annie put the sofa between them, her eyes as angry as they were frightened. "You wouldn't have cared!" she accused. "You never care about anything but having fun! I mentioned marriage and you ran."

"You never mentioned the baby!"

"I wanted you to marry me for me, not for him!"

"Damn you, Annie..." Jake made his way around the sofa, and Annie, backed into a corner, turned into it sobbing. Mark screamed from the shelter of her body.

Janessa forced herself between them, pushing against her brother's chest with all her might. He took one step back. "Stay out of this, Jan. We—"

"She's my friend, and this is my house," Janessa said with a calm vehemence that surprised even her, considering she'd just learned she had a nephew. The need to protect Annie brought adrenaline flowing through her with a revitalizing rush. She gave Jake another backward push. "If you want to continue this discussion, you'll lower your voice and sit down."

"Jannie, you..." Jake grabbed her arm, intent on moving her out of the way. As Janessa balled her fist, determined to realign his nose if she had to, a deep male voice stopped the action.

"You'd better do as she says, son. If she lays into you, I'm not stepping in to help you."

Jake looked across the sofa at the man standing in the middle of the room. "Dad?" he asked, temporarily surprised out of his anger. "What are you doing here?"

"I've left your mother," Ethan replied, pushing Jake and Janessa aside to get to the woman standing in the corner. "Now sit down and pretend you're civilized." He smiled at Annie and reached for Mark.

Openmouthed, Jake looked at Janessa, unable to frame the question. She nodded grimly. "This morning. He's staying with me until he finds an apartment."

"God," Jake exclaimed, putting a hand to his head. "I must be getting old. I think today's going to be too much for me."

Sharing the sentiment, Janessa took his arm and led him around the sofa where her father had already settled Annie in a corner. She sat Jake on the opposite end.

Ethan patted the baby's back while Mark played with the snaps on his flannel shirt; then he looked from one to the other with senatorial gravity. "Janessa and I are going to make coffee. When you two are calmer, I'll bring my grandson back."

But her father was too taken with Mark to help with the coffee. He sat with Mark at the kitchen table while Janessa prepared it and set up the tray. She covertly watched the two getting to know each other.

"I gather you didn't know about this, either?" Ethan suggested when the spoon Mark was playing with fell. Janessa retrieved it and handed it back to him with a grin.

"No, I didn't. It's a day of surprises."

"He hasn't been himself lately," Ethan said of Jake.

Janessa laughed. "Who has? Anyway, I'd have thought you were too wrapped up in your own problems to notice that Jake's been upset."

"A father always notices his children. Just because we don't fuss in the same way mothers do, doesn't mean we don't see things." He glanced at her as he continued to play with Mark. "Anything you want to tell me?"

Janessa looked up from pouring cream into a pitcher, her eyes wide. "Like what?"

He shrugged. "I'm not sure. You have a dreamy look in your eye I don't remember seeing there."

"Well, there's nothing to tell."

"Just asking. Sounds quiet enough out there. Maybe Jake would like to get acquainted with his son."

Chapter Ten

"Why are there candles in here?" Ethan was analyzing the contents of Janessa's refrigerator. He frowned at her over the top of the door as she walked into the kitchen.

"They burn longer and drip less when they've been refrigerated."

He looked at her doubtfully then turned back to the almost empty shelves. "How do they taste with ketchup?"

Janessa stood on tiptoe to lean over the door and point. "There's pancake batter in that bowl, and cheese and ham in that little meat-keeper drawer. Or there's soup in the cupboard."

He looked disarmingly helpless, and she asked quietly, "Want me to make you some pancakes for dinner?"

"Nah." He reached into the meat-keeper drawer and pulled out the cheese. "I'll just make a sandwich. You do have bread?" He closed the door and gave her a very small grin. "Or do you roll up the slices and burn them for candles?"

"Cute, Daddy." Reaching into the wooden bread box, she pulled out a loaf and handed it to him.

He read the big-lettered advertising on the bag. "Eleven grains. No preservatives. Contains sunflower seeds, rolled oats, wheat bran..." He looked up at her again with an air of martyrdom. "Do I eat it or plant it?"

Janessa poured him a cup of coffee. "Don't whine, Daddy. Simon would be disappointed in you."

A gray eyebrow rose over the upper rim of Ethan's glasses as Janessa handed him a plate and a jar of mayonnaise. "When your mother finally came home at four in the morning, she told me you were engaged."

"Four in the morning?" Janessa had a panicky recollection of her mother's plan to seduce the governor's bodyguard and wondered if she'd been successful.

He nodded. "The issue here is your engagement."

Janessa shook her head, adding a cheese slicer to the things in front of her father. "It isn't true. I called her this morning to explain. Didn't she tell you?"

"She said he put a ring on your finger in front of everyone."

"He did. But we're not engaged," she said firmly. She took the ring out of the hip pocket of her jeans, showed it to him, then put it back. "I just couldn't make him look like a fool in front of all those people by saying no."

"But everyone thinks—"

"I know!" she snapped, patting his hand apologetically. "We haven't had a chance to straighten it out yet. He's had meetings all day and it hasn't exactly been quiet around here. I'll talk to him soon. I'm sorry if you'll be embarrassed."

Ethan snorted, slathering mayonnaise on the bread. "Any amount of embarrassment is preferable to having Pruitt for a son-in-law. Oh, by the way, your mother started packing. Said she was moving to Tierra del Fuego."

Recognizing that as nonsense, Janessa met his eyes and dissolved into laughter. For just a moment, things were as she remembered them, as she would like them to be forever. When she'd been confined to bed after the accident, her father had cheered her up more than once with a silly line, delivered with an oratorial seriousness that was believable—until she paid attention to just what he was saying. "Was that before or after you decided to leave her?" she asked softly.

"Before," he replied, the mock seriousness still in place as he sliced cheese. "I told her if she stayed we might get invited to live in the White House when you become First Lady. Got any pickle relish?"

"No. What did she say?"

He slapped the sandwich together. "That even in the White House she'd probably find me intolerable. I guess I was supposed to get angry because she came home so late. So I said goodbye."

"Daddy!" Janessa elbowed him impatiently. "Weren't you upset?"

He shook his head, taking his plate and cup and moving to the small table. "If she was out that late with another man, it's over. If she wasn't and did that just to hurt me, it's still over. Anyway, it's not your concern, sweetheart. Just let it be."

Janessa was following him to the table when the phone rang. It was Clay. The very sound of his voice soothed the agitation that had been growing in her all day long. "Hi, Jannie. Do you know where Jake is? I can't find him anywhere."

"He's here," she replied, then pausing significantly, added, "with Annie. You won't believe what's happened. I'll tell him you called, but I don't think it'd be a good idea to disturb them right now."

Clay expelled a long breath and Janessa frowned at the receiver. "If it's an emergency..."

"No," he said, his voice betraying just a trace of frustration. "It can wait. How's your dad?"

"Fine. He's sitting here right now having dinner."

Ethan looked at the cheese sandwich in his hands and gave a silent but scornful laugh. Janessa rolled her eyes at him.

"So you have your father at the kitchen table and Jake and Annie...?"

"In the living room."

He laughed softly. "Do you feel displaced?"

"Just a little," she admitted. "I've had the most unbelievable day."

"How'd you like to come with me on an assignment?"

She frowned. "What kind of an assignment?"

"Safe Fowl in Oregon is lobbying against a Department of Fish and Wildlife bill. I thought I'd have dinner at the pond in the park and check out their statistics."

Janessa smiled into the receiver, knowing that watching the ducks in the park pond was one of his favorite activities. "I hope you're not going to try to put that on your expense account. Thanks, Clay, but I've got too many patterns to cut tonight. If I don't get them to my girls tomorrow, they won't be ready in time to fill our orders. The painting and stuff has put me so far behind."

"You're working too hard, Jannie," he admonished. "You're going to make yourself ill."

"I have no choice."

"Yes, you do. I'll be by in twenty minutes."

"But, I..." The line had been disconnected.

"WHERE'D YOU GET THIS?" Janessa asked suspiciously. She and Clay were huddled together under a cottonwood in the dark, wrapped in a Pendleton blanket, eating chowder from a thermos and cheese bread.

"The Crown and Anchor."

"It's wonderful." She sipped from a steaming soup mug. "Perfect fare for picnicking at night in forty-degree weather."

"Don't be a stick, Jan." Clay poured more chowder into her mug. "This is fun. Everyone picnics during the day and when it's warm."

"You're getting eccentric, Clay," she pointed out. "Aren't you a little young for that?"

"It's the sign of a good writer. If we didn't deviate from the norm, we wouldn't see things to write about."

"And how do you propose to check the Safe Fowl in Oregon statistics in the dark?"

"I don't have to," he admitted. "I have them on my desk. And you were going to tell me about the trying day you've had."

"Right." Janessa downed the last of her chowder and handed Clay the mug. He put it in the basket beside him. Tucking the blanket around her again, he listened while she started with her father's arrival just as he, Clay, was leaving her house, and continued through Jake and Annie's battle in her living room.

"Jake's baby?" he said in surprise, then repeated the question again, as though needing verification. "Mark is Jake's?"

Janessa nodded. "Apparently when Annie found out she was pregnant, she mentioned marriage to Jake, not telling him about the baby, but just sort of . . . testing the waters, I guess. She said she didn't see him for three weeks after that. She decided he wasn't interested and made other plans for herself and the baby."

"But what about John, what's-his-name? The guy in her building."

"Kennett. He was just a friend who helped her through the pregnancy. They were never intimate."

"So, how do Jake and Annie stand now?"

Janessa shrugged. "They were still talking when I left, but I think a lot remains unresolved. He can't forgive her for not telling him all this time, and she's suspicious about his intentions. Is he just trying to talk things out with her because he knows he has a son, or because he loves her and wants to be with her?''

Clay shook his head, trying to absorb the news about his friend. Then he noticed Janessa's grim expression and held her closer. ''And your parent's have really separated?''

She nodded grimly. ''My dad's living in my spare room and complaining about the contents of my fridge. I can't believe the whole world could fall apart like this in one day.''

He squeezed her hand, as though in apology for bringing the subject up. ''Did Pruitt call?''

She shook her head. ''I tried him a few times this afternoon, but he must still have been at one of his meetings. Or he's avoiding me.'' She looked at him with a wicked arch to an eyebrow. ''If that's the case, he's a very wise man.''

Clay opened his mouth to bring up the subject of his investigation of Pruitt, but Janessa was already talking again, this time with enthusiasm. She had looked so grim when she'd joined him that her smile was welcome, and he hated to interrupt her.

''Do you realize that I'm an aunt and you're an uncle?'' She rested her chin on her hand, and her delicate features softened into an expression of such mushy anticipation that he couldn't resist its snare. ''I'm going to make Mark a sweatshirt for every day of the week with a whole menagerie of animals on them. I'm going to be the most disgustingly doting aunt you've ever seen.''

Clay stared into the darkness a moment, then asked without preamble, ''Do you want to come to Los Angeles with me for three days?'' He hadn't intended to invite her along. All afternoon, while he'd pondered the problems of his job offer and his parents, it hadn't occurred to him that the trip could be anything but business and duty.

But as though he didn't already have enough complications in his day, the feelings that had been building between them every time he saw her were taking over. He had wanted this to be a simple excursion, an excuse to tell her about his plans and to listen to her troubles. But that was all changing. He found himself rubbing his thumb over the knuckles of the hand he held. It had grown quiet and gently trembly in his grasp.

"You're going...about the job?" A breathless little gasp had interrupted her question. She didn't know what she felt—excitement for him, or fear that if he chose to accept the job she would lose him.

"Yes." Some dark emotion rippled through his even voice. "And my parents called. They're going to be in L.A. to start a fund-raising tour. I'm going to have lunch with them at their hotel. I could use your moral support."

She thought of the condition of her shop. All the major painting, papering and sanding were finished, but the details of cleaning up and moving in were enough to keep her from a good night's sleep for some time yet. A three-day jaunt was the last thing she should consider doing with her time. But Clay had asked for her moral support, and in a lifetime of friendship he had asked her for so little. That was something she could easily give.

When Clay saw the vacillation in her eyes, he coaxed her with, "We'll even stay at the Disneyland Hotel so you can enjoy the park every spare moment."

She knew it was unsophisticated of her to become excited, but Disneyland was her favorite place in the whole world. Her parents had taken her and Jake and Clay twice when they were growing up, and the memories of those trips were among her most cherished. A photograph of the three of them in the teacups on the Mad Hatter's ride still adorned her kitchen bulletin board.

And then there was the enticement of three days alone with him. How did she feel about that? She wanted to go, she decided instantly. The prospect of leaving behind the problems surrounding this day and having some time alone with Clay was something she couldn't resist.

"I'll need to ride the Matterhorn," she bargained. "And have a choux fritter in Old New Orleans."

He grinned. "Of course."

She smiled. "Then I'm yours for three days in Los Angeles."

"You're going where?" Ethan stood next to Janessa as she filled the refrigerator with sandwich meats, cheese and various other foods.

She closed the door with a graceful swing and smiled into his concerned expression. "Disneyland." Atop the refrigerator, she stacked white bread, several packages of cookies and a box of crackers.

"With Clay?"

"Yes."

Ethan leaned against the counter, arms folded over his broad middle as he watched her store cans of coffee, soup, and cocoa in the cupboard. She turned to him with another smile. "There. That should keep you well supplied while I'm gone. Annie promised to call you once a day in case you have trouble with the washer or anything."

His gray eyebrows drew together in a deep V. "I'm not helpless, you know."

Janessa playfully punched his arm and began folding the grocery bags that littered the kitchen floor. "Of course you are. It's all right. You never had time for this stuff. No need to be defensive. But if you're going to be living on your own, you'll have to get used to it. This'll be good practice."

"Maybe I'll just find myself a pretty little housekeeper to see to my needs."

Janessa felt horrified, even though she knew the remark had been calculated to do just that. She pressed bags in a drawer without looking at him. "You'd have to keep up with her, Daddy. Young women are insatiable today."

Ethan expelled a hard-edged laugh and moved across the kitchen to pour a glass of water. "Middle-aged women are insatiable today."

She stood and found herself faced with his flannel-shirted back. There was a disheartened droop to his shoulders that was completely unlike her blustery, robust father. Pondering his remark, she could make no sense of it. Even her mother was sure he had no lover, middle-aged or otherwise, and as far as Janessa knew, her mother was no nymphomaniac.

Putting her arms around him, Janessa leaned her head against his well-padded shoulder blade. "I was only teasing, Daddy. I'm sorry if I said something inappropriate."

He patted her hands, still staring out the window. "No need to apologize." He was silent for a moment, then he turned to her, his eyes grave behind their wire-rimmed glasses. "Why Disneyland?"

She explained about Clay's job offer and his parents' visiting the country. "When he invited me along," she said, "I kept thinking about all the work I still have to do at the shop. But when he promised to take me to Disneyland, I couldn't refuse. Remember the fun we had there the summer after I graduated from eighth grade?"

His smile was instant and held a trace of sadness. "How could I forget? We lost you twice, Jake and Clay had to be pulled out of the water in the jungle ride, and they ate so much I thought we'd have to fly them home as freight."

"Those were the good old days," Janessa said with a chuckle.

"Your mother know you're going?"

Janessa nodded. "I called her this morning. I also told her about Jake and Annie and Mark."

"How'd she take it?"

"A lot like we did. She was completely surprised, but hopes they can work it out." She smiled. "I think she was pleased at the thought of being a grandmother."

Ethan drew a deep breath, his crossed arms rising and falling with his stomach. "I don't know. When they left here Saturday night, things were still a little tense. She said he knew where to find her if he wanted to talk, and he said he was tired of talking. Either she wanted to marry him or she didn't. She said they had a lot to consider. He said all they had to consider was that their child needed two parents."

"I agree with that." Janessa straightened away from the counter, gathering up the plastic produce bags and putting them in a drawer. "Even grown-up kids like to know they've got two parents. Keeps everything on an even keel, somehow."

"Life just isn't always as orderly as we'd like it to be." Ethan patted her shoulder then headed for the hall closet and his jacket. "Come on. Since you're leaving so early in the morning, I'll take you out to dinner."

"I've changed my mind." Janessa looked down at the almost perpendicular drop of twenty or so feet and laughed, the sound filled with fascinated fear.

"Too late now," Clay said into her ear, tightening his grip on her waist as the bobsled in which they sat teetered for one tantalizingly terrifying minute on the lip of the drop. Ahead of them a sled swept down the track with blurring speed, shrill screams and deep laughter chasing it.

"But I wanted to ride the carouse-e-e-el!" Janessa's protest ended on a scream as the sled pitched forward, dropping them down the Matterhorn. She screwed her eyes shut, clutching the arms that tightened around her, screaming again as she chanced a peek and found the sled aimed directly at a low-hanging wall.

Clay's laugh penetrated her scream, deep and rich and vibrating in the innards of the manufactured mountain. He braced his strong legs against the foot of the sled, holding himself and Janessa steady as the sled bobbed and wove through darkness and light. Sometimes they were hurled around a curve on the outside of the mountain where the park stretched out for acres and the less-adventurous visitors walked at a leisurely pace. Then they would be catapulted back into darkness, sprayed with water as they sped through manufactured streams, tossed around like debris in a flood.

Janessa's throat ached from screaming and her cheeks from laughing when the sled finally began to slow. She slumped back against Clay with a groan. "I must have been much more adventurous at thirteen. This didn't seem half— Oh, no!"

Clay laughed, tightened his grip on her again as the almost ninety-degree angle at which they climbed the highest peak pressed them onto their backs. "As I recall, you screamed bloody murder then, too."

"Oh, Lord." Janessa leaned against him. "Can't we do something slow and quiet after this?"

"What about the space ride?"

"No!" Notorious for its approximation of travel in a runaway space ship negotiating its way through a two-foot wide canyon, the ride was not what she had in mind.

As the sled chugged to the top, Janessa tilted her head against Clay's shoulder and, as much as the restraining belt would allow, turned to look at him. He turned to meet her gaze. "It would be a good time for coffee and my choux fritter."

"You promise not to toss your cookies all over me?"

"Clay!"

She slapped his knee and he laughed harder. As she looked into his dark eyes, bright with amusement and devilry, his smile just an inch from her mouth, his chin grazing her cheek, her heart seemed to coil in on itself, tautening with the near pain of too much happiness.

The sled stopped and teetered at the top of another hill, then went down the other side like an arrow shot from a bow. Her scream and his laugh followed them down.

Arm in arm they walked miles, the Southern California sun warming their shoulders as they became reacquainted with the rides they remembered, and investigated new ones on the acres of park that had been added since their last visit. They bought souvenirs, sampled tasty delicacies, had dinner in the starlit dining room of the Blue Bayou Restaurant, which abutted the Pirates of the Caribbean ride, and ended the day in the prow of the sailing ship *Columbia* as it plied the waters of an imaginary river.

The night was still balmy, but a cool breeze stirred the water, mingling with the sounds of the electronically generated male chorus that boomed a sea shanty from somewhere in the ship.

Settling his jacket over Janessa's shoulders, Clay pulled her back against his chest, wrapping his arms around her. They leaned against a railing, the beautiful flowers planted all along the nearby bank filling the night air with sweet fragrance. "Warm enough?" he asked.

She snuggled closer, leaning her head back against his shoulder. "Perfect. Couldn't you just do this forever? Play and eat and live in a place where every dream comes true. No bad guys, no threats to happiness or safety, your every need anticipated and attended to."

He laughed softly in her ear. "Would you be there?"

She hesitated one brief second, her small frame softening against him. "Of course."

"Then extend my reservation." Clay planted a kiss on her temple and tightened his hold on her.

Janessa turned in his arms, her eyes bright in the darkness. All day long they'd been hand in hand, or arm in arm, always touching, their spirits as interwoven as their bodies. They'd been racing toward this moment for hours. "Clay, I'm afraid of what's happening here," she whispered.

She didn't have to explain. The friendship that had brought them to this point in time had been changing for weeks, ripening into something that was finally demanding recognition. The affection that had always been so easy between them was now something to be treated with cautious respect. The change had given it a potential that made Clay draw a deep breath.

"Afraid or not," he replied quietly, "I'm falling in love with you, Jannie." Then he laughed softly. "And I feel like some kind of fiend admitting it."

"I know. I feel—" she paused over the word, giving him a look of wicked amusement that nearly decimated his control "—lewd yearnings for you, the man who's been like a second brother to me. I keep wondering if that can be right."

He pulled her close, his arms closing gently around her. "This doesn't feel wrong. But I know what you mean about feeling frightened. Being your friend was easy. Being the man who loves you might require a better man than I am."

Janessa leaned away from him to look into his eyes. Her own were filled with affection—and something else she didn't want to analyze too closely right now. "There is no better man than you. I'd just like to be more sure of what's motivating me."

He had done so much for her in her life that she felt as though she owed him whatever he asked of her. She just wasn't certain that was a solid foundation for taking this relationship further. And what she felt for him might simply be an adult manifestation of a childhood adoration.

Clay nodded, admitting to himself that the prospect of physical intimacy with her was part of what frightened him. He'd loved and protected her for so long. Could he love and cherish her with the tenderness she deserved?

When the boat docked, they took the monorail back to the Disneyland Hotel. Fireworks lit the sky, but neither Clay nor Janessa noticed as they sat close together in the back of the car, each lost in private thought.

Chapter Eleven

"How's your work schedule, Barclay? Are you tied up for the next month or so?"

Clay was surprised by the question, though he didn't react. In the two hours since he and Janessa had met his parents in the posh hotel dining room, it was the first question either parent had asked him about himself. He had begun to feel like part of an audience rather than part of the conversation.

"I set my own schedule, Mom, but I usually put in a full day. It's just not a nine-to-five one."

"Are you free to leave?"

He frowned. "Leave?"

"The office," Robert elaborated. "To come with us."

Clay carefully replaced the knife he held, and his eyes locked with his father's. *Come with us.* How long had he waited for this tall, professorial man to ask that particular question? Even now, though he was thirty years old, it sang through him with clarity and resonance, like a favorite melody.

Forgetting everything else that was happening in his life, everything that would have to be put on hold, he turned to his mother. Her smile was bright, her pretty face free of makeup. She reached out to pat his hand; she'd been around so seldom to do that. He felt his self-esteem swell and turned his hand to catch hers. It was small and callused in his. Only an irritating flash of common sense prevented him from shouting an affirmative.

"We understand from one of the public-relations people the foundation has hired to accompany us on this trip that you've been very modest in your letters." She took his other hand and squeezed both. "Your name is becoming somewhat of a household word."

His father and mother were both beaming at him. Words were his business, yet he could not think of one to adequately describe how he felt at that moment. As a child, he used to dream of his parents coming home to take him back with them. As he grew up and began to understand that they loved him, though they didn't really need him in their lives, he had been willing to settle for their being proud of him. But their letters to him came back full of descriptions of their work and little comment on what he had told them: he'd pulled a four point that quarter; he'd landed a job at the *Standard News*; he'd been made a columnist.

He felt as though he were perched on the brink of a cliff. The very next thing his mother was going to say was, "We're so proud of you, Clay." He knew he was a worthwhile human being, but it would be such reinforcement to know his brilliant parents thought so, too.

Robert put an arm around Sharon's shoulders and she squeezed Clay's hand. Clay could not recall a moment in his life when the three of them had been closer.

"Darling," Sharon said, "we want you to travel with us for this month and write about what we're doing."

Still Clay held her hands, reveling in the way they clutched his. "You said the foundation hired..."

"Yes, but she isn't someone who knows your father and me. She's boned up—" Sharon smiled "—pardon the pun, on her paleontology, but if we could get across what we see and feel when we work, what we're trying to accomplish, I think donors would give more readily."

Robert nodded gravely. "And more generously."

The cliff crumbled under Clay, but he didn't fall headlong into blackness. He simply sat down with a thud on what was left. This was all so familiar. Trying hard not to let his journalist's cynicism get the better of him, he held on to a little of the dream. "Would I be working with the two of you?" he asked.

"Oh, no," Sharon replied as Robert shook his head. Clay looked from one face to the other for any sign of regret, or even a glimpse of embarrassment. There was neither. "We're booked solid all day long, and evenings will be spent visiting with potential donors. But our diaries are detailed. They should be of great help to you."

Robert went on to list their stops, their accommodations, and all Clay could gain by accompanying them. "I promise there won't be a dull moment," he said, smiling briefly. "What do you say?"

Clay drew his hands from his mother's and leaned back in his chair. Feeling left him, like the wind from a spent parachute. Then a small smooth hand closed over his from the other corner of the table. He looked into Janessa's eyes and found them filled with anger and pain—his pain.

When he turned back to his parents, they were still leaning toward each other, looking at him expectantly. "You've forgotten something important," Clay said, reaching into his breast pocket for his billfold. He put a credit card on the small tray that was immediately swept up by a waiter. He went on with a kind of fatalism that suddenly felt comfortable after all the years he'd resisted admitting to it. "I don't know you, either. I know your work, but I don't know the two of you any better than your hired PR representative does."

Both faces looking back at him registered hurt surprise. "Clay," Sharon said, glancing at her husband in concern, then back to her son. "We're your parents."

Clay sighed wearily, knowing that expecting them to understand was useless. "Yes, I suppose you are. Unfortunately I'm not your son. I'm simply the product of your love, and while I admire it for its durability in holding the two of you together, I deplore it for its inability to include me." He turned to Janessa as he stood. "Are you ready?"

Brow furrowed, Robert stood, putting a hand to Clay's arm. "Son, what are you talking about?"

Clay disengaged the arm his father held and picked up the credit card the waiter returned.

"Clay..." Sharon began, reaching for him.

Clay took a step back, out of reach, and pushed Janessa ahead of him toward the door. "Thanks for letting me know you were coming. See you again sometime." There was more pain than sarcasm in his tone.

Following Janessa from the dark restaurant into the sunny parking lot, he knew he was being cowardly. He had brought the subject up, after all. And in a crowded restaurant, of all places. He had thought he was ready to spill it all, thought it would have a cleansing effect on him. But they'd looked so stunned, so hurt, that all he had accomplished was to intensify his own pain.

Robert caught him halfway across the parking lot, turning him forcibly around. Sharon caught her husband's arm with a quiet remonstration to calm down.

Janessa, her hand still caught in Clay's, put her other arm around his and said his name, the tone of her voice a plea for reasonableness.

"We did not come ten thousand miles," Robert said, his voice trembling with controlled anger, "for you to insult us."

He was insulted. Suddenly the cowardice fled and Clay forgot the pain. "You're insulted?" he asked quietly. "You came ten thousand miles to get money for your project, not to see me. You haven't seen me in over ten years and you find a lousy couple of hours for me during which you ask not one question about me, about what I'm doing or what I want, except in how it relates to whether or not I can be used to help you make some more money on this trip."

"But we asked you to come with—" Sharon began, her eyes anguished.

"No, you didn't!" Clay shouted. She flinched and the pain suddenly returned, ripping at him, but he couldn't stop. Feelings and frustrations suppressed all his life poured out of him with volcanic force. "You didn't want me. You didn't want my company. You wanted my skill as a writer to further your project. Damn it! I'm your son, and after ten years all you can think about when you see me is that I could further your project." Filled with misery, Clay's eyes moved from his mother to his father. His voice fell to almost a whisper. "And *you're* insulted?"

Sharon began to sob, and Robert enfolded her in his arms, glaring at his son. "We invited you to share—"

"What?" Clay asked, his throat, his entire being, burning with barely controlled emotion. "A month with your public-relations person? The two of you were going to be tied up, remember? You were scheduled for appearances all day and would be meeting donors every evening. I would be working with your diaries and your notes."

"Clay..." Sobbing, Sharon reached out of her husband's arms to catch her son's hand. He held hers for a moment but felt unable to spare her or himself. "In almost thirty years, Mom, that's all I've ever had of either of you—your research notes. That's all your letters to me were. At the age of ten I probably knew more about Kenyapithecus than most paleontologists. You never asked about me beyond how my grades were and my general health. You had no idea of all the fears and insecurities I harbored for so long because you'd just walked away and left me behind.''

"The Knights told us you were doing so well.''

"I did do well,'' he replied, "because they made me feel loved and important. They did all the things for me that you should have done.''

Robert squared his shoulders as though in justification of his actions. "We knew they'd love you like their own.''

"Then you mustn't be upset,'' Clay said quietly, "now that I'm theirs instead of yours.''

Sharon pulled out of her husband's arms completely and threw herself at her son. "Don't say that!'' she wept against him. "Please don't say that.''

Clay held her close, as much for his own comfort as for hers. "I'll always love you.'' He looked into his father's glare and braved it for a protracted moment. "And you. I don't seem to be able to help myself. And I'll probably always crave your approval and praise, and feel absurdly glad when you give them, like I did this afternoon when I thought it was for me and not just for what I could do for the project. But the ties that bind aren't there anymore. They've dissolved from lack of care. Ethan and Elaine are my mother and father.''

With a cry of pain and anger, Sharon slammed a fist into his chest. "That's cruel!'' she accused.

Clay drew a ragged breath. "It's true. I'm sorry.''

Robert pulled her back. "Then I guess we have no more business here,'' he said. "Goodbye, Barclay.''

Clay reached for Janessa and headed for the car, marching blindly past the lot attendant, dodging moving cars and people. He was vaguely aware that she had to run to keep up with him and that she was crying. He didn't realize that he was, too, until he opened the passenger side door and couldn't see the interior.

"Stop!" Janessa pleaded, holding him to her, resisting his efforts to put her in the car. "Clay, stop and let yourself feel it and be rid of it."

Crying, she clung to him, and he finally dropped his head to her shoulder. His breath came in painful, pointed bursts while the truth of his solitary position came home to him. With it came the realization that the Knights were his family and that Janessa was the very heart of him, but something basic in him called out to the flesh and blood from which he had sprung. He had to accept that he would probably always yearn for it.

He finally straightened, fighting against the echoes of the words he'd heard and said, and looked down into Janessa's face. Her eyes still reflected his pain. She sniffed, wiping the moisture from his eyes with her thumbs.

"God, that was ugly," she said, her voice, her attitude firming. "I can't believe they would do that to you. Are you all right?"

"Sure. You?"

"Yeah." She leaned against him again, feeling powerless to comfort him. She hugged him with every ounce of strength she possessed. "You don't need them," she said, then knowing that wasn't true, amended grimly, "at least you don't need them when they act like that."

"If that were true, it would make everything so much simpler." Clay kissed her cheek and helped her into the car. Slipping behind the wheel, he turned the key in the ignition and drove out of the parking lot, determined to put the ugly scene out of his mind. "Where do you want to go? We can check out Rodeo Drive in Beverly Hills, or go to Universal Studios, or—"

"Let's go back to the hotel."

Clay glanced at Janessa as he turned onto the street that would take them to the freeway. "You tired?" He reached a hand out to touch her knee. "I'm sorry if all that upset you."

Janessa removed her seat belt and inched closer, putting her arm around his shoulders. "Their insensitivity upset me. But I discovered something while the three of you were arguing."

He checked the rearview mirror, changed lanes, then glanced at her again. "What's that?"

"I could have killed them because they were hurting you." She rested her forehead against his temple and sighed away the pain. "Not because you're my friend, but because you're my man. I love you, Clay. I have no more concerns or reservations about it. My love is real." She nuzzled her nose against his ear. "And it's all for you."

Clay heard her declaration with his heart as well as his ears and wished himself anywhere but in a car heading to the Santa Monica Freeway.

"Jannie..." was all he could say.

"Watch the road and don't miss our turn," she instructed, nibbling on his earlobe. "We're going to make love in your room in...how long do you think it'll take us to get back?"

He got on the freeway, merged with the traffic and accelerated. "Just sit tight, Jannie," he said, pulling her knees closer to him, "and anticipate."

JANESSA DROPPED HER PURSE and Clay's jacket on a chair as Clay crossed the room to close out the view of the entertainment park and the sunny afternoon. Then he came back to her to take her in his arms. He reveled in the knowledge that, after all the years of living side by side, they would finally become one, their lives overlapped in the magic and mystery of being in love.

Janessa leaned her face against his shirt front, the gesture filled with willing surrender. "I've run after you for so many years. You've shared so many of my life's momentous occasions with me. And you've taught me so many things."

Janessa paused as her breath came a little faster and words became more difficult to form. She lifted her head to see if he understood what she was trying so hard not to say. "I'm a virgin" seemed such a discordant admission at this point in time, but she felt he should know.

The moment her eyes made contact with his, she knew he understood. He smiled with all the indulgence of her dearest friend, but his eyes held all the passion of her anticipating lover. He kissed her gently and sighed as he rocked her from side to side. "At this moment, I feel as much an innocent as you do. We're about to make love, and there is no experience in my past that compares to what I feel now. I won't be the teacher here, Jannie. We'll learn from each other." Combing his fingers through the thick loose hair at her temples, he tilted her head up and leaned down to kiss her with slow concentration.

He gathered up the bottom of her long sweater until he could reach the soft skin at her waist. Moving his lips to her ear, he pulled her closer, his hands moving up her back, finding the obstruction of her bra. He made a small sound of displeasure and unhooked it. It came off with the sweater in one swift movement. Her hair fell over her face then settled around her shoulders with a fluid swirl as he tossed the clothing aside.

Janessa trembled as the cool air of the room touched her skin. Clay's eyes went over her with wonder, his hands unable to resist the inclination to follow them. They traced the delicate bones at her neck and shoulders, moved down her slender arms then up her rib cage to the spherical swells of her breasts. His hands cupped them, his hair grazing Janessa's skin as he leaned down to kiss each one.

Feeling rose from deep inside her and began to pulse along her skin. His lips moved up between her breasts, along her collarbone to her shoulder, then to her ear. The feeling followed his lips like a shadow, warming, stirring.

Clay raised his head to remove his sweater, but Janessa stopped him. Uncrossing the arms he had placed at its hem to pull it up, she raised them slightly, away from his body. Slipping her hands underneath, she raised the soft knitted fabric. Her fingers worked with a slowness that darkened his eyes. Tossing his sweater and T-shirt with her things, she ran the pads of her fingertips from his narrow waist to the broad bar of his shoulders.

Dispensing with his jeans and her panties, Clay pulled her down beside him on the bed. For one moment he could do nothing but stare at the shadowed features staring back at him. He felt like a man who'd won the lottery, or the Pulitzer prize—as though his every dream had been realized.

Janessa put a hand out to Clay, as though reaching for focus and substance. The heat and muscle she felt on the crest of his ribs reassured her, and her hand went on to explore the concavity of his stomach, the strong-boned juncture of his hip, his tough thigh.

He pulled her closer, his hands roaming everywhere, sharpening already strained feelings to a dangerous pitch. Her hands imitated his, stroking every plane, tracing each inviting hollow.

Clay tipped Janessa onto her back, cradled her head in the crook of his arm. Her heart, poised with some knowledge her brain didn't have, ticked like a clock gone wild.

Clay placed his free hand on Janessa's waist. It began to move in slow circles down the middle of her body. The beat of her heart seemed to have slipped under his hand, following it over the slight ridge of her femininity.

Janessa held him close in an agony of wanting. He pressed his lips to her cheek, and then it rippled through her, feelings so strong, so elemental, so physically satisfying, yet with such a spirituality at their heart that she felt the reason for living had been confirmed. Love.

"Clay!" She whispered his name with such a note of awe, that he held her to him, cherishing her, for one more moment.

As feeling continued to wash over her, Janessa stroked down his body's center, as he had done to her. Drawing circles with her fingertips, deepening them with the palm of her hand, she followed her path to its warm, strong destination, exploring, caressing, loving with a sincerity and an ardor that more than made up for her inexperience.

Clay shifted Janessa and rose over her. He probed with care for her body's resistance, then whispered, "I love you."

She arched against him, then subsided as he began to move slowly. As his body's undulation began to create pleasure inside her, the prospect of experiencing it again, of helping Clay experience it, made her instinctively move with him.

It was long moments before they were able to shift their bodies to lie side by side. And then even touching didn't seem close enough. Reaching an arm around Clay's neck, Janessa pulled herself up as he nudged under her so that her breasts were pressed against his chest. He pulled the blankets over her then wrapped his arms around her back.

"I can see why it makes the world go round," she said with a sigh of happy repletion.

Filled with delicious languor, Clay rubbed a foot along her calf and kissed the top of her head. "I wonder why it took us so long to get around to it."

Janessa shrugged against him. "I guess it's just hard for friends to think of themselves in other terms. You become so dependent on each other for those things a friend provides that you're afraid to risk it."

"Risk it?"

Janessa folded her hands on his chest and rested her chin on them, smiling with a small trace of sadness Clay found unsettling. "We've put that behind us. It'll never be the same again."

He pushed the bangs back from her eyes, needing to see her clearly. "Would you have chosen our friendship over what we just shared?"

"Of course not." She strained up to reach his lips with hers. "But I'll miss it. Won't you?"

"No," he replied with a small, exasperated laugh. "Friendship hasn't the depth of love."

"Love is harder to maintain than friendship."

"Oh, yeah? How do you know?"

"My parents. Jake and Annie."

"I don't know about your parents, but Jake and Annie weren't friends first. And anyway, isn't this a hell of a time to be analyzing it?"

Janessa pinched the skin under her hands. "You brought it up," she reminded as he yelped in complaint. "You asked why we..."

She lost her train of thought as she found Clay dotting kisses down her body.

CLAY WATCHED Bill Chance close the beige vertical blinds at his office window. With the baking early-afternoon sun shut out, the office cooled instantly and seemed to grow quiet.

In the past two hours, Clay had met and been interviewed by the editorial management of the *Times*. Bill had taken him through the complex of buildings, from the deafening roar of the pressroom in the lower levels to the ivory tower of the top-floor executive dining room. He met several of the men behind the names he had admired most of his professional life and had the thrill of a lifetime when one of them quoted a line from his own column back to him. He realized with a sense of surprise that he was more than flattered by their persistence—he was interested in the job.

"Well." Bill sat behind his desk, leaned back in his chair and fixed deep brown eyes on Clay. "Now you know where we stand. We want you. I can assure you that we don't offer that kind of money to everyone. And there are already two editors fighting over the office we're holding for you. Can you give me a decision by Monday?"

"I will."

Both men stood and reached across the desk to shake hands. "Hope to have you on staff," Bill said, seeing Clay to the door of his office.

Clay drove back to the hotel through the freeway jumble. He was energized with professional excitement. He'd shaken hands with three Pulitzer prize winners. But could he ever get used to this traffic, he wondered? Could Janessa? Los Angeles was a beautiful, if hectic and congested city. And the climate had a lot to recommend it.

Pushing aside the incredible salary the editorial management had proposed, he tried to think objectively about separating Janessa from her family. She would hate it, he knew, but after the previous night, he had little doubt she'd come with him.

He smiled as he braked for a traffic jam at the freeway interchange. He had never felt like this in his life—so acutely aware of everything. As a journalist, he'd always been an observer, but this was different. He was aware of things from his own perspective, rather than from the objective point of view from which every newspaperman tried to function. It was as though Janessa had tapped something inside him that had long lain dormant.

He'd never thought seriously about having a family before. He and Jake had always had such a good time on the fringe of involvement, playing with life rather than taking it seriously. But now life seemed to have a meaning, a purpose with which he wanted to become involved. As the traffic began to move on, he accelerated and wondered if he'd be able to explain that to Janessa.

He found her in the bathtub, one not very long but beautifully shaped leg stretched out as she soaped it. Her golden hair was caught up in a carelessly knotted bun, spilling tendrils over her ears and down her neck. Perched on top of the silky mass was a pair of Mickey Mouse ears. An urgent desire took quick precedence over explanations.

She looked up at him and smiled, and his heart seemed to forget its purpose. "Mercy," he said, his tone low and seductive as he advanced into the bathroom. "A mouse in my tub."

Her eyes watched him move, their color darkening as she read his intention. "I bought them for Mark," she whispered. "Do you like them?"

Leaning over the tub, a hand on either side of it, he pulled his eyes from a lazy perusal of her supple nakedness to focus on the hat. He grinned. "They're a little small."

"Of course they are," she replied, flicking a spray of water at him. "Mark is small. Aah!" She gasped as Clay removed his jacket and her mouse ears, then tossed them all aside as he reached for her hands and pulled her to her feet.

Laughing as he whipped a towel off the rack and wrapped it around her, Janessa demanded, "What is this?"

He kissed her long and slowly then scooped her up into his arms. "A mousetrap," he said.

Thoroughly loved, Janessa settled against Clay's chest some time later and sighed heavily, as though entertaining a thought of social significance.

Clay squeezed her shoulder. "What?"

"I was thinking of all the other mice in the world," she said gravely, "who have to settle for cheese."

He laughed and pinched her silky skin.

There was a moment of silence while she leaned her elbow on his chest and looked into his eyes. His expression sobered and he toyed with the hair that had fallen free of her haphazard pinning. "Are you going to tell me what happened at the interview?"

"Yes," he replied, taking her hand from his chest and linking the fingers of his free hand with it. "It went very well. They've offered everything I could have hoped for and more."

Her heart remained steady, unsure whether to plummet or soar. She was so proud of him, but she hated the thought of life without him.

"But I'm undecided," he went on. "It's very appealing but there are a lot of considerations."

Janessa felt obliged to be supportive. "I imagine with the resources of the *Los Angeles Times* at your disposal, you could accomplish even more than you do now."

He nodded, bringing their linked hands to his lips and planting a kiss on her knuckles. "That's true, but I'm trying to be as considerate of myself, the person, as of myself, the journalist. Would I be happy here? A move to L.A. would be a considerable change in life-style. The weather's great, but the traffic's awful. There are a million things to see and do, but there are also millions of other people seeing and doing them. And this air has color and texture. The food is less expensive than at home, but every other cost of living is higher.''

Clay freed her fingers to raise the pillow behind his head. He pushed up to lean against the headboard, bringing her with him. He caught her fingers again and threaded his through them. ''And then there's the most important consideration of all.''

Suspecting what was coming, Janessa lay her head back against his shoulder to look at him.

''Will you come with me?'' he asked.

Janessa lay still for a moment, cursing the fates that always played this kind of trick: Make two people fall in love and then give them impossible choices. She loved him and she owed him, but didn't she owe herself, as well? ''I can't,'' she said finally. Feeling the surprised tensing of his body, she sat up and pulled away from him, unable to bear it.

His voice was quiet and controlled as he asked, ''Why not?''

''I can't leave my family in the state they're in right now.'' Her voice rose a little as she replied. Her frustration with the situation and with herself made her annoyed with Clay. ''My dad's helpless alone, my mother might do something totally harebrained, and Jake and Annie ... well ...'' She expressed the condition of their relationship with a desperate sweep of her hand.

There was a moment of charged silence. Suddenly realizing she had presented Clay with her back, Janessa turned to face him. Seeing the hurt and anger in his eyes, she wished she hadn't.

His voice remained even when he spoke. ''What do you think you can do for them?''

''I don't know. Just be there, I guess.''

"You have been there, and what good has it done anyone? They're all still having problems, and you worry yourself into headaches."

She squared her shoulders defensively. "They're my family, Clay."

He closed his eyes for a moment, obviously marshaling patience. Then he sat forward, putting his large warm hand over the one with which she braced herself on the sheet. His eyes were dark and deep, seeing into her innermost being. "What am I to you, Jan?"

"My best friend," she replied without a moment's thought. Then she added softly, "And my lover."

Clay leaned his shoulders back against his pillow, closing his eyes for one silent moment. Then he opened them to look at her in disappointment. "You still think of me as a friend first, and a lover second."

"You've been a friend a lot longer." She shrugged as she tried to explain herself. Grabbing her cotton nightshirt from the end of the bed, she slipped it on and began to pace. "A friend would understand about my family. Then there's my shop." She stopped at the foot of the bed, her slim knees poking out from under the shirt as she folded her arms. "I'm delighted that you got this wonderful offer. I want you to have it, but I've spent a fortune in money and effort trying to organize my own career." *I do owe you a lot,* she thought desperately, *but is that enough to hinge our lives on?*

He nodded. "I understand that. But certainly there must be some way around it. Wouldn't a shop here do as well—maybe even better?"

That was probably true, but her soul had gone into the drafty, rickety one in Salem. Afraid that was not a substantial argument, she said on a note of panic, "What about the cabin? What about the boat? What about Jake and my parents?"

With a grunt of disgust, Clay threw the blankets aside and stood, slipping into his jeans. "This doesn't have anything to do with your family, or your business, or the cabin at the lake." Bare chested and barefoot, he began his own pacing pattern perpendicular to hers. He went from the dresser to the window and back again. He stopped to stand over her and lean down until they were nose to nose. "This has to do with Disneyland."

"What?" she demanded.

"Disneyland," he said again, sweeping a hand to the window through which the whole panorama could be seen, lights going on against a dusky sky. "You said you wanted to live here always, and now I believe you really meant it. You don't want anything in your fairyland to change. You want your parents to stay together—for you."

"I—" she began, but he jabbed an accusatory finger at her shoulder and went on. "Never mind that they find the going difficult, that they need to make some kind of a change."

"They—" she tried again, but he was still talking.

"And you want Jake to settle down with Annie because that would make *you* happy. Have you wondered if it'll make him happy?"

"Of course I—"

"And you're using them as an excuse not to come with me, because that would really upset your pretty little world." Clay took three steps away and came back, his eyes bright with temper. "We've been friends a long time and you're comfortable with that. But if our status as lovers took precedence over that, things would finally change. You'd have to make concessions to me, and that just isn't possible, is it? You're the most loving little daughter, sister, friend in the world as long as we're not upsetting the way you like things."

"That's a lie!" Janessa put both hands flat against his chest and pushed with all her might. "I'm worried about my family because I want them to be happy for themselves, not for me! And I do love you, but you're selfish and thoughtless if you expect me to drop everything I've worked so hard for just to follow you and support your career."

Her angry shove hadn't rocked him, but her words did. He took a step back. "Just to follow me?" He repeated her careless phrase.

"I didn't—" she began, but he turned away to the closet, cutting her off.

"You needn't explain. I'm used to being second choice to someone else's career. I've lived my whole life that way."

"Oh . . . !" Janessa bit back the expletive and satisfied herself by grabbing Clay's arm and yanking him around to face her. His jaw was grimly set, his eyes hard and dark as he looked down at her. "Since you're so keen on analyzing everything, Mr. Journalist—" she jabbed her finger in the air, rocking on her toes to indicate the height of her indignation "—this isn't just about me following you. It's about you making a decision to move to Los Angeles so that I would make an instant, no-thought-required decision to go with you, thereby proving to yourself that you finally come first in somebody's life!"

They glared at each other in silent assessment. Then he arched an eyebrow and said in self-derision, "Backfired on me, didn't it?"

Janessa drew a deep breath and brushed a strand of hair out of her eyes. "It wasn't fair."

He shrugged and turned to continue pulling things out of the closet. "Fair or not, I know where I stand, don't I?

Somewhere behind your parents, your brother, your friend, and your business."

"Oh . . . !" This time Janessa did not delete the expletive and stormed into the bathroom, slamming the door.

Chapter Twelve

"I can carry my things," Janessa said stiffly to Clay as he pulled into her driveway after the interminable flight home and the even longer drive from the airport. "You needn't get out."

Ignoring her, he pulled her suitcase out of the trunk as she reached into the back seat for her tote. When she tried to take the case from him, he pushed her hand away, his expression changing from grimness to interest as he gestured across the street with a jut of his chin.

"Looks like there might have been some patching up while we were gone," he said as she turned to see her mother's white Mercedes parked there.

Janessa put a hand to her heart. It was such a comfort to know something might work out right for someone. "Thank God." That just left Jake and Annie. At the moment, she and Clay were too hopeless to even consider.

Janessa went around the house, deciding to enter through the basement and afford her parents some privacy. As Clay followed her into a room jumbled with fabric, boxes and all the general clutter surrounding her work, she put her tote on a dilapidated chair, bracing herself to thank him for asking her along on the trip and bid him a civil goodbye. But it was at that moment that the conversation upstairs became audible.

"You don't even care!" Elaine shouted, her voice high and angry.

Clay and Janessa froze and looked at each other.

"I damn well do care!" Ethan bellowed back. "But I'm powerless to do anything about it."

"You haven't even tried!"

"I have! It looks like I haven't, but I have!"

Against her will, Janessa felt herself drawn to the foot of the stairs that led to the kitchen. The upstairs door was open and the argument was as clear as though it were being waged right beside her. Underlying both voices were pain and frustration. Her mother sounded desperate, her father despondent.

"Just come back home," Elaine said, her tone conciliatory, almost pleading.

"You have your job," Ethan replied bitterly, "your friends, your own life."

Elaine's voice rose. "Do you know what this is doing to our children?"

Ethan's answer was weary. "They have their own lives. I'm not really that necessary to anyone anymore."

Janessa opened her mouth to speak, her foot on the bottom step, ready to race up and correct her father. Clay stopped her with a hand over her mouth, pulling her swiftly against the wall as footsteps moved across the kitchen to the basement door. The rear entrance to the house was just opposite it. Janessa hadn't realized she was crying until Clay's hand broke the tears against her cheeks.

"What I resent," Elaine said evenly, her voice vibrating with anger, "is that you're willing to just give up. To lie down and die without trying to make things better."

Ethan's voice was calm, reasonable. "Why should I put you through that? It's frustrating for you and humiliating for me."

Elaine's sigh, her last grasp at patience, was audible in the basement. "Do you think you're the only man who's ever struggled with impotence? You were a great state senator, Ethan, and generally a great man. Are you going to be defeated by such a small obstacle?"

"Six months is not a small obstacle." There was a long silence, then the sound of a doorknob being turned. "You've so much to offer now. You'll find somebody else."

There was an immediate whop, followed by a grunt, as though someone had been struck by a purse or an umbrella. Then the slam of a door seemed to shake even the basement.

There was a long stream of colorful invective from Ethan. Something was kicked across the floor, something else thrown over; then the door slammed again; and after a moment, a car roared away.

Janessa dropped her hands from Clay's arms and leaned her head back against the wall. "So, that's it." While feeling sorry for her father, she felt impatient with him for giving her mother up for such a reason. "What is the matter with him. Mom's willing to be patient, so why...?"

"Give him a break," Clay said, sitting partway up the stairs. "He's a man. Making love to his wife is a gift he gives her, as well as himself. If he feels diminished by the fact that he's having trouble, try to understand."

"But my mother's willing to be patient."

"Which only increases the pressure on him."

Janessa folded her arms and looked down at him impatiently. "So what do they do?"

Clay spread his hands. "I don't have a solution. I'm just trying to understand the problem."

"Noble of you," she said, pacing away from him. "That's just the way you've dealt with us. You understand my concerns for my family and my need to have my shop, yet you want me to move with you to L.A. You offer no solution, just a problem.''

Bracing his hands on his knees, Clay stood. ''You'll have to forgive me,'' he said, heading for the door. ''I'm running second to a sweatshirt factory. Stunts one's thought processes.''

''You're one up on me!'' she shouted after him. ''I'm second to pollution and congestion!''

He whirled at the door and stormed back to her. ''You've put yourself behind your own inability to face the fact that things have to change. I'm not going to stay here, Janessa, and be your buddy forever. As a friend, I have given you everything I can. Now, I want to give to you as your lover, your husband.''

Her eyes widened at that, her anger slipping a little as surprise took hold. Clay noted her expression and shook his head. ''Did you think that all our making love meant was that we would share an extended, more physical friendship?''

''No,'' she replied, angling her chin. ''Did you think all it meant was that you could then dictate to me from some elevated position of power? A friend is tolerant, but a lover or a husband has a right to make demands, isn't that it?''

''No, just a right to expect more.''

''The right to come first.''

She flung the words at him like an accusation, but he had to admit, finally, that it was true. ''Yes.''

Clay had always been a pillar in her life, but in two short days of sharing love with him, he had become its foundation. He was vital to every single day, yet it was impossible for her to turn her back on all her other responsibilities at that moment. Knowing there was no way to explain that to him, Janessa simply offered him a thin smile and said, ''Then I guess we'll just have to remain friends.''

Clay walked to the door, absorbing the pain of her rejection. He opened it and looked at her over his shoulder, finality in his eyes and in his voice. "I don't think that's an option for us any longer. We can't go back now—at least, I can't. 'Bye, Jan."

Janessa made no effort to stop him. Feeling like the sole survivor of a disaster, Janessa went upstairs to the kitchen. The bucket of potatoes and onions she kept in a corner as a touch of country decor lay on its side. Vegetables were strewn across the tile floor like pieces on some giant checkerboard. A chair lay on its back.

As she cleaned up the kitchen, her parents' conversation played over in her mind and she finally had to concede that Clay was right. They had all been so happy for so long—how could anyone accept that their lives would change? The Knights had always had each other, no matter what crisis had befallen them. Not the strain put upon them by politics, nor Janessa's accident, nor the considerable pressures of five strong-willed people living in the same space, had ever affected their closeness. But now it appeared to have disintegrated, and their tight little circle was torn apart by the fates, which sometimes seemed so opposed to happiness and contentment.

Clay had suggested that Janessa's concern was selfish. That was true. As they drifted apart, she knew the people she loved would no longer be moving in and out of her daily life, and that hurt. She couldn't even let herself think about Clay's parting remark.

As Janessa went to the telephone with some half-formed intention of getting her mind back on business by calling Graciella to make sure the last shipment had been sent in her absence, she noticed the messages her father had tacked to the bulletin board. One message was from Simon, and three from friends congratulating her on her engagement. Janessa put her hands over her eyes, her spurt of courage dissipating as she remembered. The three days in California had put Simon and his machinations out of her mind. His note read: "Pick you up for dinner at seven Friday. Love, Simon."

She picked up the telephone, intent on calling him, tracking him down if she had to, and giving him a piece of her mind while forcibly refusing his invitation to dinner and telling him she was returning his ring. The melodic notes of her doorbell forestalled the action. Jake stood on her front porch.

"Hi," she said, pulling him inside. She was happy to see someone who wasn't shouting. Stopping him in the center of the living room, she directed him to stay right there, and ran down to the basement where she had left her suitcase. Quickly extracting the souvenirs she'd purchased, she ran back upstairs. She offered him a folded navy-blue T-shirt with the Disneyland logo across the chest. "I brought this back for you."

As he unfolded it, smiling, she held up the smaller T-shirt and the mouse ears in her other hand. "These are for Annie and Mark. Should I . . . give them to you?"

He looked at them a moment then shook his head. "You'd better give them to Annie. So—" his expression changed subtly, taking on an undercurrent of hostility "—you two have a good time?"

Janessa blinked at him, trying to judge the reason for the change in him. Had he guessed that the nature of her relationship with Clay had changed? It probably showed on her face. "Yes and no," she admitted.

He shifted his weight. "That's cryptic. Is he taking the job?"

"I think so."

He frowned at her. "He didn't tell you, or he hasn't made up his mind?"

"He asked me if I'd go with him and I said no." She sighed. "I think he's going anyway. You'll have to ask him."

Jake looked into her eyes, saw pain and confusion and weariness. He never knew what to do for her when she wasn't behaving like the strong, scrappy sister he was used to. The past week had turned him inside out, and he'd discovered things about himself he'd never known before. Hesitantly he put a hand to her face. "Are you okay?"

She came into his arms with a sigh of relief and he closed them around her. "No, I'm not. Are you? Is anybody?" She told him about their parents' conversation she'd overheard in the kitchen that morning. "I guess it's over and we just have to face it."

Jake patted her back. "Things don't always work out as tidy as we'd like. It'll all come right somehow." He doubted that was true, but it helped to say it. "Now." He took hold of her forearms and pulled her slightly away, looking into her eyes with authoritative insistence. "About this thing with Pruitt. I want you to stay away from him until the authorities pick him up, so that you're not implicated in any way. Don't take any calls from him, don't meet him, don't..." Janessa's blank look finally registered with him and he stopped, an ugly suspicion forming.

"What are you talking about?" she asked.

The arms he held had grown tense, and he dropped his hands, the suspicion confirmed. "Clay didn't tell you?"

She was silent for a moment. Her voice had deepened ominously when she asked, "Tell me what?"

He ran a hand down his face, knowing all hell was about to break loose and he wasn't ready for it. He'd had a row with Annie only that morning and a run-in with Stewie during lunch. When he saw Clay, he was going to kill him.

"Simon Pruitt is involved with the pirating of videos. Clay's been investigating him, and we followed him the night of the party when he put you in a cab." Jake looked into her furious face without flinching. "No point in being outraged. We did it because we were worried about you, and as it turns out, we were right." He went on to list some of the things they had learned. "The police know he'll be moving a truckload of tapes in a couple of days to Portland. From there it'll be smuggled overseas. He stands to make a tidy profit. Probably enough to finance a strong campaign."

Janessa didn't know who she was most angry with—Jake and Clay for undertaking such a project on her behalf and not telling her about it, Simon for doing something so inexcusably stupid, or herself for never suspecting anything. Even the night of the cocktail party when she had seen Jake and Clay, she had suspected them of nothing more serious than keeping an eye on her because they didn't trust Simon. She'd had no idea their mistrust had been prompted by suspicion of the man's criminal conduct. "Nice of you to tell me, Jake," she said, walking to the door and opening it. "Even if it is somewhat after the fact."

"Remember the last time I tried to talk to you about Simon?" he reminded, sauntering toward her. "You know what your problem is, sis?"

"Besides the fact I have you for a brother and Clay for a...friend?"

He noted the slight pause but ignored it. "You've come through a lot and you know you're strong. So you think you can place us all where you want us and we have to stay there, because that's what you want. Well, too bad. I love you and I will always worry about you, and I don't have to justify that to anybody. And if Clay wants you to go to California with him, I think you'd better give it some serious thought. He's given you more and taken more crap from you than any of us. If that isn't real love, I don't know what is." The door slammed behind him with a resounding bang.

Resisting the urge to fall into bed with an ice pack on her head, Janessa had to content herself with changing into jeans and a sweatshirt, then heading downstairs to get her things. She'd give some thought, meanwhile, to just how she'd tell Clay her opinion about friends who lied.

Hauling her suitcase and tote bag upstairs, she unpacked, hoping the busy work would be therapeutic. The more she thought about Simon, the less she found herself able to believe what Jake had told her. Simon had too much political self-preservation to risk doing some activity that would result in a prison sentence. Unless he really did need the money for his campaign. And she did have a vague memory of his visiting a video shop in south Salem one evening after taking her out to dinner. She had opted to wait in the car while he went inside to see someone, but he hadn't seemed particularly secretive about going in. And the suggestion that she wait outside had been hers not his. She was firmly convinced that he loved himself and the prospect of a political career too much to risk it.

TIRED FROM WRESTLING a topic for his column out of a brain too preoccupied with Janessa to think, Clay closed his eyes, only to have them snapped open by the sound of his door buzzer. Who the hell . . . ? he thought.

It was Ethan. "What are you doing here?" Clay asked him in genuine puzzlement, when he let the ex-senator into his condo.

"I needed a break," said Ethan, "and I just happened to have a bottle of Irish Cream with me." He grinned as he quoted Clay's words from the night they'd talked in the garage.

"Come on in." Clay pushed the door open, seeing the discomfort behind Ethan's cheerful exterior. "Take the chair by the fire." Tossing his briefcase and jacket on the sofa, he got glasses from the kitchen and handed them to Ethan, then began to build a fire. He'd been cold since they'd touched down in the northwest this morning. He couldn't decide if it was the three days in the Southern California sun, or Janessa's rejection that had thinned his blood.

Ethan poured, cleared his throat, took a drink and cleared his throat again. "I saw Elaine today." He said the words in a rush, as though afraid he would change his mind.

Clay lit the paper under the kindling. Reluctant to betray his presence at Janessa's this morning, he asked cautiously, "How is she?"

"Angry." Clay stood and Ethan handed him a glass. "Hit me with her umbrella."

Sitting in the matching chair opposite Ethan, Clay laughed. "She never was shy about revealing how she feels."

Ethan stared moodily into his glass. "I'm in a panic, Clay," he admitted. He drew a breath as though prepared to go on, then he stopped and shook his head. Clay saw the man who could speak with conviction and authority before a crowd of thousands lower his head and blush.

To help Ethan out, Clay decided to be honest. He said, "Jan and I came back to her place this morning and saw Elaine's car. Thinking you two might be patching things up, we went in through the basement." He gave a small smile of empathy. "We heard everything."

For a moment Ethan looked horrified, then he relaxed in his chair, expelling a sigh of relief. "So even my daughter knows her father's over the hill."

"C'mon, Ethan," Clay chided. "You know what they say about going over the hill."

"What?"

"You gain momentum."

Ethan snickered and drank. "Not me, son. I've stalled."

Clay looked at the man who meant so much to him and felt almost as uncomfortable with the subject as he did. But growing up in a more understanding age, one that didn't require a man's eternal virility and unwavering strength as Ethan's upbringing and position had, gave Clay an edge. "It sounded to me as though that upset Elaine a lot less than it upset you."

Ethan shook his head again, looking bleak. "She's still a youthful, sexy woman...."

"Then let her help you," Clay said earnestly. "Get a book. Try something new."

Ethan scoffed. "I'm too old for that."

"If you were too old," Clay reasoned, "it wouldn't bother you." Ethan looked at him consideringly, and Clay pressed his advantage. "Ethan, you've never rolled over and died in your whole life. You've got years and years left to spend with the woman you love and who loves you. Don't worry about having to perform; I don't think Elaine cares about that as much as you think she does. There's so much to making love that can still give you both pleasure. And I'll bet everything would work out if you'd get your mind right. It's a new world, Ethan. You don't have to be Hercules—just a man who loves a woman and wants to show her. That's all."

Ethan was silent for a moment then downed the contents of his glass. "I'd be embarrassed to buy a book."

Clay put his glass aside and stood. "I'll go with you. We'll laugh and leer, and let the clerk think we're a couple of Don Juans trying to broaden our horizons."

As Clay settled the screen around the fire and put his jacket on, Ethan looked at him with grave blue eyes. "Have I ever told you what I think of you?"

Clay opened the door. "Many times. Hardheaded, single-minded, independent, smart a..."

"All those things." Ethan retracted nothing. "But remarkably, you're okay, son. And I've often wished your name was Knight."

Clay hooked an arm around his shoulders and led him down the hall. "In my heart, it is."

WITH HER CLOTHES UNPACKED and her house back in order, Janessa glanced at her watch and decided she had just enough time to bathe and change for the dinner Simon had scheduled in his message. Unable to reach him, she decided to keep the date and tell him what she thought of their engagement and return the ring. Her anger superseded any concern for her personal safety.

She was preparing to run a bath when Annie arrived, standing just inside the door in jeans and a denim jacket, her bright auburn hair tied back in a ponytail. "Hi," she said cheerfully. "How was California? Jake tells me you brought back presents."

Janessa gestured toward the sofa. "Sit down for a few minutes. I'm supposed to meet Simon for dinner, but I want to hear about the shop. First, though..." She took the T-shirt and mouse ears off the coffee table.

"Oh!" Unable to resist, Annie put the ears on and sat up straight. "How do I look?"

It was a moment before Janessa could reply, caught in the memory of the delicious afternoon the mouse ears had earned her just the day before.

"Charming. But they'll probably fit Mark better. Where is he, anyway?"

Annie made a production of inspecting the shirt. "Jake picked him up. He didn't say where they were going. He's done that for an hour or two every day since we had that fight." She removed the hat and folded the shirt. "Thanks, Jan. Mark will be thrilled."

Janessa leaned an elbow on the back of the sofa. "Are you and Jake any closer to a solution?" she asked quietly.

"Maybe." Annie smiled thinly, rubbing a thumb over the shiny mouse ears. "He really seems to care about Mark, and he tries to talk about us without shouting at me. I'm beginning to think that might mean he cares about me. I'd just like to be more sure that it's because I'm Annie and not because I'm his son's mother."

"Considering how bossy he is by nature," Janessa pointed out, "if he's making an effort to be understanding, you have a right to feel special—even loved."

Annie considered that, then folded her hands over the gifts in her lap. "You didn't tell me how Los Angeles was. Is Clay going to take the job?"

"I think so." Janessa's eyes clouded, and she toyed absently with a strand of hair. "He asked me to marry him."

Annie nodded. "I thought that was coming."

When Janessa looked at her in surprise, Annie arched an eyebrow. "Do you think you're the only one who cares about other people's relationships? I saw it happening. I just wasn't sure either of you did."

"How can I move to Los Angeles when the family's in chaos and I've sunk every dime I own and my entire soul into opening the new shop?"

Annie thought a moment, then shook her head. "Please. I have my own tough questions. I assume you've told him how you feel about that."

"He thinks that if I love him, I'll follow. But after what he and Jake did, I'm not sure what I feel." She explained about Clay's and Jake's investigation and what it had revealed.

"Then, isn't it fortunate for you that they did it?" Annie asked cautiously. "I mean, you could have been caught with him and had some fast explaining to do. That would have been embarrassing, not to mention inconvenient."

"They could have told me," Janessa grumbled.

Annie frowned. "And you'd have made them stop. Come on, you were never serious about Simon, anyway."

"It's the principle of the thing."

"Would you rather have been arrested with Simon for a principle? Besides, if that's true, he's probably got dangerous friends. They were only thinking of you."

As Janessa opened her mouth to offer a scathing reply, the telephone rang. "Jeez!" she exclaimed, going to the kitchen. "This place has been like the stock exchange all afternoon. Simon!" She made a conscious effort to speak calmly when she heard his voice. "Hi."

Annie, hearing the name, wandered to the door of the kitchen to listen. Janessa waved a shushing hand at her friend as Annie made a throat-cutting gesture with her index finger.

"I won't be able to make dinner tonight, after all," Simon said.

He sounded breathless and a little harried, Janessa thought, but then he often did. "A campaign meeting?" she asked, probing.

"No, just . . . a family matter. You know how it is."

"I do, but it's important that we talk about this engagement, Simon." She was insistent, hoping to force a revelation. "I was hoping we could talk tonight."

"It just came up, Jan." His voice became firm. "This was something I'd planned to do later in the week, but it . . . well, it just won't wait."

Janessa's heart gave a small lurch and began to beat faster. Suddenly she was sure Simon was somehow involved in the pirating and that there had been a change in the plans to move the videotapes. "But I thought it was a family matter," she pressed, hoping to learn more.

"It is. Jan, I've got to go."

"Simon—"

"I'll call you tomorrow, I promise."

Before she could protest, he'd hung up.

Forgetting that she wasn't speaking to him, Janessa immediately dialed Clay's number. "I'll just bet they're moving the tapes tonight," she told Annie as the phone rang. When Clay didn't answer, she disconnected and tried the newspaper only to find that he'd stopped by but left an hour earlier.

Trying to reach Jake had the same frustrating results. He wasn't at home, and no one at the tavern knew where he was. "If he calls," she told Stewie, trying to sound calm while impressing upon him the urgency of relaying the message, "tell him I said Simon's had a change of plans, and he's moving tonight instead of on the weekend."

"What are you doing?" Annie demanded, following Janessa as she reached for her jacket and searched the living room for her purse.

"I'm going to the video place."

"How do you know where it is?"

"I was out with Simon one night when he stopped there. I waited in the car."

"Janessa!" Annie followed her down the corridor and into the bedroom where she found her purse under the opened top of her suitcase. "You can't just barge into the middle of a...a pirating thing. It's dangerous. They'll catch him another time."

"They worked so hard to set him up this time."

"I thought you were mad at them about that."

"It's the principle of the thing." Janessa's father had taught her to despise crooked politicians as one of the lowest forms of life. She still wasn't sure about Simon, but if he was involved in video piracy, he wouldn't get away with it if she could help it.

"Shouldn't you call the police?"

"I don't know who Jake and Clay were working with." Janessa dug into her purse for her car keys, continuing her search as she started for the living room. "By the time I explain it all to somebody else, Simon and the shipment could be gone."

"What do you think you'll be able to do?"

"I don't know. Stop them, follow them—something—until we can reach Jake and Clay."

Annie rolled her eyes and followed Janessa back through the house to the front door. "I can't let you do this by yourself," she threatened.

Janessa opened the door and frowned at her friend. "You think you can stop me?"

"No," Annie replied, stepping outside. "But I can come with you."

Janessa turned the lock and closed the door. "Why?"

Annie tore open her car door. "It's the principle of the thing. Get in. I'll drive. By the time you find your keys in your bag, it'll be too late."

Chapter Thirteen

"Jason Knight! I am considerably past middle age, but I am not a dinosaur!" Elaine's indignant expression changed to one of wide-eyed, eyebrow-wagging silliness as she transferred her gaze from her son to her grandson. Mark sat astride her knee, clinging happily to her hands as he looked around his grandparents' living room, gurgling. Elaine bounced him up and down. "I won't settle for a comfortable, companionable old age simply because your father feels ready for one. I have my pride, you know."

"I hate to think of you alone." Jake watched her playing with his son and a wave of sadness overwhelmed him. At a time when his parents should be enjoying grandchildren, they were separated and unable to share Mark. Jake's sadness deepened as he realized the same was true of himself and Annie.

Elaine glanced at him and smiled, a wicked look in her eyes. "Then I'll move in with you, darling, and we'll swing together. I could probably even teach you a few things."

Jake laughed. "Maybe you've just become too much for Dad." Catching the subtle stiffening of her expression, Jake went on quietly. "Is that it? You've become such a presence at the museum. Is Dad jealous of that? Does he want you home?"

"That's part of it." Mark rubbed his eyes and she pulled him into her shoulder, patting his back as she rocked back and forth on the apricot-colored sofa. "He was such a powerful man for so long. I think retirement was a more drastic change than he was prepared for. I, on the other hand, had lived for his career for so long that finally being able to throw myself wholeheartedly into something I've always wanted to do has made me good at it, and successful."

"But if you understand that so well," Jake asked, puzzled, "can't you find a way to make your marriage continue to work? I mean, Mom! Forty years invested—"

"Does not mean that I have to throw away whatever years I have left on a man who doesn't care." The sound of a motor roaring into the drive followed by the screech of brakes made Elaine frown. Jake went to the window to push the curtains aside.

"It's Clay," he said, glancing at her as he went to the door.

Clay pushed the door aside the moment Jake turned the knob and strode past him into the room. "Are they here?"

Jake followed him. "Who?"

Clay looked around and, apparently disliking what he saw, turned on Jake with a grim look. "Jan and Annie."

Knowing his friend was not one to panic, Jake said worriedly, "Annie went to Jan's about an hour ago when I picked Mark up. Why? What's wrong?"

"Lieutenant McMullin called me to tell me they got word the pirates have a change of plans. The videos are being moved tonight instead of Sunday. When I called the Crown and Anchor to tell you, Stewie said you'd taken the afternoon off and he didn't know where you were, but that Janessa had left an important message for you—Simon's moving tonight, she said. I don't know how she found that out, but she's not at home, she's not at the shop, she's not at Annie's.''

"You don't really think . . . ?''

"Yeah, I do.''

"But she'd have called us," Jake said reaching to the back of the sofa for his jacket. "Mom . . .''

Elaine was sitting stiff-backed, oblivious to Mark's sudden squirming. "Are you saying Jan's in danger? And Annie?''

"It's a long story," Clay said, already heading for the door. "But they'll both be safe if Jake and I move right away.''

She shooed them out the door. "I don't understand, but go. Mark's fine here with me, Jake.''

Jake waved his thanks and ran after Clay to his car. The Camaro would be faster than the BMW.

"Jan obviously called you—she left you the message. If she tried me, I wasn't reachable either.'' They roared down the drive and onto the quiet street. The thought crossed Clay's mind that Janessa had been too angry at him to call him, but he dismissed it, not wanting to think she wouldn't call if she needed him. He wasn't crazy, either, about the notion that she had tried to contact him and he hadn't been there.

"So, where were you?'' Jake demanded, finding it convenient to have a place to plant the blame.

"With your father,'' Clay replied.

In the corner of the parking lot across the street from the mouth of the alley, in the shadows of the tall bushes overhanging from the residential lot next door, Janessa and Annie planned their strategy.

"What are we going to do?'' Annie whispered.

Janessa stared at the truck standing in the alley. "I don't know.''

"Then why are we here?"

"I'll think of something."

"Well, hurry. I feel like we're being watched."

Janessa looked up and down the street. The only other vehicle in sight was Simon's Corvette, and it was empty. "Don't panic. There's just us and Simon's car and the truck." She frowned through the windshield. "I wonder why we haven't seen anybody."

"They're criminals," Annie replied. "They do things stealthily so they won't be seen. The truck must be loaded if it's out in the alley."

"If we could get close enough, we could disable the truck," Janessa said, then added lamely, "if we knew how to do that. That would buy us some time to find a phone and call the guys again."

In the dark, Annie's small voice said very matter-of-factly, "All we have to do is remove the distributor cap."

Janessa turned slowly to face her. "What's that?"

Annie made a cuplike gesture with her hands. "It's round and has all these little cylindrical things on it. Wires feed from it to the spark plugs. If you take it off, the engine won't go."

Forgetting the issue at hand, Janessa asked with new respect, "How do you know that?"

She shrugged. "When you're single and don't have a family, you learn to do a lot of things for yourself. I bought a book."

Janessa had always thought Annie a remarkable person, and it just occurred to her that she'd never have taken the time to tell her. But that would be something for another time. "Can you take it off the truck?"

"If I can find it in the dark," Annie said hesitantly, then added dryly, "and if no one comes out to stop me."

"I have a flashlight on my key ring." Janessa, successful at locating her keys this time, pulled the ring out of her purse, held the miniature flashlight aloft and pushed the tiny button. A small circle of light flashed on the ceiling of the car. She turned it off.

Annie outlined their course of action, ''We have to pop the hood, then remove the cap. Do you think we can do that without being heard? The loading-door is open.''

''We'll go closer and see.'' Janessa was already opening her door. ''If we hear anyone, we'll go to Plan B.''

''What's that?'' Annie whispered desperately as Janessa got out of the car. But Janessa was already running on tiptoe across the street, too far away to hear.

Flattened against the wall of the Laundromat that abutted the alley, Janessa strained to hear any sound coming from the loading bay at the back of the video shop. For a moment the sound of her own deep breaths covered everything else. Then she heard it—shouting coming from inside the building.

Annie, standing silently beside her, nudged her. Janessa nodded. The sound was so muffled she felt sure whoever was arguing was deep inside the building, probably beyond another door. She decided instantly that they might never have a better chance. She turned to Annie and whispered, ''Ready?''

Annie whispered back, ''No!''

Janessa grabbed Annie's arm and drew her with her as she turned into the alley. It was twenty yards to the truck. Except for the crunch of gravel, they ran silently, keeping to the shadows against the wall. At the open bay door the shouting was louder, though the words were still indecipherable. The two women waited a moment. The distant shouting was still the only sound.

Janessa crept to the front of the truck and fumbled around the grill for the hood release, praying that there wasn't a lock. Then, with only a small metallic click, it opened effortlessly under her hand. The sound of the hood opening seemed loud in the still darkness, but there was apparently no one close enough to hear.

The adrenaline rush buoying her movements, Janessa flashed her light onto the engine. She watched Annie give it a quick scan, then reach for the desired part. Her reach too short, she climbed onto the bumper, closed her hand over something on the side and pulled. Triumphantly, she held up what had to be the valuable distributor cap, several important-looking wires spilling out of it like a dead bouquet.

Janessa heard the infinitesimal sound behind her and whirled at the same moment that a powerful flashlight picked out Annie's shapely bottom bent into the truck. A quiet, slightly accented voice said, "My, my, my. Now *that* is a hood ornament."

Unable to see beyond the light, Janessa was pretty sure there was only one man. And judging by the height at which the light was held, he was not very tall. She made an instantaneous decision and threw herself at him, shouting, "Run, Annie!"

She heard the man's grunt of surprise as she landed against him, sending both of them to the rough, rank-smelling concrete. Footsteps ran past her. Heartened by the thought that Annie was getting away, she fought the body she had pinned to the ground with determination, if not with real skill. Methodically slapping at and biting the two hands that tried to capture hers, she resisted her victim's effort to reverse their positions by pushing against his chin with all her might. Then it became apparent that her victim had four hands. She was lifted off the pavement and placed firmly aside, two strong hands gripping her upper arms as her opponent got to his feet.

In the beam of the flashlight she saw a small, but well-built swarthy man dabbing at the corner of his mouth with the back of his hand. His eyes were both angry and interested. Beside him a burly giant in a baseball cap held Annie by an arm. His meaty hand nearly engulfed her from shoulder to elbow, but she glared up at him as though she were twice his size.

The small man jerked his thumb toward the loading bay, and Janessa and Annie were dragged inside. Flung against the wall as the door clattered inexorably downward, Janessa watched it close with a sense of having made a terrible mistake. There was always the chance Jake had gotten her message, but as the small man and the two thugs squared off against her and Annie, the possibility provided little comfort.

"I'll question them, Mr. Santiago." The man who had held Annie spoke.

Santiago looked up at his companion, who was a head taller than he was and probably twice his weight, and said with weary patience, "Be quiet, Bobby." Then his eyes settled on Janessa and he rubbed a thumb along his now bruised bottom lip. "What were you doing to my truck, young ladies?"

"Stripping it," Janessa replied. "My brother runs a chop shop."

"She's lying." The accusation followed a flurry of activity at the other end of the loading bay as three men emerged from what must have been the video store. One of them was Simon.

Janessa felt hurt surprise, followed quickly by disgust. The suspicion she had refused to believe was proven.

"Her brother runs a tavern," Simon told Santiago after a cursory glance at Janessa, "and his friend's a reporter."

"DAMN!" JAKE SPAT the expletive in a paroxysm of frustration as he and Clay watched Annie and Janessa being dragged into the video store's loading bay. He pushed his car door open and would have raced across the street to the alley if Clay hadn't caught the back of his jacket.

"Think, Jake!" Clay whispered harshly. "You can't go charging in there. The police are here—" he looked around at the empty street "—somewhere."

"What in hell did they think they were doing?" Jake demanded. They had arrived only a moment before to see what appeared to be a fight in the alley. When the distant but bright beam of a flashlight had revealed Janessa being hauled up off Santiago and Annie in the grip of Billy Calderon, they had both stared as though in a nightmare.

Clay popped the lid of his trunk. "I've got some things in the back we might find useful."

The street was silent as they got out of the car and moved to the trunk. Looking around, Jake whispered, "You're sure the police are here?"

"They called me, remember? If they were visible to everyone, they'd defeat their own purpose." Clay hefted the tire iron and handed Jake a wrench. "Let's see if we can get in through the front."

"SHE'S AN EX-SENATOR'S DAUGHTER," Simon said, indicating Janessa with a jut of his chin. It was only then that she noticed his hands were tied and his chin bruised. Puzzled, she watched him move into the room. There were two men behind him, one older and pockmarked, the other probably still in his teens. The older man gave Simon a shove that pitched him against the opposite wall. Then he pushed a large automatic pistol against his temple.

Simon glared beyond the shoulder of the armed man to the boy behind him. "This what you had in mind, my hotshot little brother? Me and two innocent women killed so you can buy a Porsche and get all the girls you want?"

Janessa's disgust became confusion. Brother? Simon had never mentioned a brother. She quickly decided that, considering the young man's connections, and the image Simon was trying to project of a noble upright citizen, she shouldn't be surprised.

"I told you to stay away from here!" the young man argued, his voice high and nearly hysterical. "Didn't I? Didn't I?"

The pockmarked man cocked the pistol, the sound like a shout in the quiet room. He glanced casually over his shoulder to Santiago. "I'm gonna shut him up. I'm tired of hearin' him talk."

Simon was apparently undaunted. "If you hurt her," Simon said to Santiago, with a glance at Janessa, "her family will never let you rest. The other woman's her brother's girlfriend. He and Barrister will tear you apart, Santiago."

Santiago pushed the pockmarked man aside and smiled at Simon. "Many have threatened to tear me apart, but as you see—" he raised his hands, palms up "—I am still here. Now I have listened patiently to your accusations that I have led your brother astray. But again, as you see—" he indicated the young man standing nervously to one side "—he chooses to work with me of his own free will. I am tired of your coming here to bully him into quitting. Your presence always upsets him. Try to think of him as a professional in a lucrative business. Not unlike yourself, eh?"

"I am not a pornographer or a thief," Simon declared.

Santiago smiled in apparent good humor. "I prefer to think of myself as an artist and an entrepreneur. But we will not argue. You have threatened me and my men several times and I will have no more of it!" He turned to Bobby. "If he says one more word, kill him."

Walking to within an inch of Janessa, he said quietly, "I will have what you took from the engine of my truck."

Janessa swallowed. "I threw it away when I was fighting with you."

Something subtle changed in his eyes, and all the gracious good humor evaporated. Ruthless anger emanated from him as he grabbed her by the arm.

"I have it!" Annie shouted, without waiting to see what he intended to do. She pulled the distributor cap out of her jacket and handed it over.

Santiago looked from it to Janessa, then shook his head, releasing her. "You have a terrible tendency to lie. I think perhaps it would be best if you come with us. We will leave Mr. Pruitt and your friend here with Bobby and Figueroa. Their cooperation will ensure your safety."

Janessa looked away from the panic in Annie's eyes and tried to think clearly. She didn't relish a trip to the Portland docks in the early hours of the morning with what passed for the local faction of organized crime. But Simon was tied up, and she and Annie didn't have a chance against a couple of tough men.

Santiago gestured to Figueroa, who leaned down and pulled up on the door. When four uniformed policemen with guns drawn appeared on the other side, Janessa blinked, thinking her hopeful imagination had conjured them up.

One stepped forward. "Police. Freeze."

Janessa turned to Annie, a shout of relief on her lips. But it turned to one of pain as she was yanked backward by a fist curled in her hair. Something cold and cylindrical was pressed to the pulse in her throat. She hoped a little hysterically that it was a corner of the distributor cap, but an ominous click assured her that it wasn't.

"Gentlemen." Santiago pulled harder on her hair and she found herself staring at the steel beams of the ceiling as he inched slowly backward. Her neck feeling as though it would break, her heart beating hard enough to choke her, Janessa swallowed against the cold metal at her throat. "This impulsive young lady and I will be leaving by the front. I'm sure you do not wish to see her with a most unattractive hole in her throat."

"The hole would look much better on you, Santiago. Where do you think, Clay? Above his ear? Between his eyes?"

The sound of Jake's voice accompanied the release of pressure against Janessa's throat. She felt the hand wrenched out of her hair, and Clay pushed her aside as he took the gun from Santiago. He looked at the hood consideringly, grinning at Jake who held a wrench to the man's temple. Santiago seemed completely convinced that it was a gun.

"I don't think I can decide. You'd better do both."

"Gentlemen," Santiago said quickly, his voice a little high as he held both hands out at his sides. "You will see that no one has been hurt."

Clay glanced across the room, saw Annie plastered against the wall and Janessa, trembling and dirty but otherwise unharmed. He nodded. "All right. Just one hole."

"All right, you two." Lieutenant McMullin glanced reprovingly from Clay to Jake and shoved Santiago to two waiting officers. "There is such a thing as established procedure. That wasn't it. Where are the two officers I sent around the front?"

"They pushed us out of the way, Lieutenant," a disgruntled officer explained from the doorway to the shop.

McMullin sighed and spoke quietly to Clay. "I'll see you two and the ladies at the station. Be punctual. You're on thin ice, Barrister."

As Jake strode across the room toward Annie, Clay turned to Janessa. She was leaning against a stack of cartons, arms folded to stop their trembling.

"What in hell did you think you were doing?" he demanded.

Janessa fought an impulse to back away. She stood her ground, drawing her first even breath in fifteen minutes. Her throat felt thick and she couldn't swallow. "Stopping the truck from moving until you could get here with the police." Then she added, "It worked, didn't it?"

"Worked?" He repeated her word on a strangled sound. His eyes darkened as he stepped closer. "He was dragging you off by the hair with a gun at your throat!"

"Had you been at home or at your office," she pointed out judiciously, "I wouldn't have had to cut it so close."

"Had I..." He began to repeat her accusation, then stopped, too frustrated and too emotionally unsettled to continue the discussion. He was on the brink of either taking her in his arms or knotting her hair around her throat, and he didn't want to make the wrong decision. Finally he just took her arm and pulled her toward the door. "Come on. We're going to the station."

BY THREE-THIRTY IN THE MORNING, several things were clear to Janessa. The American criminal-justice system worked, but very slowly. Annie and Jake might one day decide that they loved each other, but they would still spend the better part of their lives arguing. And Simon had had no part in the pirating of videos, except that of trying to extricate his brother from Santiago's employ. And he would always be able to turn a difficult situation to his advantage.

As Clay and Janessa, and Jake and Annie opened the doors to leave the police station, they found Simon talking to reporters on the steps, dabbing at the bruised chin he'd received in his scuffle with Figueroa in the video shop.

"Is it true that you confronted Santiago about your brother's association with him?" A microphone was shoved into his face.

Simon squared his shoulders and showed the photographers a face exquisitely designed for the front page of a newspaper, or a campaign poster. The bruise only contributed to the drama. "That's true," he replied with quiet heroism. "Several times."

"Weren't you concerned for your safety?"

He frowned as though the question were illogical. "I was concerned about my brother."

"Do you think his association with Santiago will hurt your campaign?"

He gave a thoughtfully wise shake of his head. "I don't think so. The people of Oregon can always be counted on to think for themselves, to..."

As he went on in praise of his prospective constituents, Clay closed the doors and turned to lead the way to the building's rear exit. "Let's go out the back or they'll be all over Jan—"

Janessa put a hand to her hip pocket, felt the sharp bump of Simon's engagement ring where she had left it several days ago and stopped.

"No," she said with sudden resolve. "You three go ahead. I'll meet you at the car."

"Jan." Clay caught her arm to stop her. She'd been ignoring him all night long, only speaking to him when she absolutely had to, and then with disdain in her eyes and ice in her tone. "They'll keep you another hour. We'll..."

With a withering look she pulled away from him and went through the doors. The reporters and photographers reacted immediately, parting the circle they had made around Simon to let her in.

Clay, Jake and Annie watched as Janessa put a hand to the hip pocket of her jeans and pulled out the ring. Clay's heart rose in his throat. She had told the officer who took her statement that Simon had tried to defend her and Annie, had tried to talk Santiago into freeing them. Maybe her feelings for him had become love....

"When's the wedding?" one reporter shouted.

Clay held his breath as Simon put his arm around Janessa's shoulders and drew her to his side, raising his other arm to silence the small crowd. For one protracted moment there was no sound but the occasional roar of a passing car and the wind-stirred slap of the rope against the flag pole.

"There isn't going to be a wedding," Janessa said quietly but clearly. She looked into Simon's stricken expression and strained up on tiptoe to kiss his cheek. Then she smiled at the reporters. "I've spent so much of my life in politics because of my father. I'm not willing to give public life any more of my time. Mr. Pruitt, I'm sure, will be an active, dedicated public servant, and that's the very reason I've finally decided we have to go our separate ways."

Janessa knew it was a melodramatic statement, but Simon appeared to love it, though he maintained a look of noble pain. The reporters were madly taking notes and holding up microphones, the photographers snapping enough pictures to fill every newspaper in Oregon. Simon seemed to grow several inches.

Janessa hugged him again, whispered, "Good luck, Simon," and ran down the steps to where Clay and Jake and Annie waited. For the first time in hours, she felt good.

"Now he'll be more insufferable than ever," Jake complained as the knot of reporters tightened around Simon once more, his eyes were closed dramatically as he clutched the ring in his fist.

Annie shook her head at Jake. "You miss all life's subtleties. Jan got to pay him back for announcing their engagement publicly, by rejecting him in front of the press. But she softened the blow by giving him enough ammunition to turn the whole thing to his advantage. In the morning edition he'll be a hero, jilted because of his dedication to service. Simon could make president with that.''

Jake shuddered. ''God help us.''

Annie rubbed the arms of her jean jacket against the early-morning cold. ''We'd better go to your mother's and get Mark.''

''I called her while you were giving your statement.'' Jake opened her car door. ''She said he was fast asleep and to just leave him there till morning. Come on. I'll take you home.''

''It's my car,'' she pointed out. ''How will you get home?''

''If you were feeling generous, I could sleep on your sofa till morning.''

Annie appeared to consider that possibility. She went to Janessa and gave her a hug. ''I think we sew better than we spy, Jan.''

They giggled together for a minute. ''You're a good friend to have either way,'' Janessa said. ''Take tomorrow off.''

''But the carpet for your office and the reception area is coming tomorrow.''

''I'll handle it. You get some rest.''

Jake put Annie into the car. Then he turned to Clay and Janessa, standing about a foot apart in front of Clay's car. The entire issue of the investigation of Simon had yet to be brought out among them, and it lingered there, ripe and almost visibly present. He felt too tired to deal with it at the moment but knew it couldn't be ignored. ''So.'' He smiled and gave Janessa a big hug, asking hopefully, ''All's well that ends well?''

When she remained impassive in his arms, her expression condemning as he drew away, her brother said, "I didn't think so."

"I'll explain it to her," Clay said, opening the passenger side door of his Camaro. "You take Annie home."

Jake looked doubtful. "Are you sure?"

"I'm sure." Clay gave Jake a grim smile and a push toward his car.

Chapter Fourteen

"Some friend you turned out to be." Janessa was out of the car almost before Clay braked to a stop in her driveway. She noticed idly that her father's Mercedes was back.

Clay yanked his keys out of the ignition and got out as Janessa slammed her door, heedless of her sleeping neighbors and the lateness of the hour. He looked at her across the expanse of roof. "I'm not your friend anymore," he said quietly. "I guess that's how all this happened."

Janessa stormed to the porch and began to rout through her purse for her keys. In her haste to leave earlier, she'd forgotten to turn on the outside light. It occurred to her as her fingers made contact with makeup, wallet, lint brush and other various necessities she carried that the search could take hours. Then she remembered. She'd been using the flashlight on the key ring to light the truck's engine for Annie. She wasn't sure what happened to it when she threw herself at Santiago.

As she slumped against the wall with a groan, Clay reached past her, inserted the key he'd always had to her house, then pushed the door open. Casting him a glare he probably couldn't see in the dark, Janessa went inside and flipped on the living-room light. Hearing Clay close the door quietly, she turned on him from the middle of the room. She'd had about all his calm control she could handle.

On the way home from the police station, she'd expected him to apologize for the investigation, to explain why he'd deceived her for weeks while he sought information on Simon, to at least look a little remorseful. Instead he'd been silent, somehow implying with his attitude of temper being held closely in check, that the entire incident had been her fault.

"I suppose you can explain," she suggested, "why you chose to investigate my friend behind my back."

"Yes." Arms folded over his dark cotton jacket, he stood several feet away from her, looking her in the eye. "It began because I was asked, but—"

"By Jake?"

"Yes. But before long, I became convinced that Pruitt was involved with Santiago. He kept showing up in the damnedest places and the evidence seemed irrefutable."

She lifted her chin smugly. "But you were wrong."

"About Pruitt's involvement with Santiago, yes," he admitted, "but not about the danger you might have been in had their paths crossed while you were with Simon."

Remembering how he had found her being dragged by her hair out of the video shop, she lifted her chin a little higher. "And it never once occurred to you to tell me what you'd discovered?"

He sighed then, the first sign he'd shown all evening of feeling somewhat responsible for what had happened. "Yes, it occurred to me several times. The first time, you were upset about your parents and I didn't have the heart to bring it up. The second time, you were upset about Jake and cried all over me—only a rat could have told you then. I had planned to tell you in Los Angeles, but I got distracted."

"Even after having made love to me," she pointed out stiffly, "you continued to deceive me."

"Janessa!" With one hand on his hip, he waved the other in utter frustration. "I was wrong. I should have told you. Maybe I shouldn't have done it at all—I don't know. But don't try to make me out a villain because of it. I was motivated by the noblest of reasons—your safety. Although at the moment I can't help but wonder if a dip in the river in cement overshoes mightn't have done you more good than harm."

"Really? Then who would you have had to blame for this whole fiasco?"

"Who ran to stop a crime without calling the police or waiting for Jake or me?"

"Who set this all up and wasn't there when it all began to happen?"

Clay closed his eyes, straining to hold on to the shreds of his patience. "The police set it up. When Jake and I went to them with what we'd learned about Simon, they had already put the story together from the other end. The bust was theirs, not mine. I was invited along to get the story because I'd provided the lieutenant with some details he didn't have. He did it as a favor. The change in the date of the shipment was a last-minute one, probably because Santiago had gotten word the police were onto it. I was still under the assumption nothing would happen for another two days."

"So where were you when I called?" she demanded imperiously, as though she had every right to know.

"With your father," he replied, pleased to see her drop her haughty pose in surprise. "He came to see me late this afternoon—shortly after I left you, in fact. We had an early dinner together."

"What did he say?" she asked softly.

It was Clay's turn to adopt a superior attitude. "We spoke in confidence. Man to man."

She felt mildly impatient with that, but considering the nature of her father's problem, she could understand it. "Is he all right?"

"Physically, sure. Emotionally, he's a mess. He needs your mother."

"Did you tell him that?"

"I didn't have to. He knows it." Clay shifted his weight and ran a hand over his face in frustration and exhaustion. "He just doesn't know what to do about it. We did a lot of commiserating. May I sit down?"

Janessa frowned at him impatiently. "Since when do you have to ask?"

"Since I stopped being your friend."

They studied each other belligerently, then finally she swept her hand toward the sofa. Mabel lay curled in a corner, oblivious to their heated discussion. Clay fell into the other end of the couch. Janessa sat on the ottoman in front of the chair that stood at a right angle to the sofa.

"So you commiserated." She repeated his words with a trace of scorn in her tone. "I can just hear the two of you discussing what a trial your women are."

He arched an eyebrow in surprise. "So you do consider yourself my woman? What a wonder."

"Actually," she replied, "I consider myself my own woman. That's why I can't just go running off with you to Los Angeles as though all that matters in my life is what matters in yours. I'm surprised you can't see how selfish that is of you."

"Then you expect me to turn down the new job to stay here with you. Isn't that selfish of you?"

Of course it was and she knew it; she just didn't know how to get around it. "When you were my friend," she reminded him, "you understood how important my work is to me."

"When I was your friend," he said, his eyes dark and clear as they pinned hers across the small space that separated them, "I had no idea what it would be like to be your lover, to fall asleep with you in my arms and wake up with you still there, clinging to me, smiling in your sleep because I held you and you felt comfortable and safe." He leaned forward, elbows on his knees, his voice quieting. "You've always been an important part of my life, Janessa, but now it revolves around you. I can go on without you, but life and my work would become superficial. The heart in me would be gone."

She got to her feet in a burst of anguish. "What do you think will happen to me? That I'll just go my merry way and forget you?"

"I think you'll devote yourself to your business and the trials of your family without having to risk your personal self in any relationship." He looked boldly back into her angry eyes. "You moan and groan about them, but you don't do anything constructive, except call on *me* to help when you don't know what to do. You can continue to live through them, because you sure as hell aren't willing to live for yourself."

"You don't want me to live for myself!" she corrected, advancing on him. "You want me to live for you, because your parents wouldn't."

Clay stood, towering over her for a moment, his expression thunderous. Then he took several steps away from her as though needing to put distance between them. "That's the second time you've said that, and I deny it again." He turned toward her, retracing his steps. "I've had the greatest professional opportunity of my career placed in my lap. I want to take it, and I want to enjoy it with you. I want you to share in all it can give me. How does that make me selfish?''

Janessa put her hands on his arms. "Because it's your opportunity, Clay, not mine. It will answer all your needs, but mine are separate and distinct from yours. You worked beside me while I prepared the shop. Can't you put what you want aside for a minute and remember what it means to me?''

Clay closed his eyes and drew a breath. "Is there a reason you can't do what you do here in L.A.?''

"Several. My shop is here, my employees are here, my family is here, Clay. I . . . I'm . . .''

Clay read the look in her eyes. "You're afraid to leave," he said for her. "You're uncomfortable with the thought of me as a husband. Why is that?''

"Because you demand things from me that you'd have never asked as a friend." Then the thought that had haunted her for some time now erupted from deep inside. She heard herself voice it with shock. "I owe you, but that's not a basis for a life together.''

He studied her across the small space that separated them, as though he couldn't believe what he had heard. "What?" he asked, his tone strangled.

"I owe you," she repeated. "You're the reason I learned to walk again. And you've always been there when I needed you.''

He stared at her, all the color and animation draining from his face. "You're telling me," he asked slowly, "that what you feel for me is gratitude and not love?''

"It's love," she corrected, "inspired by gratitude. I think." Looking into his eyes, she suddenly wasn't sure. She put a shaky hand to her head. "I'm not making sense anymore. Could we talk about this another time?''

There was a long moment of silence. "I have to call the *L.A. Times* on Monday.''

She dropped her hand and looked at him, her eyes glazed with pain and weariness. "Then don't consider me when you make your decision."

Clay suddenly felt consumed by misery and anger. How could all these years of camaraderie and caring come to this? Love born of some imagined debt? Pain unfolded inside him. Somehow that kind of love seemed worse than no love at all.

She looked as despondent as he felt. Whatever had driven her to such a conclusion was very real, at least in her mind. As clearly as he had once understood her, loving her now clouded his ability to see inside her. She had become a mystery to him.

"All right." Clay put a hand to her face and leaned down to kiss her softly. "I love you, Jannie. Here or in Los Angeles, that won't change. Now or when I'm eighty, it will never change. 'Bye."

He turned to leave, but Janessa caught him, pulling him into her arms. She held him for a moment, the pain she felt at letting him go making it impossible for her to unravel the reason she had to. She pulled his head down and kissed him as gently as he had kissed her. "'Bye," she whispered.

AT SEVEN THE FOLLOWING MORNING, Janessa lay in bed, staring into Mabel's slitted eyes. She had been staring into the cat's eyes for most of the night. She had a vague memory of having read that one could see the answers to the world's questions in the eyes of a cat. But that was not true of Mabel's eyes. All Janessa saw there was near-blindness and a cantankerous light.

With a decisive movement Mabel didn't appreciate, Janessa moved the animal from her stomach to the pillow beside her. Swinging her legs over the side of the bed, she hurried to the shower and dressed quickly, grateful that her father was still asleep. She located her spare set of keys, jumped in her car and set off for the shop, picking up a cup of tea at McDonald's on her way. Sometime today, she thought, she'd have to return to that alley and search for the keys she'd lost.

There was no point in looking for answers, she decided. She was afraid of marriage to Clay and she couldn't understand why that should be. But she pushed aside the guilt she felt after having admitted that she feared her love for him was grounded in gratitude. There were other valid reasons she couldn't chuck everything to follow him. She was a businesswoman with a new shop about to open, employees to consider, orders to fill.

How she was going to live without Clay was something she'd consider later, when she had less to do. She could live with the ache inside her where his friendship had been. She'd made it through grim times before. It occurred to her that Clay had been with her then to help her through, but as she entered her shop, she dismissed the thought. Thoughts of Clay in general were disabling her this morning, and she had too much to do.

It required three trips to her car to carry in the pictures and memorabilia she had brought from her office at home to decorate her new one.

The carpet layers arrived on schedule at nine. For half an hour she entertained herself by standing on the stairs and watching them put it down. The speckled blue-and-beige, low-pile carpeting was nailed into place with amazing efficiency and precision. It brought the paint and wallpaper border to life, calling forth the comfortable, homey feeling she'd wanted.

When the men moved her desk onto the half of the carpeting that had been put down, Janessa perched on the desk to savor the pleasure of watching her dream come true. Only there wasn't any. Stubbornly she waited for it to come. She had worked so hard for this, planned and plotted every step. Where was the thrill, the excitement, the feeling of fulfillment? She didn't know; it simply wasn't there.

Jake found her leaning over the railing, watching the workmen put the carpet down in the walled-off front sales area. From the middle of the vast bottom floor, he held up a white sack. "Croissants and tea as a peace offering."

Despite her misery, she smiled down at him. "Come on up."

He tiptoed across the new carpeting and sat beside her on the edge of the desk, nodding his approval. "Looks wonderful, doesn't it? I was skeptical when you chose this pattern, but it's perfect." His eyes narrowed on her pale face and shadowed eyes. "Why aren't you pleased?"

She shook her head, staring at the carpeting as though it would eventually provide an answer. "I'm not sure. I think it has something to do with having made a selfish decision."

"You're in tune with the times," he said, offering her the open bag. "Our generation is supposed to be selfish. *Newsweek* said so."

Janessa pulled a fat golden croissant out of the sack and broke a tip off it while Jake placed a cup of coffee and a cup of tea behind them. "Whatever you do," he warned, "don't scoot your hips back. You'll get a hot seat for real."

When she didn't respond to his feeble attempt at humor, he knew he'd made the right decision in coming to see her this morning. Most of the time he didn't know how to deal with her, but this morning he knew she needed him. Maybe that would enable him to find a way. He delved into the bag for a packet of sugar and a little sealed cup of cream. "So tell me about your selfish decision."

"I'm not going to Los Angeles with Clay," she replied directly. "That's rotten, isn't it?"

"Why?"

She broke off the other tip of the croissant. "He needs me." She looked up at him as though surprised. "I think he really does."

"And what do you need?"

"To be successful, to see Mom and Dad happy, separately, if not together, to know that you and Annie are able to admit you love each other. I need . . ." Tears came from nowhere to course in two wide streaks down her cheeks. She put the croissant aside grumpily.

"You need . . . ?" Jake insisted, handing her a napkin out of the bag.

"Him," she admitted simply. "And for some reason I can't understand at all, that frightens me. When he was just my friend, I was as comfortable with him as I am with you. But now . . . I've lost all that. I need him more than ever, but it's like he's a stranger and I'm a little afraid of him."

Tears fell rapidly, though soundlessly, and he handed her another napkin. Then he set his coffee aside and put his arm around her shoulder, pulling her close. "He's never made demands on you before," Jake said quietly, "but maybe it's time he did. You proved a lot to yourself when you learned to walk again after the accident, but don't forget who helped you through. I don't mean by that that you owe him anything. I mean that together the two of you accomplished something remarkable. You're a dynamite combination. Don't let it all go because he wants something from you that you find hard to give."

"Jake!" She frowned at him. "He thinks I can just relocate my business in L.A."

"Can't you?"

"Jake . . ." she began again, unable to believe he couldn't see her point. "I—"

"I know." He interrupted her by squeezing her closer. "This shop means the world to you and you've established the business here. It would be hard to move it, but would it be impossible?"

"Maybe he's just trying to prove to himself that I'll drop everything for him, something his parents never did. Is that fair?"

Jake shook his head. "I don't know. I've never spent one day without the knowledge that I was loved by four very special people and that I could turn to them at any moment and find comfort and support and laughter. And neither have you. He's lived his whole life that way. He's had us, and I know that's meant a lot to him, but it isn't everything. If he wants a little assurance of loyalty, I find it hard to fault him. Particularly because I know he adores you. Whatever you gave up for him, he would compensate for it to the best of his ability. And what more can we ask of one another but a little give and take? Unless it's a lot of give and take."

Janessa looked into the light in his blue eyes and shook her head in wonder. "Jake, you sound like a grown-up."

He shrugged and smiled grimly. "Loving a woman who refuses to love me back has made me resort to serious thinking."

"She does love you back," Janessa said, then added in amazement, "and she knows what a distributor cap is! Did you know that?"

He laughed softly. "I read it in her police report. Great, isn't she?" He cupped Janessa's head in his hand and pulled it to his shoulder. "I love you, Jannie. I want you to be happy. Think hard about what you're doing, okay?"

She held him back when he would have stood. He looked at her, his eyes gentle. "The truth is," she said, a deep frown between her eyes, "I do feel as though I owe him."

"Is that bad?" Jake asked.

She looked surprised by the question. "Is a sense of obligation a good basis for a marriage?"

Jake smiled. "Maybe you feel you owe him simply because you love him, and not because of what he's done for you. Isn't it easier to tell yourself that what you feel is gratitude? Gratitude is so much less demanding than love is."

Janessa felt as though she were five years old again and denying she'd eaten the last of the jelly doughnuts when the evidence of her guilt was all over her face.

Jake got to his feet. "Got an appointment for lunch at the Crown and Anchor. I'm a busy executive, you know."

"Mmm." She walked him down the stairs to the door. "And the best brother anybody ever had. Thanks for coming."

He hugged her again and went out into the sunny morning.

THE BOISTEROUS Friday lunchtime crowd was thinning. Only a fine layer of laughter and cigarette smoke penetrated the long room to the booth near the kitchen where Jake conducted most of his business. Clay slipped in opposite him with the air of a man in a hurry.

"All right," he said shortly. "I'm here. What is it?"

"I thought we'd have lunch," Jake said, pouring wine into glasses already set out, "and talk about things."

"I'm on a deadline," Clay said, pushing his wineglass away after Jake moved it toward him.

"Aren't you always?" Jake replied, pushing the glass back. "When are you supposed to call L.A.?"

"Monday." Clay folded his arms on the table. "What do you want, Jake?"

"I want to talk about Janessa," Jake replied evenly. Then he cut off Clay's attempt to leave by clamping down

on his friend's wrist. Clay looked at him with a glare Jak
recognized as dangerous. But there was a lot at stake here
If he could patch things up between his best friend and hi
sister, he would feel that he had redeemed himself, at leas
in part, for Janessa's accident. "Sit down and shut up," h
said with a glare of his own. "I've ordered you a Reu
ben." It arrived almost as soon as the words were out of hi
mouth. Stewie brought it out himself, along with a secon
sandwich for Jake.

"First of all—" Jake peppered the small salad on th
side of his plate and passed the shaker to Clay "—I'd lik
to apologize for acting like a jerk."

Clay used the shaker, then put it aside, glancing at Jak
with a quirk of a brow as he picked up his fork. "You al
ways act like one. I never think twice about it."

"You were right," he went on, ignoring Clay's com
ment, "I was jealous of you and Janessa. After the acci
dent, when I felt so responsible and wanted so much t
help her, you were the one who got through to her. All th
time we were growing up, though it was always the three o
us, the two of you had a special something I couldn'
share. My father couldn't talk to me, but he could talk t
you. And just lately, when the whole family seemed to b
falling apart, I couldn't talk to you, I couldn't talk to Jan
and I couldn't talk to Annie." He expelled a long breatl
as though all that had been very difficult to say. "Took m
a while to come to the conclusion that it was my fault, and
not everybody else's. Sometimes I tend to talk too loud t
allow myself to do any listening. That's where I blew i
with Annie. Had I been listening that first time when sh
talked to me about getting married, I'd have heard wha
she was saying. I wouldn't have cut and run. It might b
too late for me now, but you've got time, deadline or not.'

This kind of soul-baring was so unusual in his friend that Clay ignored his lunch and frowned across the table. "What's the point, Jake?"

"The point is that Janessa loves you."

Clay nodded grimly. "I know that. Unfortunately it doesn't help. She won't come with me."

"Or you won't stay with her."

Clay pulled the wineglass toward him and took a long swallow. "Do you have any idea what the *L.A. Times* job could mean to me, Jake? This is the *cordon bleu* of journalism."

Jake nodded. "You know who called the shop while you guys were in L.A.?"

Clay shook his head wearily. "Who?"

"Bloomingdale's with an order for fifty dozen shirts. I guess Bloomingdale's is the *L.A. Times* of Janessa's business."

Clay tossed his fork down and leaned against the back of the booth. Jake went on, "I know you love her and that you need her, want her with you. She feels the same about you. I know how devoted you are to what you do. What she does is important to her." He topped off Clay's wineglass and looked into his friend's unhappy face, feeling every sliver of his pain. "I know you think it's heartless of her not to go with you. I just wonder if it's crossed your mind that it's cruel of you not to stay with her."

Clay said nothing, just picked up his glass and downed its contents.

"Your parents are a bummer," Jake said quietly, "but Janessa can't make that up to you. It isn't fair of you to expect that of her."

There was a long moment of silence while Clay stared at his plate. Jake watched him, prepared to ward off a blow. But when his friend raised his eyes there was only pain, not violence.

"I'm grateful that you have such insight into our problems," Clay said with a sigh. "I trust you also have a solution?"

Jake smiled and shook his head. "No. But I have great
faith that you'll find one once you get everything into
perspective."

"Thanks, buddy." Clay picked up his fork and stabbed
it into his salad. "Just what I needed. An impossible situation put into perspective—with every impossibility in
sharp focus. Helps a lot."

Jake smiled again, pleased to see the grim humor in
Clay's eyes forcing some of the misery aside. "What are
friends for?"

JANESSA SAT IN HER OFFICE in the dark, toying with the
new calendar blotter she'd bought for her desk. The room
smelled of paint and new carpet. It was the fragrance of
excitement and new beginnings, of a dream finally realized. She had spent all day accepting the fact that it
brought no thrill. Even the order from Bloomingdale's,
though gratifying, had made little impact on her mood.

Though she had always thought herself more mature
than her older brother, he had reminded her of an important nugget of truth this morning. "What more can we ask
of one another but a little give and take? Maybe a lot of
give and take."

She had to admit he'd also been right about her sense of
owing Clay. It wasn't that she owed him because of all he'd
done for her; it was that she owed him because she loved
him and he loved her.

It seemed ironic to her that she had always faulted Jake
for blaming himself for the accident and using it as a place
to hide from what was demanded of him when she had
been doing the same thing. Thinking of her growing love

for Clay as gratitude had relieved her of the demands love made on a woman.

Janessa spread her hands over the desk Clay and Jake had given her and found the answer that had been eluding her all day. That was where her success lay, she thought in wonder: she was loved. Her work was important, even critical to her sense of self, but it would never provide the spark that lit her life.

Janessa stood, love, excitement and determination coursing through her. Clay had been wrong about one thing. She wanted her family to be happy for themselves, not for the sense of security their happiness gave her. Well, she was going to fix him, she thought, reaching into her drawer for stationery. She was going to fix all of them.

IN A FLOWERED SILK ROBE, Elaine opened the front door, blinking against the early-morning sunlight.

"Sign here, please."

A young man in a brown uniform and cap handed her a small envelope and a clipboard. She juggled both to take the pen he also offered.

"Thank you." As the messenger retrieved his clipboard and took off at a run to the truck idling at the curb, Elaine backed into the house. Closing the door with her hip, she slipped a long fingernail under the flap of the envelope. A familiar, elaborate handwriting sprawled across a gold-trimmed card.

"You are cordially invited to dinner at 211 Oakglen," it read, "7:00 p.m. on Tuesday. No RSVP required as no refusal will be accepted."

Elaine felt a stab of trepidation. Two-eleven Oakglen was Janessa's address. Certainly an intimate mother-daughter dinner invitation would have come over the telephone rather than by messenger? She knew her daughter well enough to wonder warily what she was up to.

JAKE PULLED UP in front of Annie's house as the Message Movers truck pulled away. He saw Annie on the top step of her duplex, holding Mark. She was fighting the baby for the contents of the envelope the messenger had left.

Jake cleared the three steps in one leap and took Mark from her. Pride warmed him when his son gave him a de-lighted, gummy grin.

"Jake," Annie said absently, her eyes perusing the card she held. "This is the strangest thing. I think it's from Jan. It says—"

"Dinner tomorrow night at seven. I know." He re-moved an identical card from the pocket of his flannel shirt and placed it over hers. "I got one, too. What do you suppose she's up to?"

Annie closed her eyes a moment, then smiled dryly. "As the one who followed her into Santiago's clutches, I shud-der to think."

ETHAN ROLLED OVER in bed, his first thought upon wak-ing being the lamentable contents of Janessa's refrigera-tor. It was empty again, and the events of the weekend had left little time for shopping. He'd heard her leave early that morning and knew he was on his own for breakfast.

Propping himself up on an elbow, he was surprised to find a tray on his bedside table. On it was a hot pot, an empty mug and a white paper bag. Examining the con-tents of the bag, he found cranberry-nut muffins. His spirits began to rise. Then he noticed the envelope, tore it open, and read the contents.

He stared for a moment into space. Why had Janessa invited him to dinner when he lived here? Unless he was only one of several guests? He considered that possibility and felt a strong foreboding.

CLAY WAS PULLING his door closed—his briefcase under his arm, a commuter mug of coffee in his other hand—when a pretty young woman in jeans and a blue smock came whistling down the hall. In her hands was a bouquet of spring flowers in a vase shaped like the head of Mickey Mouse, ears and all. He put his briefcase down and took it from her.

"For me?" he asked in mild surprise.

"Clay Barrister?"

"Yes."

"Yep. Have a nice day."

It had to be from Janessa. Clay opened the card. He read the dinner invitation twice, then unlatched the door and put the flowers and card on the coffee table. He was already late, but he stopped a moment to stare at them. Under the invitation were the words, "Disneyland Forever!" Did that mean she didn't want things to change, just as he had accused? Or did she want what they had shared there to go on forever?

Whichever it was, he had to acknowledge that he had no sense of self-preservation where she was concerned. If they couldn't be together, and one of them was to come out of this with dreams intact, he wanted it to be her.

Chapter Fifteen

"Ethan, you're going to frighten him!" Elaine pulled on one of her husband's arms as he held Mark over his head, then lowered him to the floor in a swift swoop. The baby laughed hysterically, his reaction anything but frightened.

Ethan ignored his wife, swinging Mark up again, making airplane noises as he walked across Janessa's living room, holding the baby aloft.

"Relax, Mom," Jake said, pulling her down beside him on the sofa. "Dad used to do that to me all the time and you never objected."

Elaine continued to watch her husband and her grandson with apprehension. "It scrambled your brains, darling. I don't want that to happen to Mark."

"Not nice, Mom. Maybe you should bring him in for a landing, Dad," Jake called to his father. "I think the cleanup crew needs a little time with him."

As Ethan brought the giggling baby to the sofa, Annie reached for him. Jake pushed her hands aside. "I'll change him."

"I will." Elaine stood and removed Mark from Ethan's arms. With a sniff over her shoulder at her husband, she headed for the bedroom. "It's the only way I'll ever get to hold him."

Ethan sat down between Jake and Annie, a smile of satisfaction on his face. "She's just jealous because Mark likes me better."

Jake put a hand to his mouth and noted that Annie held a chuckle back with difficulty.

In the kitchen, Janessa checked the various components of her meal. The boisterous conversation from the living room cheered her.

"I should have brought a bigger bottle of champagne."

At the sound of Clay's voice, Janessa turned away from the relish tray she was preparing. Her hair was tied back in a fat ponytail, and her cheeks were flushed from the heat of the small kitchen.

Clay looked fresh and handsome, if a little uncertain. Janessa resisted an impulse to put her arms around him. "That was thoughtful," she said, taking the bottle from him. "There'll be plenty for a toast. Let me have your jacket."

Janessa pulled on his lapel as he turned to let her remove his suit jacket. The airline ticket folder in the breast pocket caught her eye and held it, like something grossly out of place in an otherwise well-ordered picture. She held the jacket against her for a moment, guessing what rested in the pocket—their permanent separation. It was probably a one-way ticket to Los Angeles. Her rejection of his offer of love had been very nearly complete, and she'd had no time since to amend it. She was ready to leave with him tomorrow if that was what he wanted—but, was it?

"Thank you for the flowers," Clay said as he turned back to her. Noting the sudden bleakness of her expression, he felt a stab of alarm. He opened his mouth to ask her about the meaning of "Disneyland forever," but Annie came into the kitchen, looking for milk to fill Mark's bottle.

Holding grimly to her plan, Janessa served dinner, distributing everyone around the table so that the halves of each couple were forced to face one another. Putting her parents at the head and foot, she placed herself and Annie side by side with Clay and Jake opposite them.

Jake had brought a succulent, glazed ham from the Crown and Anchor. He sliced it while she served all the appropriate accompaniments.

Her father helped himself to scalloped potatoes with a look of approval. "Not a bad table for a woman who keeps candles in her refrigerator."

Jake looked up blandly from the bowl of beans *almondine*. "Doesn't the light in your refrigerator work?"

Everyone groaned, and he passed the bowl to Clay.

"Ah...I hate to point this out, darling," Elaine said from the end of the table, pointing to the large round basket there, "but there's a problem with the rolls."

"What?" Janessa looked up from the relish plate.

Elaine tipped the basket just enough for Janessa to see Mabel curled up inside of it. "Either she ate them, or she's lying on them."

With a groan of amused disgust, Janessa went around the table to remove the basket. Settling a disgruntled Mabel on the sofa, she went to the kitchen to retrieve the now dried-out rolls she had forgotten in the oven. They looked far less enticing on a dinner plate than they would have in the basket, and Jake discovered that they made a rocklike noise when dropped against the china.

"Jake!" Annie slapped at his hand. He looked at her in feigned innocence. Then his expression softened, as his eyes were trapped in the affection in hers.

Janessa looked away, thinking that her plan for them might be executed more easily than she had thought. She turned to her mother. "Have you decided where you're going yet?"

Concentrating on ladling raisin sauce onto her ham, she sensed that everyone was looking at her. Her father's eyes were wide, her mother's blinking. "When we had lunch, you talked about taking some time to travel," she reminded. "I just wondered if you'd made any definite plans."

"No," Elaine said simply, apparently not pleased the subject had been raised.

"You're not going to give up the museum job, then?" Janessa continued.

"No," Elaine replied. "I'll keep it . . . for a while."

"Good." Janessa let the matter drop, looking across the table at Clay, who appeared to be watching her put her Machiavellian plan into operation with amused detachment. She smiled at him and offered the bowl of salad.

"I understand you're no longer engaged to Simon Pruitt," Elaine said. She sipped champagne and arched an eyebrow when her daughter turned to her. "Seems you straightened that out while helping apprehend our little corner of the underworld. Such a busy woman."

Janessa inclined her head as though that was praise rather than criticism. "Your son and his friend left the job half-finished. Someone had to step in. Annie was a little help."

"A little help?" Annie protested at the same moment that Jake and Clay exchanged a look of pained exasperation. "Who removed the distributor cap? Who turned it over when Santiago slammed you against the wall?"

Ethan paled, Jake dropped his fork, and Clay asked, his voice ominously quiet, "What?"

"Well, it was more a push than a slam," Annie interceded quickly, realizing belatedly that Janessa hadn't mentioned that to anyone. "Anyway, I saved her. You guys were a little late."

"They saved your pretty little hides, the way I heard it." Ethan lifted his champagne glass. "To timely intervention."

"Skilled and timely intervention," Jake amended, drinking.

"She did handle Simon brilliantly," Annie said to Elaine about the interview with the press on the steps of the police station. "And Simon did try to get Santiago to let us go. He's not quite the pill he seems to be."

"My engagement to Simon," Janessa said to her mother, her tone airy yet meaningful, "was one of those things that happens to all of us at one time or another. You get into something deeper than you intended, and it becomes difficult to find your way out, even if you want to. You know how it is."

Elaine looked back at her daughter, her eyes registering receipt of the message and a mild annoyance that it had been sent. "Do I?"

Janessa toasted her with her glass. "You must. More ham?"

"Thank you, darling, I think I've had enough." Elaine smiled meaningfully. "I think we've probably all had enough."

The tension around the table was now palpable. Janessa put her fork down carefully, took a last sip of wine, then pulled two envelopes out of her apron pocket and put them on the table. Five pairs of eyes followed the movement, then settled on her. There was a moment of silence while she collected her thoughts.

"If you say, 'I suppose you're wondering why I've asked you all here,'" Jake threatened, "I'm leaving."

Elaine reached across the corner of the table to pat her son's hand. "Janessa would never be that trite, Jake. Go on, darling."

"I love you all," said Janessa. She looked into each pair of eyes, finally settling on Jake's with an apologetic smile. "That's why I've called you all here. I've been accused and rightly so, of taking all your problems to heart and fretting over them, but not doing anything about them." She took one of the envelopes and put it by Jake's hand. She smiled at him again, pleased to see that though this little ritual would have embarrassed him only days ago, he was valiantly maintaining his equanimity. "I know this is presumptuous of me, but we all know that the only thing keeping you and Annie apart is pride."

Janessa put an arm around Annie. "Pride's important, but I don't think it's worth sacrificing love for it. In the envelope is your confirmed reservations for a weekend at Salishan Lodge. Graciella will take care of Mark. Please spend the time talking about important things—how you really feel and what life would be like without each other. Talk about Mark."

"Jan, I..." Jake began, but she was on her way to the bedroom to get his jacket, Annie's coat and their sleeping baby. "Are we being thrown out?" he asked as she walked them to the door.

Ethan, Elaine and Clay called goodbyes, then turned to look at one another in trepidation.

"Just for now. I have things to discuss with Mom and Dad." Janessa opened the door, then hugged each of them. "Check-in time is noon so you should get on the road early to take advantage of the whole afternoon."

Eyes fixed on her friend in wonder, Annie stepped out onto the porch, but Jake hung back. "Janessa. You...I...."

"'Bye." She hugged him again, then pushed him out the door and closed it.

Elaine stood, a rosy flush brightening her cheeks. She smiled fondly but firmly at her daughter. "If you think you're going to treat me like—"

Fueled with power, Janessa went to the table and picked up the other envelope. "Sit down, Mother," she said, her tone gentle but authoritative.

With a small gasp of indignation, Elaine continued to stand.

"I'd sit, if I were you, Elaine." Ethan grinned, looking more amused by his daughter's activities than chagrined. "She might have the floor under you booby-trapped or something."

Elaine looked down at her feet as though considering that a distinct possibility. She sat.

Janessa handed her father an envelope. "You and Mom have reservations at the Shelburne Inn where you spent your honeymoon." With the first hint of discomfort that had shown in her expression all evening, she looked at her mother, then back at her father. "Quite accidentally," she said, "Clay and I overheard your argument in my kitchen the other day." Ethan reacted with a simple nod instead of the angry embarrassment Janessa had expected.

"Clay and I talked about it," he explained.

Elaine looked stunned, while her daughter said, "Yes. Clay told me you'd talked, but he didn't really give me any details. So, uh, did you ... I mean ... ?" Unsure now how to proceed, Janessa looked at her father for help.

Ethan smiled with the kind of thoughtful serenity that had always convinced the press he knew things even the governor didn't know. "He told me," Ethan said, his voice slightly unsteady as he stared at his plate, "that it's a new world. He thinks that having a little trouble with the—" he paused only an instant "—mechanics of making love, only presents me with the opportunity to explore—" he raised his eyes and looked into Elaine's as he drew a shallow breath "—new ways of expressing what I still feel very strongly."

"All right!" Janessa cheered, then realizing her parents were staring at each other, her mother with tears spilling over, she covered her mouth with both hands.

Across the table, Clay watched her with a look that made her heartbeat accelerate. He got to his feet and headed for her bedroom. "I'll get your mother's coat. I presume you're throwing them out, too?"

Watching her parents walk into one another's arms was a relief that temporarily unburdened Janessa of all her other concerns. For a moment, everything was right in the world. Clay helped Elaine into her coat while Janessa hugged her father.

"So now you think you're Dr. Ruth?" Elaine held Clay close for a moment, the lightness in her voice belied by a faint waver.

He laughed, walking her to the door. "Hardly. But I've learned a little about love myself in the past few days, and I felt the need to share it with the people who've given me so much of theirs."

Elaine looked at him, her eyes shrewd. "Just what are your intentions toward my daughter?" she asked in a whisper.

"Some honorable," he whispered back, "some not."

Elaine hugged him again. "Good luck on both counts."

As Clay and Ethan shook hands, Elaine took Janessa in her arms. "Thank you for being such a busybody, Jan."

Janessa hugged her mother hard. "I have my talents. Enjoy your weekend."

"We will." Ethan drew Elaine out the door. "Come along, my love. We have work to do."

Elaine turned back to wave at Janessa and glance heavenward in gratitude, her eyes and her smile bright.

"I'll bring your things by the house when you come back, Dad!" she called after them. Apparently concerned about other things, her father didn't even appear to hear.

Janessa closed the door after her parents with a sense of having single-handedly carried a freight train forty miles.

"Has it occurred to you," Clay asked, "that you could end up with another brother or sister out of this?"

Janessa laughed at the thought, but sobered quickly as her eyes settled on his. He stood beside her at the door, looking down at her with the same careful vigilance with which she had watched him all evening. Then she recalled what her father had said about talking to Clay and realized that she hadn't accomplished her parents' reconciliation all by herself at all. She went to the table and began to stack dishes to ease the tension. "So you really got into my father's 'problem' with him," she said.

Clay stacked glasses on the empty dessert tray. "Yeah, we did. And I told him what I thought."

"And that was?"

"Pretty much what he told you." He glanced up at her and added with a small smile, "And a few other things you probably would rather not hear about how women can be so confusing to deal with that it's amazing a man's entire body doesn't stop functioning."

When she stopped stacking to frown at him, he carried the tray into the kitchen and called over his shoulder. "I'm sorry, but it's true." Janessa followed him with the stack of dishes and they faced one another down the length of the cluttered counter. "Not because men are more intelligent, and not because women are inferior in any way. It's ust that those of us who love you want so much to give you the best of all we have." His expression sobered and his deep, quiet voice filled the tiny room. "Sometimes the strain of that makes the brain, as well as the body, function poorly, and we make bad decisions."

Janessa stared at him, afraid to believe he was saying what it sounded like he was saying.

Clay looked into her eyes and tried to analyze what he saw there. He could feel the love in her, but lack of love had never been the problem. The day before, when he'd been on the brink of making the decision that would change his whole life, he had tried to dig deep within himself to find all the other things she would need from him besides his adoration. He had been surprised to find that he'd been able to be selfless and put her first. He wondered how to explain that to her without sounding just the opposite. He chose to avoid that question temporarily. "So," he said, taking the tray back into the dining room. "Where are you sending me? I didn't see a third envelope."

She pulled out the chair where her father had sat and fell into it, suddenly feeling tired and emotional. "Good thing, isn't it?" she said. "I noticed when I helped you with your jacket that you already have travel arrangements." Before she lost her nerve, she said with great determination, "I want to go with you. I know I told you to make your plans without me, but I was being selfish and perverse—and scared." She stood and took the tray out of his hands and put it aside. Wrapping her arms around his waist in a shameless effort to have a physical effect on him, as well as an emotional one, she asked, "Can I go with you, Clay?" His arms had closed around her, but for one awful moment he said nothing.

It took him a moment to remember that there were air
line tickets in his breast pocket. He then understood wha
she had presumed. Considering the decision he'd made, h
couldn't help but be amused. Clay finally looked into he
eyes and saw her confusion and tortured uncertainty and
was immediately remorseful. With a shout of laughter h
pulled her close. "Sure, you can. If you really want to g
to Butte, Montana."

Her face crushed against his shirt, Janessa thought sh
hadn't heard him properly. She was tired and upset de
spite the successes of the evening. She tipped her head back
and looked at him. "Butte, Montana?"

He nodded. "My parents are there on their tour," h
explained. "I thought, before I settled down to life with
you, I should make peace with them. Your parents will al
ways mean more to me, but I can't shut mine out com
pletely. They're so involved in their work that they had n
idea what they'd done to me. They'll never be my family
but maybe I can be their friend."

Janessa struggled to absorb what he'd told her. Hi
generosity pleased her; she would have hated to think o
him alienated from the Barristers for the rest of his life
But something else he had said was flashing in her mind.
Before I settle down to life with you . . . "Then we'll go t
Los Angeles together?"

"No."

His answer rang with discordant finality. Janessa felt the
world fall away from under her feet.

"I'm not going," he added. "We'll stay in Salem to
gether."

"You didn't turn down the *Los Angeles Times*?"

He nodded, walking her into the living room. He sat in
an overstuffed chair in the corner and pulled her onto his

ap. She pushed against his chest, resisting his efforts to settle her in his arms.

"Well, first thing in the morning, you'll call them right back and tell them you've changed your mind."

He rested his arms on the chair, letting her sit there stiffly on his knee. "But I haven't."

"I'll come with you," she insisted. "I called a customer of mine in L.A. this morning and she put me in touch with a realtor who's going to look for a small office space for me downtown, near the newspaper."

"Well, first thing tomorrow," he said, "you'll call her and tell her you've changed your mind."

She looked back at him stubbornly. "But I haven't."

Clay leaned his head against the back of the chair and closed his eyes, a faint smile on his lips. "Great. Now you're going to L.A. and I'm staying here. I guess that means you'll have to write about politics and I'll have to design sweatshirts."

"I'm serious, Barrister," Janessa said. Her expression fierce with determination, she shook his shoulders, forcing him to open his eyes and look at her. "I'm going to leave Annie in charge of the shop, and I can design in L.A. just as easily as here."

"Jannie—"

"In fact, L.A. will probably be sort of inspiring."

"Jan—"

"'Course, we'll have to get a big house so everyone can come and visit." She was staring at nothing, smiling at the prospect. "Near Disneyland, so we can—"

A large hand over her mouth stopped her. Wide blue eyes looked at Clay over the silencing fingers.

"I'm going to have something written into the marriage contract," Clay said, finally lowering his hand, "guaranteeing me equal time to speak. I'd like to tell you why want to stay here."

She folded her arms, sitting stiffly again. "Go ahead."

This time he ignored her pose and pulled her down into his arms. She nuzzled into his neck without a struggle. "And I don't want you to speak," he said firmly, "until I'm finished."

She wrapped her arms around him. "Yes, Your Grace."

"You're happy here," he said softly, running a hand gently up and down the slim back curved in his arms. "And I'm happy here. I hadn't seriously considered the job in L.A. until I'd seen my parents. They always have a way of making me feel less than adequate, unimportant. The offer became a boost to my ego, a way to prove to myself that I'm worth something to people who have no truck with mediocrity. Had you agreed to come with me without having to give it a second thought, I'd have considered myself almost divine." He laughed softly, kissing her cheek. "Fortunately for me, you've always been an ego stabilizer."

Janessa lifted her head to look into his eyes, all the love she felt for him visible on her face. "It took a while for me to come around to the realization that I have this strong feeling of owing you because I love you, not because I feel indebted for all the times you've been such a buddy. Clay, I'll leave with you now, tonight, if that's what you want."

He pulled her back against him, wrapping both arms around her with crushing strength. "It isn't. It never was. The *Times* would be a great career boost, but I've given it serious thought over the past twenty-four hours. It simply doesn't mean that much to me. I love my work and I'm happy to continue to do it at the *Standard News*. Your family has taught me the value of a loving circle, united against all the pressures of the world, large and small.

want to devote myself to it, and it would be hard to do that under such big-league pressures."

Janessa tightened her grip on him, her face buried in his neck. She could feel his warmth and his pulse and the vibrations of his voice. "I can't let you give me that much," she whispered.

"You must," he insisted. "It's what I want. The world is a vast and wonderful place that offers limitless possibilities to those with drive and energy and the will to seek them out. But everything I want in this world is right here—" he squeezed harder "—in my arms. I'll be happy just keeping Oregon politics honest. Just promise you'll stay with me."

"I promise." The reply came instantly, sealed with kisses that roved his face, his neck, his hair. "I promise. And if you ever change your mind, all you have to do is tell me. Do you promise?"

"I promise."

Janessa lay quietly in his arms and asked gently, "What made you decide to go to Butte, Montana?"

"Oh," he sighed. "I got to thinking about everything I dumped on my parents in Los Angeles."

"They had it coming," she said staunchly.

He shrugged. "At least I guess I deserved to unload the way I've felt all these years. But strangely, once I was purged of it, I found myself wondering how they were, whether they'd gotten over the hurt, if they hated me."

"And you have to know."

"More than that," he admitted, "I want to try to mend the fence. Since I left you after the episode with Santiago, I've been thinking about all the phases of my life, trying to establish some order to them that would enable me to move ahead. Once I decided I didn't really want the L.A. job and planned to stay with you, I started to work on

what I really wanted out of my relationship with my pa
ents.''

"And what is that?'' she asked softly.

"I want to be friends with them. I care about them
Everything I told them was true and I won't retract any o
it, but maybe there's a connection there we can still hol
on to. Anyway, I have to try.'' He smiled down into he
eyes, his filled with love and promise and the warmin
strength of a caring man. "So, do you really want to g
with me to Butte, Montana?''

"Yes,'' she replied. "When?''

"Tomorrow afternoon. Maybe Graciella could keep th
shop open for you for a day or two. She could bring Mar
with her.''

She laughed. "I'll have chaos in two languages when
come back, but what the heck.'' Her laugh turned sud
denly to a frown of concern. "What if they don't war
what you want?''

He nodded, apparently willing to accept that as a pos
sibility. "Then at least I've tried.''

"Maybe they'll understand the principle of give an
take.''

"Pardon me?''

Janessa kissed his cheek and smiled. "Give and take
Jake has this theory that a little give and take is all peopl
can ask of one another. Sometimes a lot of give and take.'

Clay laughed softly, rubbing his hand along her spine
"So he had a talk with you, too, huh?''

Janessa's eyes widened in surprise. "He talked to yo
about us?''

"Yes. He opened my eyes to a few things. Good old
freewheeling, fun-loving Jake has a very wise side to him
now that he's a family man.''

Janessa settled against Clay with a small sigh of satisfaction. "It's kind of a comfort to know that it's still the three of us against the world. The lineup may have shifted a little and our roles have developed, but you and I are together because of Jake."

"And Jake and Annie," Clay said quietly, "are together because of you."

"And my mother and father are reunited," she said, tightening her grip on him, "because of you. What a tangle!"

Clay closed his eyes, thinking that he'd never been more comfortable in his life than he was at this moment, with Janessa filling his arms. He felt a little in awe that he was now entitled to this for a lifetime. "What a lot of love," he said.

"Disneyland forever," she murmured against his lips.

He was no longer in doubt about what she meant.

Epilogue

''Happy fortieth anniversary, Ethan and Elaine! To for[
more!''

The reflected lights of the Crown and Anchor winke[
off champagne glasses raised in a toast. Surrounded by [
boisterous circle of friends, Ethan and Elaine hooked arm[
and drank from their glasses.

In the family booth in the relatively quiet corner near th[
kitchen, Janessa raised her glass and prayed that Mar[
wouldn't wake up. He lay with his nose against her nec[
his plump hand tangled in the off-the-shoulder ruffle [
her pale blue dress. A soft snore issued from his lips an[
she tried to relax, scanning the crowd for Clay.

But relaxing was difficult. Of all the nights for him to b[
late. She was bursting with the news she'd kept to herse[
for hours, but Clay had been closeted in the capitol all a[
ternoon. Sharing it with him had had to wait.

Then he was coming through the crowd, being stoppe[
by her parents, then by friends, then by Annie, who put [
champagne glass in his hand. He made his way to th[
booth and slipped in beside her. He had showered an[
changed, but his eyes were tired and, when they settled o[
hers, watchful.

''Well?'' The question was swift and anxious.